THE
OTHER
END

THE
OTHER
END

JOHN SHIRLEY

OPEN ROAD

INTEGRATED MEDIA

NEW YORK

Copyright © 2007, 2010 by John Shirley

978-1-5040-2180-7

This edition published in 2015 by Open Road Integrated Media, Inc.
345 Hudson Street
New York, NY 10014
www.openroadmedia.com

For Micky.

*Special thanks to Mrs. Shirley and to
Paula Guran for helpful input
and to Jim Baldwin for Very Important Data.*

An Important Remark from the Author*

(*anyway, the author thinks it's important)

A CERTAIN pair of writers have co-authored a series of best-selling novels about Judgment Day, written from the viewpoint of ultra-conservative, dominionist, Biblical-literalist "End Times" Christians. They draw on a misguided interpretation of the Revelation to John, suggesting that people not in alignment with the so-called "values" of the extreme-right segment of the population will be punished by God by being Left Behind and then chucked into the lake of fire. (Said co-authors wrote the book cynically, since they know it's all a lot of hogwash.)

It strikes me that if the landlord of this property we call Earth returns and discovers how we've treated it, and how many of the better tenants have been treated, then he—or she or something beyond gender—may indeed wish to do some evicting and rebuilding. But a mythology cooked up in a narrow backwater of the world is unlikely to provide the blueprint for that Day of Judgment. Hence, alternative End Times tales are called for, for the sake of balance, at least—and because we have to hope for the beginning of a paradigm shift. This novel offers that alternative judgment day.

The reader is warned that this is a novel with a clearly defined point of view; it is unapologetically partisan. Let novels of Christian apocalypse bloom—but this novel is written from the Other End of the philosophical spectrum. It is for people who would prefer to imagine another end, a more just end. I cannot be alone in this. For a while I thought the novel might have a subtitle: *A Wistful Dream*.

But perhaps it's more than a wistful dream—perhaps it's a kind of existential protest too, and one that is much overdue. It feels like the time for it.

Speaking of time, *The Other End* is set a year or two, or three, from whenever you are reading it. If, for some reason, you've come across the book at some library's old-books fundraising sale, many years from now, then you'll just have to assume that in the next year or so after you read it there was a big fashion for retro. Keep in mind, too, that the President mentioned in the story is not the current President, he's some future President, possibly the result of the sort of vote tampering we saw in Florida in 2000. He's a neoconservative.

The tale, then, is set a year or so ahead of whenever. A year's not so long, but things can change quickly. Minor inventions spread; big ones are announced; new expressions spring up.

Then again, the important things, any time, usually aren't so very different...from right now.

PHASE ONE

AN EPIDEMIC OF JUSTICE

"If I had possession over Judgment Day..."
—Robert Johnson

1

(From *Avant Science Report*, April 10, 2---)

...Radio astronomers writing in the online academic journal, *Interferometry Studies*, have announced the detection of an unusual "quasar-like" series of radio pulses from "multiple sources." Normally, quasar signals come from distant galaxies. Hammond Terrence, Professor of Astronomy at the University of Calgary, and his colleague H. Mahwjee, Professor of Astrophysics, made the announcement. "The radio signatures are more like those of pulsars than quasars in some ways, but the amount of energy involved is very much like that of a quasar," Terrence said in a brief statement. "The energy pulse also seems to be reaching us much faster than it should. We attribute this to some miscalculation in our readings. We are asking for confirmation from other astronomers, as well as alternate rate calculations. There are indications of charged particles traveling with the pulses, which are highly directional, apparently aimed at this solar system, hence we think it appropriate to turn significant

*astronomical resources toward some of
the sources. The center of our galaxy, for
example, is one of the stronger sources."
Asked by email what he meant by "aimed,"
Terrence said that he was sure the "aiming"
was "only an appearance. But it is so
striking an appearance I felt the term
'aiming' was appropriate."
Terrence refused to elaborate.*

*Another researcher at the University of
Calgary, preferring anonymity, insisted
that the sources, initially thought to be
emanating entirely from the center of the
galaxy, are in fact coming "from nearly
every direction at once and much faster
than any model could have predicted. It's
all coming from thousands of sources in
the universe, symmetrically separated.
The impression is that the universe itself
is sending the signal. We have to assume
these readings are the result of some
massive, incomprehensible breakdown of
our equipment."*

LOOK down, from high in the air, and see: a trailer park
from above, like circuitry under a microscope. Pull back
farther, about 28,000 miles farther out, to show the planet
itself...

Our world, Earth: with its thin coating of rock and dirt,
unevenly coated with organisms, tracts of saltwater, all of it
wrapped around a great ball of molten lava seething atop a
nickel-iron core.

On the exterior skin of the ball, rock shoulders from
the sea to form regions called "continents," coated with a
biosphere. The biosphere includes colonies of anthropoidal
organisms, said colonies linked by "freeways" and by

atmospheric personnel-transfer devices, known as "aircraft" and by transmissions through the air, and through cables; the colony is locally termed a "city".

Focus again on the trailer park, one small angular detail on the brittle tapestry of the city.

Pull back into the fourth dimensional perspective, see the city over the course of *time,* shaping and collapsing, forms rising and falling under roiling condensations of atmospheric moisture; while beneath the city, tectonic plates shrug, begin to buckle...

Pull back to the fifth dimension, encompass the first four—and here consciousness itself becomes visible: millions of flickering consciousnesses, reacting through spectra of colors. From some of them, the colors are harsh, and dark. These are the particular colors of suffering.

West Fresno, California

"Hey Reynardo—how you doing?" Jim Swift asked, taking out the pack of chocolate Newports. He didn't smoke, but he knew the kid smoked flavored Newports so Swift was going to pretend he smoked today.

The teen looked up from sitting on the plastic fold-up steps under the door of the old Econoline, squinting against the late sun slashing between the rows of house trailers. He was mixed black, Asian, Latino; a spindly teenager, not especially dark but not Caucasian, head shaved and tattooed tag-style; wearing a polyester trans-jacket imprinted with Oakland Raiders watermarks, the jacket having lost its see-through from grubbiness; under it he wore a football jersey, number eight, big floppy green military pants, and Nike Dunkmasters. The sneakers looked too big for him. No chance to try them on when you're running from the store.

The boy shaded his eyes, which flicked immediately to the cigarettes. Swift had a teenager himself and he felt a little guilty playing this card, feeding Reynardo's habit, but what the hell, hooked is hooked and the kid could help him and maybe later he could help the kid some other way. "Hot as all fuck for early May, isn't it, Reynardo?"

"What you want?" Reynardo asked, looking sharply away from the cigarettes. He was careful not to seem friendly to Swift—who was a big middle-aged white guy, after all. Swift was sandy-haired, blue-eyed, expression almost invariably some version of sardonic—and he looked more like a bounty hunter sent by some Bail Bondsman than a reporter for *The Sacramento Bee.*

Swift had the pack of flavored cigarettes already open, just as if he'd been smoking. He tapped a cigarette up, lipped it out, struck it alight on the static-charge lighter on the side of the pack. He puffed to keep it going, not breathing in much, that would've made him cough. He let the chocolate-flavored smoke drift toward Reynardo without seeming to blow it at him. "Can I sit down, man? I've been tramping all over West Fresno, brewd, I needa sit."

"Sit, brewd, whatafuck I care," Reynardo said carelessly.

Swift sat on the steps beside the boy, making them creak. He was a big man, almost six-four, and bulky. He held the pack of flavored Newports out to the kid, while looking through the lines of doublewides toward the projects. Reynardo took the pack, expertly plucked a cigarette, stuck it alight, handed the pack back, all in less than two seconds— several motions gracefully combined, like the motions of an orchestra conductor's baton.

"What you looking for, all over West Frez?" Reynardo asked, watching the smoke swirl in the declining sunlight. "I heard you was on the avenue."

They knew each other a little, because Swift had done a piece about the West Fresno projects involving Reynardo's older sister, Terese—about a projects cop sexually harassing her—and he'd got the kid to trust him. For awhile.

"It's all about right here, what I heard," said Swift. He hooked a thumb toward the back of the trailer park. "Behind that chicken wire. Those trailers back there."

Reynardo's face hardened, as Swift expected. Talking

about what might be in those trailers, even to a reporter anonymously, was too much like snitching. Twice in "West Frez" he'd seen graffiti reading. SNITCH—DIE YOUNG, MF.

"Them peeps is Cambodes that run that shit, they kill you soon's look at you," Reynardo said tonelessly. "Why you comin' at me with that boosht?"

"It's all good," Swift said, falling back on an outdated expression. "But I heard some children died in one of those trailers. That's pretty fucked up, don't you think, Rey?"

"I don't think nothing about anything, and you can offer a truckload of fucking cigarettes and another truckload of cash and you *still* get nothing."

"See you shoulda told me you wouldn't help me after I gave you all the cigarettes and money, not before, what kind of tactic is that?" Swift chided him, trying to get him to smile.

The kid glanced away to hide the smile, he shrugged.

They both knew he'd already told Swift what he wanted to know without seeming to. "Cambodes", in this context, was short-hand for Cambodian gang. The local Cambodes specialized in immigrant smuggling scams. They had something to protect back there...

"I don't have a truckload but I got a Franklin," Swift said. He did have a hundred dollar bill in his wallet—he'd had it there for six months.

"Fuck off," Reynardo said, leaning back, blowing smoke at the sky.

Swift shook his head, said loudly, "Well if you don't wanta tell me, you don't wanta tell me."

He put the pack of cigarettes on the stairs—though it hadn't really been about cigarettes—punched the kid gently in his skinny shoulder, and got up, wandering off between the trailers just as if he wasn't sure where he was going.

Swift figured to circle around in the trailer park awhile, keeping his eyes open, and then cut back toward the fenced off section in the back. His cell phone chimed "Ode to Joy"—he kept thinking he was going to change the ringtone because it always sounded sarcastic—and he reached into his black leather blazer and found the phone, saw from the number it was Ed Galivant calling. Ed's whole trip was something Swift only rarely had time for. The guy wrote for *The Fortean Times,* and for online sites about the paranormal. Swift liked Ed Galivant but he didn't take the guy's "research" seriously.

He closed the phone, started to put it away, but it gave out another bleep, as if reproaching him for not answering. He grunted and looked, read a text message from Galivant.

Jim, para phenom in our
back yard, call me,
too big for FT. ED G.

Swift shrugged, tucked away the phone. He let his mind wander as he wandered physically through the trailer park, and his thoughts inevitably turned at this late afternoon hour to beer, preferably dark beer, the culprit, along with sweet and sour pork, in the substantial gut he was beginning to show.

Next thing to crop up in his mind was always his daughter, Erin. The girl's name had been chosen by her mother, when Linda was going through her "goddess worshipping" period, before the born-again thing. He wondered what Linda was saying about him to Erin this week. Every week there was a new slander. He hadn't found out yet if she'd let him see his daughter this weekend.

Theoretically, visitation was court scheduled, but there were always excuses: Erin has to go to a school field trip early tomorrow; Erin hasn't been feeling well, I need to make sure she gets to bed on time; Erin has to focus on homework for a test and I'm helping her study, Jim, don't you understand that?

I understand that a teenage girl needs her father, he thought.

He needed a couple of beers, thinking about Linda. An

Anchor Steam draft would hit the spot. Even a Michelob or a Red Stripe.

He circled around another Econoline doublewide, nodding to a fat white lady in curlers and flowered housedress. She looked at him blearily as she snatched sail-sized underwear from the line. He passed another trailer chattering out the sounds of a daytime talk show—then he angled back, cutting across someone's little patch of lawn grass. They'd yell at him if they saw him, though the lawn was barely a lawn, hardly big enough for a dog to poop in.

Swift turned into the gravel road between the rows of mobile homes. A freeway rumbled and hissed and groaned nearby, beyond a scruffy field. Two small white boys in an empty trailer, taking turns with a pellet gun, were taking potshots at a raggedy yellow cat. The cat gave them the slip, ducking under a white Econoline, and the boys watched Swift pace by. He half expected a pellet in the back of the head—not lethal, but painful.

They elected not to shoot him. People sometimes mistook him for a plainclothes cop.

But the sun was cooking the back of his neck, making him sweat, as he got to the end of the road where the trailers stood behind the chicken wire. They were set a couple of empty lots away from the others. Another fifty steps and he stopped in the shade of a magnolia tree near the chicken wire fence. Magnolia trees were from the Deep South, weren't they? But then people transplanted everything into California, on purpose or not. And some smuggled in illegal immigrants, near starved by the time they arrived, people packed in the holds of freighters almost the way slaves had once been brought in wooden vessels sailing from Africa. Only now, instead of taking them to a public slave auction, they shoved them into the backs of covered pickups, and took them to places like Fresno...

Were they in there? The six medium-large trailers on the other side of the fence were shuttered, silent, inscrutable. The fence gate was padlocked. He saw no trashcans outside, no sign of occupancy. The caretaker of the trailer park had insisted that these trailers were empty; that they were being stored here by someone planning to sell them.

But Swift could almost *feel* the people inside the trailers. The nearest of the trailers was about fifty feet away from him, beyond the fence. He watched for a while, saw no one patrolling the area; caught no movement at the papered-over windows. He listened close, and thought he heard a noise from the trailer. Hard to tell, since they were nearer the freeway here and the groaning of semi-trucks obscured most anything else here.

Was that a baby crying?

If there was anyone in those trailers, they were thoroughly locked in. Maybe chained down. They were waiting to be moved somewhere. The men would be put to work, without pay, at one thing—the women at another.

What next? He hadn't planned to take any serious risks. He just wanted to get some sense that the rumors were right, the Cambodes were smuggling immigrants in, lying to them about what they'd find in America. Once they got here, they forced them into indentured servitude, into slaves—into corpses, sometimes. Rumors said one or two died every week, because of "you know—conditions." If he could confirm the rumor with enough proof to get Beckwith at Sacramento PD on it, the detective would call his contact at Homeland Security or the FBI, and they'd raid the thing. In return, Beckwith would tip him on the raid and he'd be right there with an exclusive story.

But getting enough to bring Beckwith in wasn't so easy. He could hear it now. So you heard a rumor and saw some trailers? And?

He needed something more. Maybe a couple of photos. Anyway it could take the cops time to move on it. Meanwhile, maybe someone else dies in there. He needed to make a move...

He looked around, couldn't see anyone watching him, and started along the edge of the fence, as if he were walking past the trailers to the field—though there was nothing back there except trash littered weeds. Beyond the field of weeds was a concrete-block wall hiding the freeway.

Going to get my ass shot, he thought. And not with pellets.

The chicken wire fence was topped by a sloppily strung double length of antipersonnel wire. But a determined person could get over it.

Swift spotted an old, half-soaked piece of tan carpet someone homeless had used as a mattress in the vacant lot. He waded into the knee-high grass, grabbed the edge of the carpet, and dragged it over to the back fence. He tried not to think about lice and the pee smell from the carpet as he slung it onto the top of the fence, wooly side down. He clambered up the chicken wire, feeling it start to tear under his weight, pulled himself onto the reeking carpet, cursing under his breath. "Come on you fat fuck, get your big ass over..." He finally got a leg over the carpet, drew the other up, feeling muscles scream in his back—thinking: so big deal, later you'll take aspirin.

He was poised on the top of the fence, legs drooping inside its perimeter, wondering how much noise the fence would make if it collapsed—it felt like it might—unsure how to drop, afraid he'd break an ankle. Momentarily afraid to move...

Something glinted nearby. A sunshine-yellow glimmer rippled the air. It shifted hue, becoming sunset-violet. Then yellow again.

Oh shit, he thought. I'm having a stroke. They can start with seeing lights and halos.

Still clinging to the top of the buckling fence, Swift looked around for the source of the light. He was trying to verify that it wasn't just in his head. There—in the yard close to the trailer: two big, vertical, luminous cones sang to one another with soft humming sounds; one pointed down, the other up, so they met at their points. Each translucent, glowing cone was big as a six-foot Christmas tree, but somehow infinitely extensive, too. They extended away from their intersecting points, into sky and Earth, to fade into some unbounded realm of space—it was impossible to tell how big the cones were. They were as symmetrically opposed as the halves of an hourglass. Slowly rotating in opposite directions, the cones were floating in the air near the corner of the nearest trailer. Something seemed to pulse, to emanate with a purple-violet light, from the place where conical point met point...

Startled by this luminous apparition Swift lost his hold, and dropped onto the ground inside the chicken wire, landing heavily on his feet.

"Fuck!" His feet stung, but he decided he was unhurt. He turned and looked for the luminous cones—and they weren't there. He didn't feel weak or sick or paralytic, things he might feel if he'd had a stroke. Some effect of the unusual exertion, he decided. He'd been hallucinating—some kind of illusion.

Wheezing, Swift walked through gravel and weeds to the nearest trailer, pressed an ear against the aluminum siding, plugging the other ear with a finger. He heard a woman sobbing, almost immediately. Then he caught the clear, thin sound of a child crying, and voices in Chinese—or something close to Chinese. He reached into his inner coat pocket, took out his little digital camera, set it and stepped back, got a picture of the trailer, then went to the nearest window. Brown packaging paper had been used to block off the window from the inside. In one corner the paper had been folded back, just a little, and peering through, at a certain angle, he could make out a mass of human beings lying in a room inside. He thought they were dead, till one of them moved.

Swift pressed the digital camera to the little opening and took a couple of pictures, unsure if anything would come out. No time to check now—he wanted to get the hell out of here. He turned toward the fence, and froze. At the nearest corner of the trailer two compact Asian men were coming toward him, one of them with a baseball bat of silvery metal in his hand. They were both wearing hooded sweatshirts, the hoods up; both had homemade tattoos on the backs of their hands. The one without the bat wore small-lensed blue-tinted glasses.

Swift slipped the camera in his coat's outside pocket, but they'd seen it.

"Motherfucker, you made one hella mistake," said blue glasses, with a slight accent, as he reached around behind him. There was a gun back there in his waistband or back pocket, Swift knew.

"Heard you guys had girls for sale here," Swift said, backing up, smiling, raising his hand conciliatorily. "Wanted some of that." Hoping to divert them with the pretense of being a customer.

They kept coming, the shorter one raising his baseball bat, smiling, shaking his head—and Swift played his last card. "Okay, I'm a reporter. Looking for a story. Just my job. If something happens to me, *The Sacramento Bee*'ll send the cops looking. I'm not just some random asshole to disappear—"

The bat jabbed out and caught him in the belly and he folded up, gasping for air—someone else, a third guy, grabbed him from behind by the collar, jerked him back so he fell heavily on his ass. The man behind him pressed a gun, its muzzle cold, against the skin behind his ear.

Swift knew what the Frez Asian gangs were like. They weren't going to be scared by *The Sacramento Bee*—which, anyway, had shrunk to an online publication and a Sunday print edition. They'd kill anyone who got in their way, short of a SWAT team in armored cars, and maybe fuck with them too.

He closed his eyes, thinking: *Here it comes.*

A piercing light penetrated his closed eyelids. He thought it was the bullet passing into his brain, letting light into that darkness at last, but his eyes snapped open and he realized he was unhurt. Feeling a strange buoyancy, Swift jumped easily to his feet.

He looked around, the pain in his stomach suddenly distant, and everything he saw seemed to stand out in sharp relief, as if all this time he'd needed special glasses and just this second got them; he saw clearly every textural detail of the ground, every grain of dirt—there was the skull of small bird half hidden in the trampled soil—and the faux woodgrain on the trailer's siding seemed exquisitely sculpted; when he looked at the chicken wire fence he saw its pattern as something suggestive of the whole history of wires and fences; and a few paces away three Asian men were standing in a group, arguing: Baseball Bat, Blueglasses, and a third older man, wearing an off-the-rack suit. The man with the suit had a gun in his hand.

It seemed to Swift, in that moment, that there was an unbelievable poignancy about the three men—and, in strobelike flickers, he gazed upon their lives:

He saw them as the children they'd once been, and his heart ached for them. He glimpsed their harsh upbringing, their dilemmas; confusion turning to violence...

Then he saw them as they were now; saw this place now, the trailers, the fence, the stony ground. Everything had a yellow cast to it. Not a sickening yellow, more like the color of a new yellow rose. As if one of those old translucent color wheels had rotated in front of the sun, the cast of things suddenly changed from yellow to energetic violet; the violent was followed by a indigo-blue; after that, a glamorous emerald, then that living yellow again, and so on.

They were *within* the colors—within a cone of shifting color. He seemed to hear a high-pitched pulse accompanying the shift in colors, and when he looked up he saw the colors converging into a point that led to another cone that opened upward, infinitely wide. Those cones again...

And the cones were spinning, the lower one to his left, the upper to the right.

They spun faster, and faster, too fast to see anymore, generating an indefinable emanation from their convergent points—and then the cones vanished.

A sweet smell rolled over the four men, like pure oxygen blowing over a field of wildflowers. The Asian gangsters groaned—the younger ones wept. The oldest Cambode raised a gun and shouted and pointed it at the other two—

the guy with the baseball bat struck at the gun, knocking it onto the ground. Weaponless, the older man in the suit turned and stumbled away, holding his head.

Feeling stoned yet strangely lucid, Swift found himself walking toward the front of the trailer. He saw the front gate was now standing open. The older guy in the suit was going through the gate, muttering to himself in the local dialect of Mon-Khmer Cambodian.

Swift was thinking: I should be trying to get the fuck out that front gate...

But he went up to the door of the trailer and tried the handle. It was locked

"Move," said someone behind him. He turned to see Blueglasses there, with keys in his hand.

Swift stepped aside, his mouth open, staring as the man opened the front door of the trailer. The smell from inside the trailer made Swift step back; made him forget the sweet smell that had rolled over him moments before; made him forget the poignancy that had seemed so obvious in the three Cambodian gangsters.

"Take pictures, you want," said Blueglasses dully. Then he went inside and began to unlock chains, muttering a few hoarse words to the prisoners.

Baffled by the change in Blueglasses, Swift took out his camera and took pictures of the people in the trailer. They were chained together, lying side by side. Some of them showed sores from the perpetual contact. Packed in, row after row, hundreds crammed into a trailer. A few were children; some of them were dead.

Swift's stomach convulsed and he turned away, almost vomiting. He gagged, and gasped—and got his breath back. Then he straightened up, and clawed his cell phone out, dialed 911.

"He already called 911 for them," said Baseball Bat, coming around the side of the trailer. He said something else cryptic in Mon-Khmer.

Swift called the number anyway, and explained to the dispatcher that numerous ambulances were needed...

The immigrants that Blueglasses had unchained came whimpering, muttering, blinking, staggering out into the light.

"I've called...we've called..." Swift began, trying to tell them that help was coming. He could hear sirens in the distance already. Fast for the local cops.

He turned to Blueglasses, who was going to another trailer, to open that one too. Swift trailed after him, asking, "Why'd you suddenly...I mean..."

Swift was a reporter, he worked in words, but right now he couldn't find any.

"Because...I *saw* it, man," Blueglasses said, pausing by the second trailer. "I saw more than I ever saw. You can't look away, you see that way. I saw it, and felt it—I felt how they felt. Couldn't you feel it? My sister was in there. She's dead for three years in Los Angeles, buried in Encino—but she was in there. My aunt, who took care of me when I was a kid, she's dead —she was there, too, with all those people we put in there. We were all in there together, all of us chained up. *I* was in there...I don't fucking know, brewd...I just..." He shook his head, and said nothing else—he simply turned around and began opening locks.

2

East Hollywood, California

A S Dennis Boyce loaded the .38, he was so aware of
its weight in his hands it was as if the gun had more
gravitational pull than everything else in the room. He
looked at the nickel-plated, snub-nosed pistol, and he looked
around at the motel room, and he thought:

*Is this really the last thing I'm ever going to see? A bad
landscape painting on the wall? These dust-coated curtains;
the big painted-metal door; the burnt-sienna carpet?*

He could faintly hear a song being played, out in the West
Hollywood evening: a hip-hop song on someone's radio.
Song was, "Gotta get my wobble on."

That was the last thing he was ever going to hear? Thud,
ka-thud, thud ka-thud, gotta get my wobble on?

Wouldn't it be better at the beach, where, in his last
moments, he'd gaze at the beautiful sea, listen to the sound
of the ocean?

But the idea of dying on the beach—where some kid
might find his body, where crabs would march up and tear
it to pieces; where seagulls would sup on his eyes...

No. And he couldn't die at his mom's house, didn't want
the old girl to find his body, that'd be a cruel thing to do to
her, and God knows she deserved better. And he'd sold his
car so he could leave his mom a little cash—five hundred
bucks in an envelope on her dresser—so he couldn't do it in
a car. So it was, like, an alley or some fucking place.

Or this. A sixty-dollar-a-day motel half a block off Sunset Boulevard. A dump where hookers brought their tricks.

The staff was used to cleaning up messes here. Probably wouldn't be the first suicide in this place. Calling the cops, mopping the blood—part of the service. Bedding so cheap they wouldn't care about having to throw away blood-soaked coverlets, sheets.

And then again, he should die where it was appropriate, shouldn't he? Look at who he was: a fifty-two-year-old failure. Where would a failure go to die but a room like this, really? He was a songwriter with one hit—anyway, it got to number fourteen on Billboard—and two songs that'd just barely charted. He had been a radio DJ and they'd fired him because he kept relapsing into dope and not showing up. Then he'd gone to live with his mother for a while, "just to recoup, retrench" and it had turned into five years, then six years, now almost seven working in a succession of retail gigs. He was clean from drugs—but where was it getting him? He had two half-finished movie scripts in a drawer, and one lame novel about the music industry that had been rejected from about everywhere. He had a girl child, grown now, who wasn't interested in talking to him. He had an ex-wife who pitied him. He had those things—he had nothing.

He had...enough severance pay to buy a gun from Paco, and to rent this room.

So, to review, he thought, you have every reason to blow your fucking brains out, you failure, you loser.

He had known Leonard Cohen, who recommended Zen, but Leonard was a legend, he had art, he had fans, he had a life, a daughter who loved him.

Too late for Zen. Dennis had mostly concentrated on getting women between the ages of eighteen and thirty to give themselves to him. That took up all his free time. So he was empty inside, nothing to keep him going. He didn't have success, he didn't have meaning, he just had a room at his mom's house.

Depression. *It's just depression.* I could take Prozac again, he thought.

But what was the point? So he could cheerfully live with his mom, cheerfully make less than a living wage? Cheerfully accept being a failure?

He never slept through the night anymore, and sometimes, late at night, he'd wake up and go to the window and look out from his mom's little cottage in the Hollywood Hills, and see LA's illuminated body, the scintillations from the scales of the bloated anaconda, and he'd think: I'm so small, I'm...so...*small*.

Dennis put the gun to his temple. Then he thought: Hey, at least do it a little differently. Have one last interesting experience.

Why not try—he'd always wondered about this—why not try to see the bullet coming out of the gun, right before it hit him in the forehead? His perceptions would be heightened by the intensity of the moment. Time would slow a little. He might see the bullet coming at him...

Oh, probably not. But it was worth trying.

He turned the revolver around so it was aimed at his forehead from about two feet away. He could just see the tip of the bullet in the snub nose barrel. In a moment that shiny little projectile would fly into his head and it would shatter all his memories, blow his identity to smithereens—because all those things were just constructions in his brain cells. He wouldn't exist except as a few blurry impressions in other people's minds, and those would be gone soon too.

Get it over with, man. Do one thing right.

He stared at the tip of the bullet, and squeezed the trigger. "Goodbye Dennis," he said, aloud, to himself.

In the space of time between cocking the hammer and its falling onto the firing pin, a multicolored presence came into the room—and time *did* slow down, so that when the gun went off he *did* see the bullet coming with impossible slowness, spinning toward him like a space capsule with a long ways to go yet before reaching the moon.

But long before the bullet got to him it began to incandesce, like a match that's been struck, but there was no real flame— there was only light, rays of light emerging from the bullet, spreading across it...until the bullet had become a packet of light, a bullet-shaped, shining compression of light filling his eyesight, filling all the world.

The bullet did not exist anymore. In its place was a projectile made of information. Within the bullet of information was life; was a complexity of thought and memory and intention...flying toward Dennis's forehead.

And just before it struck him, he heard someone say, "You have surrendered your potential to me. You have forfeited. You will be pushed into the next place, and I will make the equation closed, and complete."

The bullet of light struck his head and he felt himself caught up and carried away through a tunnel of darkness into what might be non-existence—and into what existence might be.

Dead but undamaged, the body fell back, its heart ceasing to beat—and then the bullet of light exploded within his skull; exploded not into destruction, but into construction.

The body contracted, once, then lay still. A moment passed, the time it takes to exhale a single breath. Then the body's heart twitched—and began beating again. It was beating a little too fast, and this was noticed. The one who'd taken the body over caused the heart to slow down.

Dennis's body sat up. The entity now occupying Dennis's body consulted the memories that he'd chosen to keep within the brain. They were just a copy of what had been there, really. But they gave him a name, and an address, and a language.

What more did he need?

Sacramento, California

Swift and Galivant were sitting on barstools in the bar at Charlie's Card Room and Lounge, Swift fighting the impulse to blow that Franklin playing poker in the next room—he could feel an almost physical tug from the tables, the call of the rattle of chips, the drone of bored dealers. Galivant was nursing one of his perpetual margaritas. Swift had known him for years and had never seen him drink anything else. Straight up, no salt.

Galivant, gazing musingly at himself in the mirror behind the bar, was a stout forty-six-year-old man with shoulders that seemed a little too wide for his height; his head was big and shaven bald and remarkably round. He wore the heavy black horn-rim glasses and slightly-ironic goatee that hipsters had been affecting for some time, and that seemed to go with his bowling shirt—he never wore anything but Hawaiian shirts or bowling shirts—and the Maori tattoos wreathing his arms; tattoos to which he had no authentic cultural connection, being white, French-Canadian Catholic.

"At the time," Swift said, hoisting his third beer since nine o'clock, "it seemed to make perfect sense. I never asked for any more explanation. I was in a strange state of mind. Later on, I went to the precinct, just sitting around there in Booking, I lost all connection to that 'it all makes perfect sense' feeling. I mean, the precinct smelled like Booking and there was a prostitute on a bench across from me scratching what I'm pretty sure was scabies on her thigh. So then I asked the gangbanger to explain further why he did it, why he let me go and let them go and turned himself in, but he just said, 'You going to see, brewd,' and after that he wouldn't say anything except in that Khmer dialect..." He shrugged. He yawned and rubbed his eyes, still tired from the stress of the day and the long drive from Fresno.

"The game's afoot, Watson," Galivant said, at last, sticking a stubby finger into his margarita, licking it.

"You don't clean your nails enough to be sticking them into your drinks, 'Holmes'," Swift said, puffing up his cheeks as if he were going to throw up. He had known Galivant long enough he could say things like that to him. When they were in high school they'd been arrested together twice, once for underage drinking and once for vandalizing the

school—stenciling it with political diatribes, really—and
when you've been arrested with a guy twice and remained
friends you can say most anything to him.

"Fuck you," Galivant said cheerfully. "Okay, tell you
what, you've got three hardcore gangsters going from 'I'm
gonna kill you' to 'Let's release the immigrants we're keeping
locked up and we'll call the cops ourselves and you can take
pictures and go your merry way.' Right?"

"Yeah. Well one of them, the older guy, was against letting
them go, I think, but he seemed to be too dazed to really
stop it, and he just wandered off. They bring these people
in, hold them hostage while their family works their tails off
trying to raise money to buy the hostages out. Some of the
trailer people get transferred into prostitution..."

"So these gangsters were making real money."

"Yeah. And they just gave it all up."

"Okay, Swift, and you explain this sudden change of
heart—how?"

Swift winced. He had a standing argument with Galivant
on the validity of the paranormal. "I guess—if you have
a few thousand gangsters around, in a city, some of them
now and then are going to have a change of heart and...
that change of heart becomes infectious. For some reason.
Mass psychology or...something. And I...just...happened...
to..." He spread his hands in a shrug of helplessness. "...to
be there." It sounded liked rubbish to him, too.

"Uh-huh. You file the thing about the colors, the cones?
Describe that in your article, did you?"

"What? No! That was...No, I just mentioned it to you
because I know you like to hear about crazy shit like that. It
was just some neurological incident with me. I should be in
the fucking ER instead of here drinking with you."

"Best treatment you could have, drinking with me. You
ask the gangbangers about the lights—in case they saw
them too?"

"I was going to. I didn't get the chance. They wouldn't
talk to me except a little at the trailers, barely at the police

station. They just sat there at the precinct smiling like a couple of hooded Buddhas." He shook his head.

"Tell you what, Swift," Galivant said, taking a pack of cigarettes out, tapping a cigarette free, toying with one—not allowed to smoke in here, this not being an Indian casino. "You might fall back on that feeble 'the occasional chance anomaly' explanation—and sure, it's often right—except that, *huh*, there were three *other similar incidents* that I know about, at roughly the same time today, in geographical alignment with this one."

Swift blinked at him. "Boosht."

Galivant gave one of his sudden, loud spurts of laughter that seemed to rebuke disagreement with him like an adult laughing at the foolishness of a small child. "No it's not bullshit! Tell you what: it's for real. Where's my briefcase. Somebody steal my fucking briefcase? Where's my..."

"Here your stinky old briefcase," said Maggie, the Filipina bartender, barely tall enough to operate the cash register's top buttons. She handed him the old brown leather briefcase. "You asked me to keep it back here an hour ago. You brain's gone bad now."

"Right, right, there it is," Galivant muttered, opening it up.

"You need a new briefcase," Swift observed. "Look at that thing. Duct taped together."

"This thing has been my beloved albatross for many a voyage through the stormy seas of chaos," Galivant said, chuckling. He could say things like that with just enough irony so that you didn't sneer but enough assurance you didn't laugh it off either. He rummaged through the briefcase. "Where is it...where is it..."

"Don't show me any more abduction crap, Ed," Swift said. "No more. I've said all I'm going to say about that stuff. Even *Fortean Times* is bored with it."

"That's 'cause it's all boosht, man," Galivant said, still rummaging. "Tell you what, alien abduction's...all boosht."

"What? That's what I've been telling you for ten years and you're coming at me like, 'Oh didn't you know it's boosht?' You fucking..."

"Hey you were *right* about the UFO abductions, okay? I finally wrapped my head around it. Where is that folder... Here it is," Galivant added, slapping a manila folder of computer printouts on the bar.

"Where'd these files *come* from? Your online 'sources'?"

"Came from what you'd call 'reputable' online sources: AP, Reuters. Posted online just a few hours ago. Fresh, fresh, fresh. Not in the dailies or on the national news yet. Read it and gape."

Swift opened the folder, held the printouts up so he could see them better in the meager, colored light of the bar.

DISTRICT ATTORNEY COPS TO HISTORY OF WRONGFUL CONVICTIONS

Kings County, CA—At a surprise press conference arranged just two hours before it was held, County District Attorney Harrison N. Marlbury, listed five prosecutions dating back to 1992, which he said resulted in wrongful convictions. "These people were innocent and the District Attorney's office knew it," Marlbury stated. He was District Attorney in only two of seven cases, while in other instances he was an assisting attorney. "In each case both the D.A. and the A.D.A. knew that the accused was innocent. But we needed convictions for political reasons and, having taken certain steps, we felt we could not go backward..." The agencies cited by Marlbury have denied the allegations...

"Look down here," Galivant said, tapping a paragraph part way down the article. "Read this bit."

"Uh okay—so his secretary is hinting he's going crazy."

"Look there, that line. She says, '*He was seeing lights and things, we think he might've had a stroke...*'"

Swift blinked and re-read the paragraph. "Huh. I'll have to call Marlbury, see if I can get him to talk about the story to me..."

"So you *do* think there's something there!"

"What? No, I'm just curious. What was the other one?"

"Read this one..."

FOSTER CARE PARENT CONFESSES TO CHILD MOLESTATION

Santa Barbara, CA—Norman Gilmour, a longtime foster parent in the beachside suburb of Santa Barbara, turned himself in to the police department yesterday evening, providing a signed confession of thirteen incidents of molestation of children consigned to his care, dating back to 1988. "We were honestly startled," said Desk Sergeant Reginald Inchman, "because there was no investigation of the guy. He just got fed up with himself and turned himself in. But he claims he won't need therapy, says he's cured by the vision."

There was no immediate comment from Gilmour on the "vision" that he'd mentioned to the police, but his lawyer, Public Defender A.R. Chavez, suggested in a brief interview that the comment might indicate a mental state that could bear on the case.

Gilmour's wife, Patricia, would say only, "Thank God it's over." She refused to make any other comment.

"These children trusted me," Gilmour said in his statement, "and they needed me. I know for a fact that some of them told social workers, and nobody in County did anything about it. I used to wish someone

would come and arrest me. Thanks to
God's intervention I can stop myself now."
He gave no further details on the nature
of the intervention...

"Okay, well, that's a coincidence," Swift said, aware that his voice was shaking a little and hoping that Galivant didn't notice it. "Jeez, I just wish this happened more often."

"It *has* been happening! I've got four more, from four other countries—all in the same week. But I'll tell you what, bro, these three here—I'm counting yours—are all connected in another way. Call it coincidence if you want, but look at this..."

He took another sheet of paper from his briefcase, a photocopy of a map of central and southern California. On it was drawn a vertical line in red ink.

"You see that line? It connects Fresno, this place in King County, and this spot just outside Santa Barbara, straight up and down. I'm willing to bet when I get a more detailed map, I'll find it connects them street address to street address. They're in a direct north south line. So the question is, what's further north of that line, and further south? And are these events, when they happen in other countries, connected by those kinds of lines?"

Swift swallowed. He'd been feeling odd and disoriented all day, since the incident in Fresno. The beer wasn't helping that much. "You Fortean guys like to 'connect dots' and that's what you've done here. But it's an arbitrary connection. It's chance."

"Is it? I've known you a long time, man. And you are *lying* to me, buddy. You are not telling me everything you felt—you are not coming clean with your feelings on what happened down there, Swift. You're being vague and dismissive and you're hiding something. You're hiding how scared you are, man."

Swift said nothing. He just stared into his beer, and watched the little bubbles fizz up to the top of the yellow fluid.

Galivant sighed. "So how's that daughter of yours?"

"With my ex. Who's gone all Christian Fundie."

"Sounds like ex-husband Hell, man."

"It is," Swift said. He drank the rest of his beer. Thought about another one. He didn't want to talk about his daughter...

Finally he said, "I'm gonna play some poker."

He could feel Galivant watching him all the way into the card room.

3

The Congo, the Continent of Africa

IT was yet another hot, humid day, with the air like a heavy hand pressing on a man's shoulders, when Sergeant Pierre Orac of the Lord's Resistance Army trudged, with five of his soldiers, into a village on the Alima River. He'd been attracted by the noise of children playing. There were many young ones in this village; there must be a school of some sort.

The main body of the Lord's Resistance Army had moved into the forests a few miles away; they couldn't stay there long. They must hit targets in Uganda again, and soon. But they'd lost a good many men. They needed fresh blood. General Kony counted on him to choose well.

The village was a few rows of white-washed houses, thatched roofs, gravel streets, a community hall, a steepled church with a large outbuilding that might be a school. The boxy plastered houses overlooking the river were flanked on the east by sunflower fields, on the north and south by forest. There was mahogany in the forest—that was worth something. Orac was trying to persuade Kony to send men to do some logging, sell the timber for guns and supplies. But General Kony was more interested in sorting through the girls they forced to come to his camp. He had killed a wife for running away; another had taken her own life. Kony was in need of new wives, and Orac needed new boys to learn the LRA's ways of killing; to grasp the expediency of terror.

The six soldiers turned a white-washed corner and found themselves face to face with three children, two boys and a girl. Orac judged one boy, about eight, to be too young. Some of Kony's officers would take a boy that young, but Orac never did. The other boy was perhaps thirteen, the girl just a little older. This was very convenient, really, a boy and a girl, it would do for today.

Orac didn't have time to winnow the others in town. The local constabulary might escape, inform the Federal troops or the UN troops, and that could be inconvenient. Kony didn't like delays. The General had cut off the legs of a good friend of Orac's—the last time he'd chosen to have a friend—for delaying in a village, drinking banana beer. "Now," Kony said, "you have an excuse for being slow."

Everyone had dutifully laughed at that. Orac's friend was left in the bush, perhaps to bleed to death, but Orac slipped back and killed him, as a favor to him, and then caught up with the army. He didn't know anything else but the army.

The children stared at Orac and his men. They gawked at their guns and tattered fatigues. The youngest showed only wonder, interest at this strange phenomenon. But terror gleamed in the eyes of the other two. They knew exactly who the soldiers were.

They knew that for over twenty years Kony's army had kidnapped thousands of girls, and forced them into sexual slavery, mutilating or killing those who resisted or tried to escape; they knew that thousands more young men had been abducted, forced at gunpoint to kill and maim their friends and family, to break them of old loyalties; to shear away any shreds of fellow-feeling they may have had for anyone but the Army.

Orac had been one of those young men; he had been forced to kill his little brother.

But I am alive! I am one of the commanders! I...am alive. My body is intact. I survive!

These children had seen victims of Kony's army. General

Kony had released some mutilated children so others could see them and be warned; it was edifying to see children with their hands cut off, their noses removed, their lips cut off. There was something particularly terrifying, Orac had noticed, about having one's lips cut off. It seemed worse than losing a leg. It was the disfigurement. Knowing people would never want to look right at you again.

One of the children muttered to the others and they turned to run, dragging the youngest one with them. Isaac Mimbala, Orac's long-legged corporal, quickly overtook them; he scooped up the bigger two, gave the small one a kick to send him on his way. He turned grinning back to Orac with the boy and girl struggling under his arms, the girl weeping, the boy gasping, looking desperately around. The children were clean, the boy in a white linen shirt and trousers, the girl in a flower print shift, all three in sandals, with soles made from tires. They were slender but not emaciated. They would survive the trek in the bush.

A man stuck his head out of a house, and shouted in Lingala, a dialect Orac didn't much know—Bantu and French were his native tongues. But it didn't matter, Orac had swung his AR-15 toward the little house and fired a burst to send the man back inside. Perhaps he hit him, perhaps not, but the man would not emerge again to distract Orac from his work.

Mimbala dropped the two children and Orac's other men expertly bound their arms behind with strips of leather. The boy was babbling about his mother needing him so the corporal kicked him in the head to shut him up, and the other men laughed...

The boy looked up at Orac, recognizing him as the leader of the group, and their eyes met.

Orac was indifferent to the message in those eyes; he had a job to do and his mind was already in the forest, with Kony, wondering how the General would like this girl, skinny as she was. But in time...

The light shifted. He glanced up at the sky, expecting to see clouds, but there was nothing, just the brassy sun, the sky of glaring tin. He glanced down at the boy, drawn to look at him, somehow, and was aware that the light was changing, going a peculiar yellow, a living yellow, and then an electric blue, casting everything in that hue, and then an orchid purple, and then the crimson of blood, and then an emerald green, and then the yellow of sunlight captured in ajar and concentrated like honey,. And the only other color Orac was aware of was the boy's eyes, the deep dark brown of those eyes, the life in them...

He saw the boy's whole life, then. He saw his birth, he saw him carried on his mother's back; he saw him ritually enjoined with the tribe; he saw him on his first day in school; he saw him reading a book; he saw him fishing on the river; he saw him walking happily hand in hand with his father...

Oh, what became of my father?

...the boy in church, the boy singing, the boy chasing a wild pig, the boy riding in the back of a truck, pointing at the sights in a town, the boy rising in the morning, the boy eating breakfast, the boy playing with his brother, the boy talking to his sister, the boy walking with sister and younger brother down the street, the boy encountering five men...and a sixth man, with an AR-15 rifle in his hands. Sergeant Orac.

And Orac saw himself as the boy saw him. He saw his hard face...

Orac was not a believer in witchcraft. He sneered at it, but this must be witchcraft, this was surely some devil's work. A light had come and disordered his mind and put it in the mind of the boy.

His heart was pounding and he was distantly aware that the men with him were weeping.

He saw their lives, too, when he looked at them, as if looking down a long corridor made of a single human being in thousands of phases and postures; he saw the girl, and what would become of her in the keeping of General Kony. He looked at the boy again—and didn't see that boy anymore. He saw himself, Pierre Orac, as a child, bound and carried off by Kony's men...

Something awoke in his head and his breast, something

painful and powerful and gorgeous at once. He could scarcely bear it—he was burned up by its presence, and yet it was only a part of himself, blazing with light. One part of a man cannot crush another part, can it? But some part of him had clubbed other parts into dozing submission, long ago.

He looked up and seemed to see a big, high cone of light that stretched out toward its point, the point converging with infinity, from which, somehow, another cone emerged, or perhaps the same one, duplicated; a mirror of the duality that underlay all being. He saw it spinning and shining...the cones were very big and then again they were no particular size. A sweet, living smell seemed to surround him as he looked at them.

A thousand feelings and memories seethed in him then and he swayed in place, weeping.

"Mimbala!" he said. "Cut the children loose..."

Mimbala was already doing it; the order was a superfluity. "What do we do now?" Mimbala asked.

"We will find the Federal men, and we will ask them to arrest us, and perhaps they will help us."

"No!" Corporal Oruna shouted, waving his gun, staggering in confusion. His confusion extended to the amalgam of Bantu and Africanized French he was speaking. "Someone has poisoned me! I am poisoned! My mind— something is in my mind! We must not let them go—Kony will kill us!"

Mimbala struck Oruna down with the butt of his gun, and took the Corporal's Uzi away. "You go back to Kony then, Oruna," Mimbala said.

The children were running back to their family, and Orac watched them. He was weeping silently as he watched them go. The strange lights were gone—or perhaps they'd taken their place within his breast, because he was still certain of what he must do...

"Come, my friends," he said to the other soldiers. Three of them, counting Mimbala, came with him. The others, helping Oruna to stagger between them, wandered off dazedly, muttering to themselves.

"I feel like I've awakened from a long, long bad dream," he told Mimbala.

"Yes," Mimbala said. "I wish that Kony would be erased from the world now. I wish that everyone could feel what we have felt, and know."

"I think..." Orac said, shivering strangely in the heat of the day. "I think...this is just the beginning."

Sacramento, California

Swift rang the bell. A few seconds passed, and Linda answered the door. Her frosted blond hair was piled up on her head, something she did for church; that and the long pink dress were clues, and Swift, cluelessly hung-over that morning, was still stuck in the inward hollowness of being down almost three hundred bucks playing poker—as if there was some inner place the three hundred bucks was supposed to be, and the casino had yanked it out and left a gaping hole. Swift could only blink and stammer at her, "Oh hi, going to church, huh? Is uh, Erin, ready to head out with me?"

"Erin is *supposed* to go to church with me. That's what we've been talking about all morning, and, what a coincidence, here you show up, to take her somewhere *else*—"

"I did talk to you Friday about coming this weekend, you said okay—"

"I said *Saturday*, Jim."

"We didn't say which day on the weekend, I tried to call you—"

"—but it doesn't matter, does it, because your daughter apparently doesn't have *time* for God, and I'm not going to leave her here alone so she'll just have to go with you."

It seemed like years since Linda had let him finish a sentence. She was a small woman, who should be intimidated by a big man like him, but who always seemed to loom over him in sheer pent-up fury. Her green eyes glittered; her eyebrows, over-plucked since she'd become a Christian, seemed to arch warningly. When they'd dated, years ago, he had ignored her tendency to press her lips to a thin line when she was tense; the way she pulled her hair so tautly from her forehead—she inevitably complained of headaches; the gnawed cuticles on her small fingers. Hadn't she always been like that? Hadn't her eyes always darted around like that?

But she'd been such a sweet little bundle in his arms, once— needing protection, desperate for affection, charmingly chattering on. Days on the beach, her in a bikini, when she'd allowed herself to wear them; her small perfect breasts, her tiny little feet.

"So, uh Linda, does that mean she can—"

"I don't care, I have to go, if you guys want to spend a couple of hours together, today, this time I guess it'd be good, I don't want her here alone, she'll call that Shontel, and I don't trust Shontel."

"Who's Shontel?"

"Ask her, she says he's not her *boyfriend*, because she's too young to have a *serious* boyfriend, he's too old for her, but she's sneaking around with him, doing the Lord knows what, I'm thinking of taking her to the doctor to see if she's still—"

"Mom, Jeez!" Erin said, coming to the door, peering over her mom's shoulders. She'd dyed her hair jet black, he saw, and wore it short and spiky. She wore an oversized "Fittin' to Wobble" Keith Courage T-shirt, and jeans, no shoes. It was an "I'm not going to church today" sartorial statement.

She'd gotten taller—had it been that long? She was taller than her mom now. She was starting to hunch over to hide it. She had inherited his tendency to height and heft.

"I have asked you not to say 'Jeez'," Linda said sharply. "It is a contraction of Jesus and that's taking the Lord's name in vain."

Erin rolled her eyes. "Oh God."

"That's just as bad, Erin Eileen!"

"What*ever*!"

"Do you hear, that, Jim? This is your influence."

He bit off an *"I hope so."*

Linda was glaring at her watch. "Oh Go—gosh, I have to go, I'm going to be late, I'm a greeter today too. Do the right thing today, Jim, for once, will you please?"

She pushed past him, like a Mini Cooper darting past a semi-truck, trotted up the sidewalk to her little car, got in, and was away in seconds. "You'd think she was going to her dealer," Swift muttered, remembering Linda's hand-trembling, hardcore addiction to cocaine-and-Oxycontin circa 1987-1989. She didn't even drink now, of course. It was all about her religion, and her job—and hammering Erin into shape.

"What do you mean, her dealer?" Erin asked.

"I mean, she acts like her church is her jones, her addiction," Swift said, feeling a twinge of self-dislike for giving into the impulse to smear his ex's churchifying. "But you know, it's been a big help to your Mom, her church, I was just kidding. About the addiction thing. What, uh, what church is it?"

"The Church of the Revelation in Christ."

"Now you're kidding."

"No, I'm not kidding. And it's like, hella huge. They rent a stadium and it's always full—you feel so tiny in there. They have rock bands."

He looked at her deadpan. "Really? Those devil-worshipping rock bands?"

"Very funny. They have Christian rock. They have this one band that plays there all the time—"

"That's called a house band."

"No, it's called The Dangels. Dad, I'm hella hungry."

"You want to go get some breakfast?"

She was getting too chunky to be eating waffles and bacon, he thought, watching Erin burning her way through a stack of carbs at the Old Swisse Wafflehouse. Swift imagined Shontel saying, "That's good, I like a big booty!"—and then was ashamed of himself for the racist stereotype. He didn't even know what Shontel looked like, or what he was into. For all he knew the kid was a 4.0 student.

Anyway if she was getting fat it was likely his side of the family to blame. His brothers were fat, his Dad was fat, and he was on his way there. Only his hiatal hernia prevented him from eating too much as it was. It didn't prevent him from drinking calories though. Was it too early to have a beer? He supposed it was. They didn't have beer at the waffle house anyway...

Hangover brain, he thought. That's what I've got. Meandering, seeing shadows everywhere. Drink more coffee, drink more water. Maybe the waitress has aspirin. What *about* this boyfriend of Erin's? God she was young to have a boyfriend. But nowadays...don't think about it.

"So uh," he began, "uh—"

"What?"

"You've got a new friend, I hear."

"Can I have a mocha or a latté?"

"A latté? At a waffle house? When did you get into fancy coffee drinks?"

"There's a Starbucks next to school, we all go there. Mom doesn't give me enough money for that and lunch too so I just skip lunch and buy a coffee drink. Those double mint extra-espresso mochas, that's my favorite, you just feel, like, 'Oh yeah I'm alive, I forgot'."

He smiled at that, though this drift toward strong stimulants so young worried him. But she had a flare for expressing herself—which came from him probably. *Oh yeah I'm alive, I forgot.* "I know the feeling," he said, toasting her with his coffee cup before taking a sip. Then he noticed that she'd ducked his question. "So I can't hear about the new friend?"

"Oh, Janine? She's—"

"No-o, not Janine. Come on: Tell all about Shontel. About Shontel, tell."

She almost smiled. "Can I have coffee or not?"

"Sure, I guess. If you tell me about Shontel." He signaled

the waitress and he got a refill, got Erin a coffee, which she pumped up with sugar and cream.

Finally, after half a cup, she sat up straighter, and said, "Shontel's my boyfriend, but don't tell Mom, she doesn't want me to have one, and especially not a black one."

"Your Mom's never struck me as racist." But he knew what was going on. Black kids are fine until one wants to date your daughter. Any kid wants to date your daughter better be a white kid and not just any white kid; better have a career picked out already.

"She is *so* racist, she says he's a gangbanger, and he's *not*, he's going to get me to ignore my homework and he's *not*, he tells me to do it. He helps me with it! She says, 'Look at how many single moms those people have…'"

"'*Those* people'? She didn't say that…?" "I swear."

He shook his head sympathetically. "I'm willing to give the kid the benefit of the doubt." He thought about asking if Shontel smoked pot but he knew it was racist to ask—he probably wouldn't ask it if the kid was white—and she wouldn't tell him anyway. "I don't care what color he is, Erin—but you're too young to…get intimate. With any color."

"Dad, Jeez! We're not doing anything." She pursed her lips and looked at the clock, as if suddenly very interested in it.

She and that kid were doing *something*, all right. How far did they go? She wasn't going to tell her Dad. It would only make things worse to browbeat her about it. "So—look, Erin, it's not important what he looks like but there is reason to worry about where he *lives* because there are guns in some neighborhoods." Actually, this was Swift's indirect way to ask, *Are you sure he's not in a gang?* Memories of the Cambodes coming at him with guns and baseball bats were fresh in his mind.

"He lives two blocks from our house, Dad. He's not in a gang. He just turned eighteen. He likes hip-hop, yeah, but not gangsta rap. He's not doing that great in school but he's smart. He takes care of his little sister and his brother, a lot."

He watched her as she spoke, seeing the little girl who'd rushed to his arms.

Erin wasn't a little girl. Theoretically she could have a baby. Okay, he thought, wincing, it's not theoretical.

"So what about Janine," he asked, changing the subject so he could think of something else. "I remember you and her hanging out a lot."

"No. That's the thing, she thought I was really lame because I wanted to be in the choir at the other church, the one we went to before, but I really *like* choir and I said, 'Shut up, I really like choir, I don't care what you think.'"

"Good for you. You were always good at singing. You going to do the talent show again at school?"

"No. I don't know. Maybe. I might do the choir at Mom's mega-church though—or try out for it. It's really a big deal; they get on TV and stuff. But I just...I like *singing* in choir. I just like singing, especially with other people. It feels..." She shrugged. Showing some embarrassment now. "It feels good. Things make sense when you're singing with people."

He nodded. A young, good-looking Asian busboy passed the table pushing a cart, glancing at Erin; he had floppy pants and his hair cut short on the sides of his head. She sat up a little straighter, her expression shifting to both demure and arch for him. Was she really having sex with this Shontel? "So this Shontel's like...the man of the family? His dad's not there?"

She opened her mouth to say *that was a racist assumption, Dad*—another black mother abandoned by her man—but then it occurred to her, he guessed, that he was not wrong about this particular family. She hesitated, then admitted, "Shontel's dad's not around. He left or something."

He nodded. "That's a hard thing for him to deal with. Well—I'd like to meet him."

She shrugged. She was in no hurry for Shontel to meet her Dad. "Some time."

In many respects, she was sequestered from him; compartmentalized, in her mother's house, in her bedroom, in her mind, and there were compartments where Dad was not admitted. He didn't like that—but it didn't really bother him because he could feel her being with him, right here, at breakfast. She was keeping things back—but there was a sense of unspoken companionship. Dad and Erin, Erin and Dad, he could feel that. It was an invisible nourishment for both of them. He felt it at home, when she was with him, when she was rushing past him to get to the bathroom, when she was distractedly watching TV while he was reading *The New York Times*. There was an "I'm with you" feeling—it only vanished when she was mad at him, and she rarely was. She worked hard, too, at being a teenager, eye-rollingly distant from whatever he was into. She insisted on liking bands she knew he'd hate. Sometimes, like many teenagers, there was an illusion she was mentally vacant, or psychologically absent. But all the time he felt her mind as a living thing, biding its time. He could simply *feel* her here, being with him...

Every time she came to his apartment, she did something to irritate him. But he missed her painfully when she was at Linda's.

"Do I have to go to church with Mom?" she asked, at last. "I mean next time—any time?"

"I thought you wanted to be in their choir."

"I think you have to be, all church-y, with them first. It's not worth it. I'd do it if I had to be there anyway—but I *really* don't want to go. Do I have to go, Dad?"

If he let her recruit him into getting her out of church, Linda would restrict his visits even more. Maybe he could equip her to tolerate church...

"You're barely fifteen, Erin—and you live with your mom most of the time, which means you live by her rules. It won't kill you to go. But if you hate living with your mom, I told you before I can maybe get custody—but you'd have to go with me to court and tell them you can't stand living with your mom. You'd have to complain up a storm—"

She shook her head firmly. Doing that in court would hurt her mother too much. She loved her mom. She just didn't like her mom's latest little obsession.

Swift nodded. "Okay then. You live with her, then you live with her rules. It's just for a while, Erin. The people at the church are probably nice people."

"They're okay but they make me say I'm taking Jesus into my heart. Make me say it a *lot*. They won't leave me alone unless I say stuff like that. And they talk about the end of the world and the Rapture. I hate that. Like, I'm fifteen and I'm supposed to be all psyched for the end of the world, as if." She was pushing a lonely left over piece of waffle around with a spoon, making it ski across the butter and syrup as she spoke, "I'm like, 'Oh, the end of the world, I can't wait for that, *brewd*.'"

"You called them 'brewd'?"

"Yes." She looked at him with conspiratorial delight. "They had a cow."

He laughed softly. "Anyway—just pretend their little mythology trip is real, to make your mom happy. But to yourself, keep in mind 'the end of the world' already came many times—all kinds of 'religious authorities' predicted it a bunch of times, and *uh-oh*, it never happened. Then again people said, 'Year two thousand, the end is coming for sure.' Guess what? The end never showed up."

"They have all this stuff about Israel and Russia and Gog and Magog or something, they make it sound like, 'Look how the pieces fit'."

"You can take the pieces and assign them names and make them fit the way you want—that's how most so-called prophecy works. Jesus himself says in the New Testament that fire's coming out of the sky and all hell's gonna break loose, all 'before this generation has passed'—but it didn't happen. These people like to ignore that one. He did get one right about the Temple in Jerusalem being pulled down— the Romans got mad and knocked it down—but that wasn't hard to predict, with all the trouble between the Jews and the Romans. The Revelation to John—some people call it the Book of Revelations—that was written a little bit after Jesus' time, and it was about the Romans, about Nero and his boys, Rome was the Whore of Babylon—"

"Jeez, Dad, talking about ho's now!" she laughed.

"—and all the Judgment Day punishment was going to happen to the ancient Romans, in that time. You can go over it point by point, if you look at books by Biblical scholars, and see how it connects to the Romans and not to our time. I had a class on it in college. So they're just *wrong*. Only— just play along, for a while. For your mama."

She nodded gravely, sucking at her coffee. Her knee was jouncing in the aisle from the caffeine. "I've gotta pee. But Dad, couldn't there be another end of the world?"

He looked at her sharply. "Why do you say that? You mean like asteroids hitting the Earth?"

"Maybe. I mean—couldn't people...predict something but be wrong about the time or...what it all means?"

He leaned back in his chair, impressed. "You remember Ed Galivant?"

Yeah—How's Uncle Ed? I liked him."

"We'll go have dinner with him sometime. Or go fishing, he likes to fish."

"Ugh, I fucking hate fishing." Her eyes darted at him to see how he'd take the expletive.

"Hey whoa, did you pick that kind of talk up from..." He'd started to say something that just might be racist, cut it off just in time. "Come on, I'm not uptight like your mom, but you sound like white trash talking that way. You'll be marrying your cousin and moving into a..." Almost said doublewide but that made him think about what'd happened in the trailer park, all those people, all that suffering—and the impossible outcome. He didn't want to go there. "... moving into a shack with 'Bubba Joe'."

"Sor-rr-ry, already. Jeez. Everybody talks that way."

"Anyway Ed Galivant likes to say that a prophecy can be wrong and right. Like what you said. You know—they can feel that some end-of-the-world is coming and they just interpret it to fit their own religion. If there's an end coming, and if you're Muslim you see the Muslim end of the world and if you're a Sikh you get theirs and so on. But what it really would be like..." He shrugged. "No one would be able to predict that...How'd you get me talking like this?"

He shook his head, amazed at himself. He normally would automatically reassure his little girl that no apocalypse of any kind was coming, that she could grow up and get married and be a famous whatever-she-wanted and have children and marry Keith Courage. But—maybe it was the dream he'd had the night before. Couldn't remember it now. The only residue from the dream was a feeling—like someone was hammering on the door at three in the morning, and you didn't know who it could be, and you were afraid to answer the door but they *kept hammering* on it and...you *knew* you had to go see who it was...

"Anyway," he said, "it's just weird that you repeated what Ed likes to say. 'You don't know what a prophecy really means'—he likes to be cryptic. But the end isn't coming, Erin. This world's been here many millions of years. And civilization, in one shape or another, has been here for thousands of years. So don't even stress about it." Had she followed all that? He couldn't tell. "How's school?"

"Sucks."

"Good to hear things are consistent. See? The world never ends. Too sucky to end."

"Can we get me some new shoes, on the way home?"

"New shoes already?"

"Mine are, like, falling apart. And can we get me a new..."

New York City, New York

They'd only just finished building the skyscraper three months before. It still smelled of paint and rug glue and the coating they put on furniture that keeps it shiny till it's been used for a while, and Frank Birch found that agreeable, like a new car smell—the scent of thriving business.

He took a deep, contented breath as he got off the elevator, coughed, ignored the burning in his eyes, and walked down the seventeenth floor hallway, between panes of glass that served as walls for offices and conference rooms, to Conference Room 17-D. They were already in there talking. He could hear them as he approached the open door, and he glanced at his watch, wondering if he was late. He was Vice President of Marketing; he was supposed to be on top of things. But actually, according to his watch he was early.

He hurried in and found Michael O'Hanlon, the CEO, just sitting at the head of the table. He liked to be called "O'Han", awkward though it was—something to do with his fraternity. Birch was alarmed to see O'Hanlon's red, beef-fed face swelling, almost purple with barely contained fury.

"Somebody forget to tell me the meeting time was moved up, O'Han?" Birch asked, remembering to smile.

"Nobody moved the meeting," O'Hanlon said, jabbing a pencil at a donut on a plate next to his coffee cup, punching small holes in it as he spoke. "You don't have to cover your damn ass—"

Yes I do, Birch thought. And you're the reason, you prick.

"—I just pulled Turner and Hoestine out of their offices and yanked 'em in here, to hear what Griffin has to say. Sit down, I'm gonna ask him to repeat it because I didn't understand it anyway. Have a goddamn donut and open your ears."

So he isn't mad at me, Birch thought. Keep your head down, Frank, till you find out what it is.

O'Hanlon loosened his tie, as he did at every conference; his shoulders were hunched, his eyes slightly yellow, his teeth yellower, as if to go with the brown suit jacket—and a brown toupee as unconvincing as any Texas senator's. Birch had been startled on meeting him, at his hiring by O'Hanlon Business Machines; OBM had lured him away from Apple-Google a year earlier. The relatively youthful, vigorous execs at Apple-Google, demanding but not without a sense of humor, had ill prepared him for OBM's O'Hanlon.

Birch poured himself a cup of coffee from the carafe on a little side table thickly arrayed with donuts and bagels and smoked salmon. He carried it to his seat between Turner and Meredith Hoestine.

Turner was a small, tanned, athletic man with a perpetually bemused expression, and a tendency to talk cross-country skiing and rock climbing; Meredith was a willowy blond woman with a remarkably long neck that made Birch think of an illustration in *Alice in Wonderland*, and long spidery fingers. Her fingernails were too long for her fingers—how did she type those interminable memos? She wore a severe navy blue dress suit, a small flag pin on her lapel. Her eyelashes and eyebrows were so blond they were hard to see.

Birch looked idly at Hilly Griffin, at the end of the oval oak table across from O'Hanlon. He was the only one not in a suit; he wore a white Polo shirt with a fresh coffee stain down the paunchy front, jeans, and high-top sneakers. He had a self-satisfied smirk on his wide, cunning face, and dirt under his fingernails. Hilly was supposedly a scientist, but actually more an engineer.

Do they clone these engineer guys? Birch wondered idly, sipping his coffee.

"For me, it's all about Nikola Tesla, right now," Griffin said, smirking, his voice like a midget's. "Especially his work in Colorado Springs, May 1899 to 1900. Terrestrial stationary waves. Now I propose—"

"Maybe we should take pity on poor Birch here," Dudley Turner said, smiling condescendingly. "He's not up to speed."

"I confess to being in the dark here, yeah," Birch said. "Could we scroll back a little? I've heard of Tesla—competitor with Edison, did important work on radio waves, invented the remote control plane, got screwed by Edison and Westinghouse, inspired an electric car company...Croatian genius, a bit flaky maybe...I saw a Science Channel doc." He shrugged. "That's all I remember offhand. He was ahead of his time—but we're ahead of him now, aren't we?"

"In some ways, yeah—but in some ways, hell no," Griffin said.

O'Hanlon waved a pencil dismissively and then in almost

the same motion stabbed a jelly donut, pulling the pencil out to watch strawberry filling drip from the hole onto the plate. "Thing is, we've been talking about aspects of this for a couple of weeks here, uh, Birch, and we thought we had the committee pretty much organized but Ms. Hoestine here, she decided—"

Meredith blushed at that.

"—you were needed here, for some damn reason—"

"We just need a creative perspective," Meredith said quickly. "We just need...the lateral thinking thing you bring to problems, like..." She looked at her untouched bagel, finishing lamely, "...with your work on the o-Pod..."

"Well thanks, I endeavor to give satisfaction," Birch said, then winced inwardly seeing Griffin grin, looking back and forth between him and Meredith. He could almost hear Griffin thinking, I'll bet you give her satisfaction.

Birch was well aware that Meredith had a "thing" for him—something more than the oddball attraction he felt for her. Meredith's eyes lingered on him at meetings, and she found unconvincing excuses to drop in at his office, where, perching on the edge of his desk, she had a tendency to show substantially more leg than in conference rooms. She was about four years older than Birch, teetering close to forty, and maybe she felt her biological clock was ticking and, sorting through the men around her, she'd picked him. That's how it felt to him, anyway, though they'd never had an intimate conversation. Just coffee a couple of times, and a drink together at an office party when he'd first come here. "How does Mrs. Birch feel about your new job?"she'd asked. He'd dutifully confirmed for her that there was as yet no Mrs. Birch. Contemplating a liaison with Meredieth affected him alternately with fascination and revulsion. There was something almost perversely sensual in the possibilities of that swan neck, those long, long legs, but he was a politically moderate and she was well to his right, a neo-Reaganite, and, despite her careful restraint, he felt a kind of predatory desperation in her. Still, she was a major stockholder in the company, a daughter of one of the founders, and there was no doubt a relationship with her could have its material rewards.

"So, can someone catch me up on what these...these particular meetings have been about, the past couple of weeks?" Birch asked, extracting a smartphone from his inside coat pocket. He liked to take notes.

"You aren't to use that 'phone," O'Hanlon said, his voice low. "This is very confidential stuff."

Birch nodded. "Sure thing, O'Han." *So damn awkward to say 'O'Han'.* He quickly pocketed the smartphone.

"What this meeting is *about*," O'Hanlon went on, "is that everything has been going wrong. And not in the usual ways the shit hits the fan. Stock's not in such bad shape. But..." He flicked his hooded, yellowing blue eyes at Dud Turner. "What's the latest?"

Turner looked at a screen flush with the table in front of him. "Latest thing, and right in the geo-pattern too, some barge captain off the coast of Argentina refusing to dump defunct electronics. He glanced up at Birch. "Before you came here, Birch, about a year before, we had to settle a lawsuit, fifteen years of the damn thing, about recycling our hard drives—we *weren't* recycling, and of course there are millions of tons being dumped in India, Congo, Ghana, all kinds of places—"

"The point, Dud?" O'Hanlon interrupted, jamming the point of his pencil into a cruller.

"Point is, we've got to get rid of a certain amount of this stuff, and only some of it is recyclable in a way that makes any economic sense for us, so that leaves all this stuff with cadmium and arsenic and lead and mercury to be dumped, got to go somewhere, and we get these third world countries to take it in, for a price, and I guess the people close by where it's dumped started complaining, claiming birth defects or cancer or something—"

"Angling for lawsuit money, lot of fucking liars!" O'Hanlon barked.

"Oh-h, probably so," Turner said, managing to sound supportive and noncommittal, at once, "and anyway we've got to get rid of this stuff somewhere. But now we're stuck with a captain, a guy who's dumped the shit for people for years, till now this guy's always been all business all the way— supposedly threw somebody overboard for talking union on his ship!—and *suddenly* he's all bleeding heart with us, says the stuff has hurt people and he won't deliver it. Insists we take it back."

"There is a pattern of these kinds of events, you see," Meredith said.

"Tell him about the clean rooms," O'Hanlon said, shaking his head in disgust. "If that one doesn't just chap my ass..."

"Our clean rooms," Turner said, "where they're working up prototypes of our new hand-helds—we've got three supervisors saying they won't go on assigning workers because they feel the techs are at risk of cancer there. These guys have worked in this job for years and suddenly they're saying it's 'irresponsible' and why don't we spend millions of dollars redesigning the clean rooms so these guys aren't at risk—"

"Hell I take a goddamn risk every time I get out of bed!" O'Hanlon snarled, stabbing a banana cream.

"I see..." Birch said faintly. He had heard that the so-called 'clean rooms' were giving tech workers cancer, with exposure to gallium arsenide and the like, going back to the 1950s. But he'd assumed that companies like OBM had re-designed them for safety.

"It isn't just *us*," Meredith put in.

"Sure as hell isn't," O'Hanlon snorted. "LenScutter over at International Chemistry—he told me this morning, they got people blowing whistles and whining and quitting right and left. Latest one's about their export of banned pesticides— Hell what are they supposed to do with 'em? They can't sell a banned product *here*, so they sell 'em in Brazil, Africa, what have you, or they *did*, but the three guys in charge of that said they can't do it anymore, not going to take part in giving 'poor third world people' birth defects and cancer just for the sake of a little more profit, blah blah blah, *God* what self-righteous poppycock!"

Not knowing what else to do, Birch shook his head in sympathetic amazement.

"Happening all across industry," O'Hanlon said. "Well the damn list goes on and on," he continued, throwing a pencil at the stack of paper—oddly enough, though, it hit at an angle, stuck, and waggled there. "We're doing a takeover of two smaller companies and now we've got stockholders alluvafuckingsudden saying we can't downsize people out, and we've got people saying that our new burrowing landmines are immoral or something—"

Birch was startled. "Our *burrowing*—?"

"Oh, it's a new thing in Electronic Armaments. The mines are fitted with cameras, chips, they watch for people out walking and they move on these little rollers to get in their way, before they're close enough to be noticed, and they burrow down—"

"They were supposed to be able to tell a soldier from a civilian—" Meredith put in, sensing Birch's discomfort.

"Well that was too expensive, as it turned out," O'Hanlon said, waving a hand dismissively. "Anyway, a lot of stockholders started in howling about it—the very people who pushed us to get into armaments before. And people at Electronic Armaments refused to work on it anymore. And it goes on. What the *devil* happened to loyalty! Same pattern—it's coming out of the blue. We've got rebellion, people pretending big-ass moral outrage everywhere we turn. It's a pattern, Birch!"

"Uh, well," Birch said, trying to wrap his head around it and failing, "could be there's some, uh, *propaganda* reaching these people. An email campaign or something..."

O'Hanlon and Turner shook their heads with eerie simultaneity, and Griffin, sneering outright, said, "You are so very far off the mark, my friend. There's way too much of this pattern. I mean, we had people bombarding us with emails, pamphlets, petitions for years, and no one cared. Then all of a sudden on their own, people change course—turning into bleeding hearts."

"They don't explain it, at all, themselves?"

"They're claiming to have had visions and psychic experiences all starting with 'cones of light' and colors and...so on. We think it's a mind control device devised by terrorists—or maybe the Chinese. Maybe trying to undermine our economy. They've got a lot more technical know-how than they like to let on. They steal what they need. And they could've had some breakthrough we haven't gotten onto. I mean, think about it, all those political prisoners they've got—an almost infinite pool of experimental subjects." He sighed in envy.

"And Christ what rigmarole our partners at ChemFutures go through to get people to test anything on," O'Hanlon said, his face twisted with disgust.

"So," Griffin went on, licking his lips with excitement, "we started looking for a pattern, see—and we've got *geopatterns*, for one thing. The thing manifests in specific places, literally every thousand miles, east to west, and in lines running north and south. In between, nothing—so far. We've tested the water and food in those areas, nothing special. So we got our particle-scan satellite to watch for any indication of unusual energy sources, any anomalous transmission—"

"*What* kind of satellite?" Birch asked.

"I had to ask that one too," Meredith chuckled.

"I don't understand the damn thing either," O'Hanlon shrugged.

"See, it's part of our system for improving Wi-Fi," Griffin said. "We're trying to figure out how we lose signals on the edges of hotspots. There's so much electronic interference out there, it's hard to sort through it all, right? So we got a satellite up there that watches for all kinds of unusual magnetic, electrical phenomena, solar storms, all kinds of atmospheric high-energy particle phenomena—even neutrinos."

"That was tricky," Turner chimed in. "Those neutrino things are hard to detect—they used to have these big underground facilities for it—"

He broke off his unconvincing attempt at sounding

as if knew something about the subject, seeing Griffin's contemptuous glowering.

Griffin went on, "Anyway, there were bursts of neutrinos detected in exactly those areas. You know—where people are giving us problems. They seem to be *locally generated* instead of coming from some supernova on the other side of the galaxy somewhere, like they usually do. We think the neutrinos are actually epiphenomena. Just an outward reaction from the real wave that's having this effect on people..."

"So uh, what's the *real* source?" Birch asked, just as if he were keeping up.

"We don't know—exactly," Griffin said, suddenly irritable. "We think it's... there's a theoretical particle, one that's supposedly everywhere you find sentience, a particle special to brain activity, called the 'IAMton'. Only a relative few IAMtons in a spider's brain; more in a cat's brain; a lot more than that in a human being's brain. That particle, when it's transmitted along a carrier wave, maybe along a stream of neutrinos, can affect how people *think*. It can affect you like LSD, almost. Only...more specific. Anyway you could maybe use it to carry ideas right into someone's head."

Turner shrugged. "If this IAMton thing even exists. It's theory."

"Sure," Griffin conceded. "But this thing behaves like the IAMton is predicted to behave. But there you're getting into quantum physics. Not my specialty."

"And the *point* anyway is just to put a goddamn *stop* to it," O'Hanlon insisted. "Some kind of mind-control's being spread that hurts business—we stop it, bingo, simple. We block it."

"Right," Griffin said. He looked at Birch. "This is sensitive. A few years ago, we paid some guys at the FBI to photocopy Tesla's papers for us."

Birch rocked back in his chair a little at the offhand revelation of bribery. "The FBI?"

"Yeah. When Tesla died in the 1940s, J. Edgar Hoover seized his notes and diagrams because Tesla was talking about making death rays and the like. Tesla's nephew got some of the notes but the Feds kept some of the juiciest stuff. There were diagrams for generating something he called 'terrestrial stationary waves'. The whole Earth's used as a conductor, see, it's like a tuning fork reacting to certain frequencies—you can transmit power right through the planetary crust. Could be the Chinese are using it themselves. Maybe they discovered it independently—and maybe that's what's causing these effects. Psychological fallout from electromagnetic attack, see. But Tesla gave us a possible method for blocking this...this impulse. Got a place up in the mountains I'm setting up, site of our new company retreat. No housing up there but we can use the property for tests...."

"I see...I think," Birch said. Electromagnetic attack? Mind control? It all sounded like ranting to him, conspiracy theory, an organized panic. He'd never heard anything like it at OBM before.

A thought occurred to him. *Is this a gag?* Were they pulling his leg, testing his credulity?

He looked around at the others, each face in turn. There was none of that tension, the effect of holding back laughter, that would go with a practical joke.

Meredith seemed to divine his thinking—which startled him a bit in itself. "He's serious, Frank, if that's what you're wondering," she said gently. "All this is for real. I thought they were pulling my leg at first."

"Hell yes it's serious!" O'Hanlon barked. "We're losing money! Check the damn newspapers! Oh we've kept most of it out of the big media—managed to hide the fact there's a pattern. We don't want people jumping on any bandwagons. But you can see a lot of reporting on those items that Turner's got there—it's for real, all right! Too goddamned real!"

Birch nodded. "But my part in this is...a little murky. I'm—in marketing."

"Thing is, in order to set up the shields," Meredith said, "we have to go right into communities and—that'll be noticeable. So we have to think of some way to...market

them, in a sense, though the public's not going to pay for
them—"

"We'll get the government to pay us for them later,"
O'Hanlon said. "We're working that out with them.
Halliburton's going to miss out on this one."

Meredith nodded, waited to make sure O'Hanlon was
done, and went on. "So we need to create a...an impression
it's something else. I mean, we don't want to just say 'by the
way we're sending some experimental electromagnetic wave
patterns into the planetary crust' or we'll have the EPA all
over us and the Sierra Club demanding tests and there's no
time for that."

Birch toyed with a piece of bagel. "The obvious, uh, cover
story is, like Griffin mentioned—Wi-Fi. Improving Wi-Fi is
the Holy Grail for us right now anyway. So we can maintain
these things are harmless boosters for wireless."

"That's not bad," Griffin said. "Might fit into the need for
a control group, for the first experiment."

Birch sipped his coffee and asked, "Control group?"

"Sure," Griffin said, abstractedly, thinking it through on
the spot, "someone to test it on, at the retreat. We can say
we've tested the thing on some volunteers."

"You mean—volunteers from OBM?"

"No, no, they're too inquisitive, tendency to chatter on the
Internet. I want some group of clueless...Well, I've got some
people in mind. We'll do this first test in the mountains,
then get the things distributed around the country. We'll
have to put them on trailers, or something, park them, for
the time being."

"Long as we can make it sound like something the EPA
doesn't care about," O'Hanlon said, tapping another pencil.
"We used to have the EPA under our thumb but..." He shook
his head sadly. "Another thing going to hell in a hand basket.
The business atmosphere in this country is just...just *toxic*."

"If we say it's very low-power transmission," Birch went
on, "that should work. Possibly it could be a *fait accompli*,
just a done deal, before the EPA even notices. We could work
up the explanation for people who ask..."

"I think it's a brilliant...a brilliant stroke," Meredith said, smiling dewily at him.

"Yeah, run me off a proposal, get it on my desk tomorrow morning, there, Birch," O'Hanlon growled, getting up and checking his watch. "I've got a meeting over golf this morning. Going to close a big acquisition—got to remember to let the son of a bitch beat me at least nine holes!"

They all remembered to laugh at that—not too much and not too little—as O'Hanlon headed out the door.

Griffin was next to go, muttering about checking some particle stats, whatever that meant. Turner gathered up his papers, and went out with him, talking neutrinos.

Birch was left alone with Meredith and an inner cauldron of mixed feelings. He was appalled, confused, intrigued, and tense with worry, all at once. He could feel Meredith watching him.

He glanced at her and she busied herself putting papers in her briefcase. While she was closing it, she asked, as if as an afterthought, "Frank—would you like me to help you put the proposal together? This evening—at my place?"

He cleared his throat, hesitating. Then he thought, When was the last time I got laid?

"Sure," he said. "Sounds good."

4

Sacramento, California

SWIFT flipped through his Rolodex, found Kellogg, Sam, Lt., SPD. Glancing at his watch, seeing it was 2:23 p.m., he decided that Lieutenant Kellogg might be in his office about now—he worked two to ten p.m.—maybe getting his warrants together. He dialed the Sacramento Police Department, extension 107, leaned back in his squeaking chair, putting his feet up on his desk as the phone rang on the other end.

Swift was tired, and sick of this cubicle. Tired of sitting here hour after hour making calls.

He'd spent some of the morning making the calls he was supposed to be making, following up on the new gang task force, and some of it calling around on "the Galivant story" as he thought of it. Only, it wasn't just Galivant anymore. A *Bee* correspondent in Southeast Asia claimed sweatshops were closing "by the dozens".

Supervisors walking out on them, people saying they were "going home to wait" but not clear about what they were waiting for.

"Kellogg here."

"Yeah, Sam, it's Jim Swift over at the *Bee*. Listen, can you give me anything on that task force, my editor's—"

"I'm off the task force, as of about five minutes ago." Kellogg's voice sounded odd, as if he was thinking about something else entirely. "I quit it. I've got to go home and think. Just have to think."

"Why, they didn't like your methods? What happened?"

"No, nothing like that, nobody took me off, I'm taking myself off. Things are strange out there. We don't know what we're dealing with anymore. I guess it's good but—I don't know. Some of these kids—you can see how they got there. Sometimes you just look at them and see it. I just never saw it before..."

"Sam—you have some kind of...experience?"

Kellogg hesitated. "I don't want to talk about it, Swift. I don't want to talk to anyone. I want to find my wife."

"I thought you were divorced."

"I am. I sure as hell am. But she's..."

To Swift's amazement, he realized that Kellogg was weeping. He had never met a more hardened cop than Sam Kellogg. Was he drunk?

"You been knocking a few back at work, bro?"

"No, no nothing like that. I just need to go home. Maybe see if I can find Maria. I don't want to wait alone."

"Wait for what, Kellogg?"

"You looked at the sky, this afternoon, Swift?"

"The sky?"

"The sky, over Sacramento. To the east."

And Kellogg hung up.

A State Park Near Sacramento, California

"Galivant!" Swift called. "You here or not?" There was no immediate reply from the small crowd gathered on the hilltop. A few people glanced at him and then looked back at the sky. "Galivant!"

Then a bald head popped into view on the other side of one of the granite boulders that cragged the top of the hill. "I'm over here, Swift!"

Swift looked at the sky once more, wished he'd brought

his digital camera, then walked toward Galivant over the slippery, uneven turf, thinking it was pointless, there was already a TV camera crew here. The images would be all over TV and the Internet, and people would say they were Photoshopped, a hoax, or something. Before today—he'd have thought it was a hoax too. Before today—he'd be right.

He wondered if the images would be suppressed.

Christ, Swift thought. I'm thinking like a conspiracy theorist. They're always wrong. *Almost* always.

He found Galivant sitting on the ground, leaning back against the boulders, legs sprawled out. Galivant was smiling faintly, eyes glistening in the late afternoon light as he looked up at the sky. On his lap was his ubiquitous patched-together briefcase.

Beyond Galivant was a group of people with the look of a church outing. One of them was vaguely familiar. Was that tall one, with the long hair, the guy from The Church of the Revelation in Christ?

After he'd taken Erin home, Swift googled the Church of R in C, because Erin had talked about it. He hit an elaborate tithe-demanding Web site with pictures of the church's movers and shakers. One of them was a man with a neat beard, long white-streaked hair tied back, a wide friendly, lined face: the Reverend Elmer Colbertson; another was George Colbertson, Elmer Colbertson's son, a young man with a lean, exactingly tanned face, a self-deprecating smile on his dark red lips, and blond hair that looked like a rock star from the 1990s, not too long or too short or too straight or too wild. It was as if they had gone to pains to select a look that distinguished them from the usual helmet-haired televangelists. And it was that young man, Swift thought, who seemed to have gathered the group of sixty or so people with him, all of them gazing at the Signs and Portents in the sky. The Signs must have caught him by surprise, since there were only sixty people out of his mega-church here. Colbertson seemed quite surprised by what he was seeing.

Swift sat beside Galivant and gazed at the Signs too. They

had to be a sign of *something*, he thought, looking at them. But of what?

The clouds...

The clouds, a range of cumulus, were spontaneously re-shaping—a vast expanse of cloud was breaking up, instantly forming into symmetrically arranged spheres, almost like bowling pins awaiting the ball; but now the rows and stacks of spheres rearranged into the shape of a pyramid, *two* pyramids meeting at the base, one upside down pointing at the ground. The whole thing was a diamond comprised of interconnected spheres—it collapsed, re-forming into a shape that was almost a face. It was a three-dimensional design, something like a head but with almost cubistic angles and switchbacks in it. This cryptic figure rearranged itself in a labyrinthine pattern of cloud-stuff, with a spinning gyroscopic figure whirling up the channels of the labyrinth— and then rearranged itself again to become something like a cube of buzzing bees, but the bees flew apart to form a shape that was almost galactic...till it re-formed into a tetrahedron.

Then he saw the birds: a great flock of starlings, flying up to mesh themselves between the viewers on the hill and the vision in the sky, the birds flying with a precision that made Swift think of the US Navy's Blue Angels, the flock exactly dividing into two halves, one going north, the other south, then curving down into spirals that spun to either side of the cloud display, clearly a part of the overall composition, while large flying insects gathered, closer at hand, to give shading and definition to the abstractions, the shape now like a circuit board but then again like a cityscape—but on the other hand really something more like a coral reef of unusual regularity, until...

"You know, Jim, what this makes me think of," Galivant muttered, "is when I took peyote with Terrence McKenna and Mike Kawitzky. When I was in my whole 'shamanism' period. This is like the stuff you see when you close your eyes, when you're on peyote or psilocybin. Maybe stuff you see at a time like that is just messages we don't know how to decrypt."

"How long's it been doing this?" Swift asked.

"About an hour," Galivant responded. "You should've come right when I first called. Seen the whole series..."

"It's got the most amazing patterns," interrupted Lymon Fuji, coming up behind them. He was an unusually tall Asian-American guy wearing a baggy army surplus jacket. Galivant and Swift had known him almost as long as they'd known one another. More than once Fuji had charged into Swift's office at the *Bee*, claiming to have a world-shaking story of the paranormal for him. Swift had only gone along once, to see some fairly shabby "UFO landing circles" on a farm near Redding. A waste of a whole day Swift had never forgiven him for. There'd been footprints around the circle, a few feet from it, where you could see someone had walked as they'd pulled weighted boards to make the "UFO landing" mark.

Gazing at the sky, Galivant shook his head. "It's almost like it's going through endless variations on a theme—a long, long exposition of some kind."

"Those are crop circle shapes, man," Fuji said, his heavy eyebrows bobbing. He shivered as a chilly wind fluttered his lank black hair, and buttoned up his army jacket as he spoke. "The same style of ideograms—if that's what they are—but faster, because we've come to a key moment. Something the aliens are warning us about." The glum, humorless Fuji, Galivant remembered, published an occasional semi-professional magazine called *Spokesmen for the Beyond*.

The crowd moaned and *ooh*ed and whispered and wept...

"I agree that we're at a key moment," Galivant said, "maybe even a critical-mass moment. But I don't think it has anything to do with aliens—or crop circles. Crop circles are hoaxed, man."

Swift turned to him, open-mouthed. "How many times did I tell you that and you said, 'No way, they can't *all* be' and I said—"

"I know, I know. I was wrong. I was checking it out in England all winter. It's all hoaxes. They use computer programs to design the things and they have a system for making them and they pretend there's something unusual about the grass afterward but there really isn't—"

"Galivant how can you say that while this is happening right before your eyes?" Fuji demanded.

"Because this isn't the same thing. It's...hard to describe why but I'm sure of it. This is a whole phenomenon to itself."

Swift shook his head, watching the display in the sky, shuddering with each new configuration, muttering to Galivant, "It's like when you didn't have something miraculous you had to believe in anything that came along. But when something really miraculous is there you suddenly see the other stuff was bullshit."

Staring at the sky, Galivant shrugged. "Maybe. None of it matters now. This matters. This *is* miraculous."

"That's right," George Colbertson said, strolling up to them, smiling. "He works signs and wonders in heaven. Daniel 6:27. But can you read the signs?"

Fuji snorted and walked away, shaking his head.

"No," Swift said, "can you read them, Reverend?"

"Yes," Colbertson said, turning to look at the sky. "That one says 'Submit to the Will of God.' Now it adds, 'The True Christ returns, the False Christ will make a great noise. Heed him not!'"

"Really? How'd you get that out of it?"

"The voice of God resounds in my heart!"

"I gotcha," Swift said, nodding noncommittally. "I've been wondering, though...could it be an artificial thing, like, created by lasers or holograms or...?"

"The animals too?" Galivant asked, glancing at him, eyebrows raised. "The insects, the birds?"

"It's stopped!" someone shouted.

It was true—the clouds had subsided into ordinary cloud shapes, the symmetrical figures in the sky dispersing in the high winds...

"I know you need a beer, Swift," Galivant said.

Swift nodded, getting up, feeling overwhelmed by the charge of unexpressed emotions. "My heart's pounding, man."

The younger Colbertson was regarding them gravely.

"Come with us, instead, and pray. Thousands will gather there, and you'll find that your heart is thumping for glad tidings...the great question is in the air!"

"'Draft or bottle?', that's the great question," Swift said, ignoring Colbertson. He followed the crowd as it began to move down the slope; it was dispersing like the clouds, the shape of the crowd pulled apart much the same way, people drifting back into the comfortable, much-maligned predictability of the mundane world.

But as he and Galivant went, they found Colbertson's followers around them, heading the same way, chattering happily. "It's finally come!" "It's really here!" "It's scary but it's beautiful!" "Praise God! Praise Jesus!"

"It's exactly as predicted!" said a chirpy, plump middle-aged woman with a cap of dyed-blond hair and a wide, flexible mouth. "We should never have questioned the Good News."

Galivant gave another of his derisive spurts of laughter. "You people are going to distort this and who knows what that's going to lead to. Look, the Bible is all muddied up! There were conflicting translations, scribes interpolating their own notions, texts chosen for political reasons and other texts, just as valid, got discarded. You can't be literal-minded about a mess like that." He stumbled over a hummock of grass, cursing under his breath, catching Swift's arm to keep his footing.

"A mess!" the woman burst out, shocked. "How can you even bring yourself to say that about the Bible?"

"Do you even *know* the Bible, lady?" Galivant asked. He looked pale, to Swift, shaken by what he'd seen. He was trying to get a grip on this thing. Process of elimination—start by eliminating what it isn't.

"Of *course* I know the Bible—"

"Do you? What was on the stone tablets Moses brought from God?"

She solemnly and proudly recited the Ten Commandments as most people think of them. "You shall have no other God before me. You shall not worship a graven image. You shall not take the Lord's name in vain. Remember the Sabbath..."

When she'd done, Galivant said, "No, uh-uh, that's a list from Exodus 20, verses 2 to 17. But Moses just says that stuff out loud, he didn't provide it carved on stones. The stuff carved on stones is from Exodus 34, verses 14 to 26. You know what the last one is? 'You shall not boil a goat kid in milk'."

"Technically that's what it says," said Colbertson, bringing his group to a stop at a flat place partway down the hill. "But—"

"So have you ever worked on Sunday, lady?" Galivant demanded, ignoring Colbertson, glowering at the woman.

"Well..." She reddened.

"If you have, we have to stone you to death. Says so in Numbers 15:32-36. Moses had a man stoned to death for working on the Sabbath. You have any children? A son?"

"Yes," the woman said distractedly, rubbing her temples. "I have a son."

"He ever rebellious?"

"They all are sometimes..."

"You have to stone your son to death, if you're a Biblical literalist. Says so in Deuteronomy 21:18, if your kid is rebellious you stone him to death. Don't believe me, look it up. And if you're not a virgin on your wedding night, you have to be stoned to death. Look it up, it's in Deuteronomy chapter 22."

He was surrounded by gaping faces; he blurted all this in a single long impassioned rant, his face blotchy, his hands shaking, a purging of pent up emotion.

"In another part of the Old Testament, God tells us it's okay to sell your daughter into slavery. You know what? Apparently incest is okay too: Lot was approved by God, he was beloved of the old boy, right? And Lot had sex with his daughters in a cave after they left Sodom! Look it up!"

Colbertson's followers hissed reproaches; eyes narrowed. Galivant lumbered onward.

"How about the murder of entire tribes by God's chosen people—except the captured virgin women given to the priest as his due, of course—that's in Numbers 31, look it up!"

"Oh surely that's not..."

"Oh but it is! And lady, did you know you're worth half of what a man is worth? Says so in Leviticus. Look it up! Want to talk about the New Testament? How about where the four gospels contradict one another—like what happens after Jesus resurrects varies from gospel to gospel! So how is that *literal* truth?"

"How can he say such things, after what he's seen today?" a buttoned-down college-age boy demanded. "He's got to be working for the other side!"

"A false prophet!" Colbertson agreed, nostrils quivering. "Turn away from him!"

But some of them were turning toward him—eyes flashing, teeth bared, and Swift began to be afraid for Galivant.

"How about your book of Revelation, then!" Galivant shouted, spinning, waving his arms, to include them all in his diatribe. "It says only a hundred-forty-four thousand out of the whole damn world will be 'saved' and they're all males! That doesn't include you, girlfriend! *Look it up!*" The woman was backing away from him, white-faced now, stumbling on the slope, but Galivant continued, shouting at the angry faces arrayed around Colbertson, "If you're Biblical literalists then you'd better start looking around for the Roman Empire—the prophecies in Revelations are all about Rome! Any Biblical scholar will tell you that! The 'Beast' that 'comes out of the sea' in Revelations is Rome coming across the Mediterranean and the guy marked '666' was the Roman Emperor Domitian! *Look it up!* And what's the last thing they say in Revelation, written almost two thousand years ago? 'Behold, I come quickly!' Is two thousand years quickly, you idiots?"

"This man—" Colbertson glared at Galivant, "—was sent here to test our faith—to cast aspersions on the Bible—" His hand chopping down to emphasize the words, as it did when he was on the big stage of the enormous mega-church auditorium: the auditorium where Linda herded Erin into the audience, pushing her into their doctrine, Swift thought, like a goat-kid to be boiled in milk.

"These aspersions, these insults against the sacred—" Colbertson was shouting now. "—are just the beginning of what you can expect as the Antichrist sends his followers to beat the drum for him!"

There was a general hostile milling toward Galivant at this.

"He's not insulting your beliefs!" Swift shouted, slipping between Galivant and the increasingly belligerent crowd around Colbertson. "He's just saying the Bible can't be taken too literally!"

"If Jesus did come back he'd kick your ass, Colbertson!" Galivant shouted, as Swift dragged him away. "You and the other hypocrites are distorting his message!"

"Galivant, shut up, man," Swift hissed, as they hurried down the path to the parking lot, "or they're gonna get back to old-time religion and stone your ass right here and mine with it!"

Galivant turned to Swift with a shrug of apology. "It just...it's like Colbertson's the first lemming over the cliff, brewd, and they're all following him!"

"Yeah I know, come on..."

"Hey Swift, yo—isn't that your daughter, getting in that bus?"

They'd gotten to the screen of eucalyptus around the parking lot, walked across the dry, curling leaves to find three small school buses loading Colbertson's followers.... and then Swift saw his daughter.

Linda and Erin were getting on the farther bus, the last passengers to board it.

Swift ran toward the bus, shouting, wanting desperately to talk to Erin—but the bus doors closed, and the bus drove away. His own car was blocked by the traffic leaving the parking lot, and Colbertson's people refused to talk to him.

No one would tell him where the buses were going.

5

Peshawar, Pakistan

THERE was this to say for the prison, it was usually dry. But Akbar didn't think he could elude the men much longer, in this new cell. There were many of them and they would beat him, and worse, given the slightest imagined provocation. He had learned to make sores on his skin, with scratches and feces, so they'd not want to touch him. The fever he got was worth it. He had heard that in other countries children were not put in with men, in the prisons. He wished he could be there. There, or dead.

Sometimes he thought he might be willing to put out one of his eyes, in trade, if only someone would let him see the sky. How long had it been?

He was always hungry but he had always been hungry outside the prison. His father had sold him to al-Jalud, to work, to offer his rear if needed, and he'd thought that he was at the bottom of life, the very bottom, till coming here; he lived with a feeling like being stabbed all the time, after his father sold him, but he couldn't feel much now, except he wanted to see the sky, and perhaps a parrot, there was an African parrot he'd seen in the market...it was blue and red...

Hassim stood over Akbar now, a great reeking lump of a man, bristling with beard, his teeth black, one of his eyes gone the color of a fish long dead. "Boy," said Hassim, "they bring the food soon—you will give me your food. Every day you will give it to me."

Akbar knew he should refuse or negotiate, but he felt a deadness this day that frightened him. First the deadness then fear at the deadness. Like he wasn't there at all but floating somewhere, watching. He wanted to ask Hassim to kill him. He had asked a man to kill him here before but the man said, "If you get me some money or tobacco."

He did not have those things.

Hassim's fingers closed around his throat. "Do you agree, boy? Your food?"

"*Hassim Jahwunal!*" came a voice, sharp with warning, from the front of the cell. "Move away from the boy!"

Hassim released Akbar and turned, with the others, to see who had bothered to interrupt the robbing of a child in this prison.

The head jailer approached; two other guards stood behind him with their submachine guns in their hands, both looking equally bewildered. The jailer, one al-Khan, was a hunched sallow man in an ill-fitting uniform, with pitted skin and thick glasses; he had barely acknowledged Akbar the one time Akbar had tried to speak to him.

Now al-Khan approached with tears streaming from under his thick rimless glasses. "You will come with me, boy," said al-Khan.

"The guards will sell the boy into another slavery!" someone jeered.

Al-Khan addressed the men in the cell. "I wish I could put you all to death as a kindness to end your miserable lives, you walking dead," said al-Khan, astonishing his guards even more than the prisoners. "Now—move aside! Let the boy through!"

Ahbar came hurriedly to stand by al-Khan. It appeared he was to be sold to another owner, to work as a servant or in a factory. Such a life could be as bad as prison, but Akbar walked eagerly out of the cell ahead of them, glad at least to be free of it for a few minutes.

There was a discussion of some kind between the guards and al-Khan, the men daring to argue with him. They used words Akbar didn't understand. One of the words was unauthorized, which Akbar thought meant something like "forbidden".

Al-Khan told the guards to shut up and do as they were told.

Akbar was led through a series of corridors, then across the prison's courtyard, to the gate. The astonishment mounted, so that Akbar himself was soon feeling it, as al-Khan, unaccompanied now by the guards, ordered the gate opened and guided Akbar through it to the street.

Akbar trembled with disorientation—and then was thunderstruck to see the hazy blue of the sky overhead.

"Oh!" he cried, hardly aware of the words. "Oh but Allah is great!"

But his common sense returned and it came to him that al-Khan was likely planning to sell him to someone. He looked around for the buyer, but saw only a truck trundling by a few old women, their heads covered in scarves, hunched in the shadow of a wall selling meat pastries.

"Boy," al-Khan declared, "Allah has come to me today, and said 'Look about you! I lift the veils from your eyes!'"

Akbar looked at him. "Did Allah do that, boss?" He knew he should run, before this madman came to his senses and realized that he was a man and men did not wear veils, and it must have been a waking dream. But he thought the man would only grab him if he ran.

"Allah showed me how things were with me and those around me..." Al-Khan raised his trembling hands, gesturing grandly. "I saw every detail of my life and those around; I saw the destiny in a fly as it flew past me! I saw every particle of dust whirling by! I saw all of us asleep, all of us dreaming dreams of cruelty to satisfy our hungers, and, as if drawn on a string, I went to look at the prisoners and I saw you through the bars, squatting there, and that Hassim coming to beat you! And I knew what I must do, though I will surely be jailed for it. I know something of your case— you came from a man who bought you from your father. But that man caught you stealing food, and you ran away and the police arrested you for theft and so you came to me. But yesterday there came a man looking for you, and he had no money, so we would not release you to him..."

Akbar dared not imagine...

"—the man professed to be your father. I said to him, 'You who sold your son, why do you now come to claim him—is it so that you can sell him again?' He said to me that he had a vision of lights, turning lights, which carried the voice of Allah, and I mocked him and struck him across the face and had him thrown out on the street. And behold— today, the same lights come to me...and look, here is the man, come again, as he said he would..."

Akbar was almost horrified to see his father—because that meant either he was dreaming, or his father would soon sell him again. He really should run, now...

But his father was saying, "I only have a little money, but I can give you that, Supervisor al-Khan, and tomorrow—"

"No need! Like you, my eyes have been opened by Allah! Take the boy! Take him home and only there! I go now to see who else deserves to be freed from my darkness! Go!"

Akbar turned to run, not wanting to be taken in by such lies and sold again, but he was confused, and stumbled, and his father swept him up in his arms and kissed him and said, "No boy, do not run, I will take you home to your mother, and pray to Allah to forgive me for the unforgivable..."

Akbar suffered himself to be carried, and waited for the good dream—so rare, anymore, a good dream—to end. But it did not end. It was the world that ended, in a way, for nothing else could make this glory a reality.

Thank Allah, the world was ending...

Van Nuys, California

"My name..."

The man hesitated for a moment, eyes squinted. Obviously he was going to make up a name, Ama decided.

"...my name is Dennis Boyce."

"Is it? Do you work for Silk Scents?"

"For whom?" He looked at her attentively: a man neither young nor old, in black turtleneck and jeans and sneakers, his face showing some wear, some softness around jaws a day late for shaving, a blueness smudging the skin under the brown eyes; curly brown hair, speckled with gray, falling over his collar. A handsome face, really, but tired—and yet the eyes showed a startling energy.

"This company—the one I'm—" She pointed to the building she was standing in front of, a big concrete warehouse structure, grayer than usual in the thin, unseasonable morning rain. "You saw my sign, right?"

Ama held the sign up:

SILK SCENTS
TORTURES!

"Yes I...ah, now I read it. You will forgive a certain hesitancy, there seems to be some damage here, pathways disrupted. I suspect a use of intoxicants. Shortly I'll have made other connections, and absorbed the dialect and my speech will be quite...standardized."

Okay, he was insane. Time to walk around the building again. If he followed she'd whip out the cell and call 911, fast.

"What derivation are you?" he asked, as she turned away.

"What?" She turned back to him but was slowly backing away. Keeping him happy, as she beat a retreat.

"Your...ancestral..."

"What race? I'm...a mix. Ama's a Japanese name, my dad's Japanese, but my mom was half black, half Hispanic. She was a professor," she added, wondering why it was important to say that. And then wondering why she wondered it. This man had a strange effect on her. For one thing, she had stopped backing away from him, though he was a stranger, one who seemed mad, in a place where she was all alone.

"I see you more clearly now," he remarked.

Yes, he was definitely insane—the megalomaniacal

variety. She started backing up again. "'Kay, I'm gonna go on by myself."

"I can feel the suffering from this building too," he said. "It's why I stopped here. I was passing through the area, on a bus, and I felt a great mass of suffering concentrated here in one building, and walked to find it. What is the nature of the torture you mentioned?"

"They torture small animals with acrid chemicals, they spray them into their eyes, inject them into their skin. They keep the animals in small cages. Mostly dogs and cats and some mice. Some get cancer and die slowly, some die quick, some survive and go insane in the confinement."

"I suspect...the dogs and cats...no, the cats...would like to get at the mice. Is that right?" He seemed to be asking the question experimentally. He remembered—that's how it seemed—to smile.

"Uhhh...whatever. Got to go."

"Would you like to stop the suffering in there? Show me the entrance, so that I can save time, and I will go in..."

Ama stopped backing up again, now about ten feet from him. "Okay, look, our policy is, we just demonstrate. Normally I have three other people with me... they'll be here soon. But we—we don't *do* that...that disruption stuff. They'll call it terrorism, and nowadays...."

Oh—I see a door, there! That's a doorway, is it not?"

"It is...yeah. And it's locked. They get deliveries there and if you mess with it the security guard will come around and kick your ass. There's a camera up there, above it, see? Got to go. Good luck..."

But she found herself lingering, watching as he walked up to the door, and put his hand on the knob, seeming to caress it.

The door popped open. The sounds of dogs barking, animals yowling, came out onto the empty sidewalk.

She stared, waiting for whoever'd opened it from the other side to come out. Probably the security guard had seen the guy coming at the door, on the camera, sent somebody to chase him off...

No one came out. The man who said his name was Dennis Boyce—had she ever *asked* his name? No, she hadn't—smiled at her and gestured awkwardly for her to come, and then he turned and walked into the building. After a moment, she walked up to the door and looked in, just to see what he was going to do.

This is stupid, Ama thought. I should get out of here. They'll arrest me with him, they'll assume I'm working with him...

An incongruous silence reigned in the big room. The dogs had stopped barking, the cats had stopped yowling. The room was unsettlingly quiet. Most of the dogs were smallish terriers; there were a few beagles, dozens of mutts; they were all staring from rows of steel cages not quite big enough for them to turn around in; cats were caged on other aisles, all of them tattered like moth-eaten fur wraps, their eyes as dead as the eyes of stuffed animals. They stared. The sight wrenched Ama's heart.

The smell of the cages hit her, then. She stopped, blinking. Boyce didn't seem to notice the silence, the staring, the smells, but only stalked through the room, smiling faintly, looking from side to side.

"So these animals are for medical experiments?" he asked. "To find cures for diseases?"

"Diseases? Not at all," she said, stepping through the door, into the warehouse-sized room. "At least you could *argue* that kind of animal testing is necessary—though there's usually an alternative. But this is all about perfume and cosmetics, that kind of thing. They develop new cosmetics, test them on animals...they use extreme amounts of raw chemicals. Completely needless stuff. We have enough cosmetics in the world. We don't really need them at all, really."

He nodded, looking into the eyes of a small terrier nearby. "The suffering emanates from the constraint—as much as the pain of the experiments," he said. "They're becoming..." He seemed to think for a moment. "Psychotic. Becoming psychotic from feeling trapped in a small space day after day, endlessly. It's worse than the physical torture—such things always are, as they reach into the creature's Substantive Being."

"Their what?"

But then a supervisor in a lab coat burst into the room, with a security guard close behind; the guard had a gun in his hand, held down at his side. A spindly man with thin hair, the security guard had a look on his face he'd probably seen in a movie about commandos. The lab supervisor, a stocky graying man with a close-cut beard and a bulbous, red-veined nose, wire-rim glasses, seemed to shiver in icy fury as he stumped down the aisle between cages toward them. "You people are under arrest! You don't want to get shot, you put your hands on your heads, *right goddamn now!*"

"You should let me say that," the security guard grumbled. He pointed the gun at Boyce and bellowed, "Come on, hands on your heads!"

In a movement that seemed more polite than frightened, Boyce put his hands on his head. "Like this?"

"That's...well yeah." The supervisor broke off, shaking his head. He had an ID badge hanging around his neck that said, *Silk Scents* and below that, *Roger Capwell.*

"Okay now," the security guard said, "You too girlie, hands on your head." Everyone ignored him.

"Mr. Capwell—" Ama said. "The door just opened so I thought we could come in. We're bearing witness to...to..."

She broke off, shuddering, as the pulses spread through the air, seeming to come from the space directly over Boyce's head. She felt the vibrations palpably, in flesh and bone; felt them humming between her teeth, making her feel nauseated and elated at the same time.

Suddenly the dogs began barking and the cats began yowling again. The cages clamored with their sound.

Exactly then, the room came into focus. It had *seemed* in focus before. But she had only seen it fuzzily.

She saw the dust on the spider webs on the orange girders overhead; she saw paint bubbles on the girders; she saw cracks in the concrete floor, and powdered concrete accumulated in those cracks; she looked into a cat's eyes and saw the workings of its iris, the crystalline lines, the simple, translucent glow of life itself. For the first time she saw life as a separate thing, as a field emanating from the animals in the cages and the four human beings standing between them; she saw pores on Capwell's face; she saw small bits of foam gathered at the corners of his lips; she saw dandruff on the security guard's shoulders; she saw fear and sadness in the guard's eyes; she saw cat fur wisping by in the air, blown on the air conditioned breeze; she saw a faint tremor in Capwell's hands; she smelled bourbon in the air, too, from Capwell; she saw a dog in a cage lying stiffly with its tongue lolling to one side, and she realized it was dead; she saw a fat fly buzz overhead and she saw the iridescent detail of its wings, their each beat visible. She felt her nervous system as clearly as a guitarist feels strings under her fingers; she saw her thoughts, like faint neon images, superimposed over her vision, one pursuing the next...

She turned to look at Boyce, saw the outline of a man and, within the outline, as within a man-shaped bottle, she saw a shimmering, living void; a thinking emptiness transmitted from another world.

"Oh fuck!" she blurted, and the two syllables seem to echo with endless ramifications. Oh as the *Oh!* of orgasm and the *Oh!* of surprise and the *Oh!* of pain and also the O of 0, zero, emptiness—and the "fuck" was coupling, with a reverberation through its Germanic roots, and...

The security guard was running away, shouting, firing the gun into the ceiling, and the booms resounded, bullets ricocheted, while Capwell fell to his knees, covering his eyes with his hands. "They're all yelling in my head! The animals are screaming in my head!" The dogs howled; the cats yowled and Capwell babbled, "They're all clawing and biting in there! No no no no no no they're all in pain, I can feel them all in pain, I can see them, *I'm in the steel box*, and I can't...get ouuu—!" He never quite said *out*, the word instead protracting into an animal yowl that partook of cat sound and dog sound and ape sound, a sound so piteous that Ama went to Capwell, patted his shoulder.

Boyce lowered his hands and the vibration ebbed and their perceptions dulled; Ama felt headachy and tired but somehow exultant.

She helped Capwell to his feet and he started immediately toward the nearest cage. "I must let them out...oh, I'm going to get fired but..."

"If we let them all out at once," Boyce said, "there will be terror and chaos and disorientation among them. Ama, call your friends, your...your *activist* friends...and ask them to call their friends, they have a...a means of mutual organizational contact?"

"Yes. A phone tree. I'll call them..."

She fumbled out her cell phone and called her friends, who didn't believe her at first, but in time they began to show up, van after van, emptying the cages one at a time, Capwell helping, taking the animals away to animal rescue shelters, to much bigger spaces where no one hurt them; to a hope of freedom.

Then as they stood in the alley watching the last van drive away, the man who went by the name Boyce said, "That's done. Let's go, then, Ama, if you're coming with me."

Was she going with him? She shouldn't, should she? She wasn't sure what had just happened. Except—that it was a very good thing. The kind of miracle she'd prayed for—without actually saying the prayer—all her adult life.

She couldn't turn her back on that. She was aligned with this man, now. She had to go with him. Dangerous? Maybe. But it felt right to do it.

She watched the last van drive away, and then wearily, resignedly, she trailed after Boyce, as he started down the road, his head held high, alert, listening.

Sacramento, California

"Never order Chinese food at a card room," Swift said, shaking his head and pushing away his plate of greasy fried rice. He'd only eaten a few bites. He was off his feed, anyway. Partly it was the smell of fresh bug-killer that wafted from the card-room's kitchen whenever the flyspecked door swung open. Partly it was because his mind was still on the hillside where he and Galivant—who was now seated across from him in the booth, absent-mindedly shoveling down his Egg Foo Young—had watched the sky dance with the most cryptic of all cryptoglyphs.

Swift felt divorced from his body, unreal. The feeling had troubled him since that afternoon at the trailers, in the strange living light of the cones. The only thing that grounded him was thinking about his daughter, Erin—and that sent a jab of anxiety through him every time. Linda's custody of Erin made him feel so powerless.

"So you're still saying, Swift, you don't know what you saw that day?"

The words were difficult to make out, filtered mushily through the noise of chewing—Galivant had a habit of talking with his mouth industriously full.

Swift shrugged. "I don't know what the hell it was. Neither do you. Unless there's something you haven't told me."

"Like you believe what I tell you anyway. You want another beer?"

"That's a dumb question."

"True. Maggie! Can we get two more? Thanks. Yeah, Swift, you're right: I don't know for sure what that stuff in the sky was—but somehow it's got to be related to the bigger pattern of anomalies. To the so called 'epidemic of justice'."

"That your cute little term—'epidemic of justice?'" Swift shifted on the creaking, faux-leather seat of the cramped booth. The plastic tape they'd used to repair the slashed seat under him was crimping up, poking him.

"Look here." Galivant dug in his tattered briefcase, pulled out a thick sheaf of paper overflowing its brown folder. "Got so many they barely fit in my briefcase. Here—look at this one first." He pushed the plate of fried-rice aside so peremptorily the platter almost slid off the table and Swift had to catch it, handing it to Maggie after she put their beers down. She rolled her eyes and walked off, shaking her head, as Galivant laid the sheaf of printouts down in front of him. On the top sheet, the headline read,

AN "EPIDEMIC OF JUSTICE"?
Reports of Miraculous Changes in Behavior Worldwide

"But don't read that article, Swift, it's shallow stuff—it's shallow stuff. Superficial reporting. Here, read this..." Galivant slapped a typescript down. "I've got Fortean contacts all over the world—my guy in Beijing sent me this—a pretty good translation. A guy, there, Xao something, he jumped in the Yangtze River, trying to commit suicide. Whole bunch of people saw him go under holding an armful of bricks; he was under water for a good ten minutes. So if he survives, he's brain damaged from oxygen deprivation, right? But he came up perfectly coherent. Here, read these paragraphs, the quote from the wife..."

> *"When I got there, my Xao was wrapped in a blanket on the riverbank and he was smiling. I said, 'Xao, I found your note, did you jump in the river and change your mind? Come home, your son needs you.' He said, 'I will take care of Xao's son, but I must tell you that I am not Xao, he surrendered his body when he gave up this life. I will do all I can for you and I am sorry for your grief.' I saw that his brain must have been hurt by having no air in the water. I wished to take him to the hospital,*

but he would not go. He said he had to go into the orphanage. There is a very big orphanage the Party operates, near the river, with many children. He dropped the blanket and walked to the orphanage. The orphanage security men did not stop him, which was quite surprising. I followed and saw he was in the dormitory with the many crying children, reaching out and calling, 'Mama, Papa,' such a thing as breaks your heart to see, very small children reaching out—but some just staring, with their eyes so empty, it is a great sadness. He looked around and the children grew quiet and then he went out again, and I followed him, asking him to come home, and he said, "In good time." Then he went to the market and spoke to people and I was amazed to see some of them follow him. They put down their packages and followed him. And my husband went back to the orphanage with a great crowd and they went into the room with the children and took some of them. The Party Officials came in to stop him, but a strange light filled the room and men from the Party began to weep, and the guards walked away, and Xao comforted everyone, and then went to another market, and returned again with more people, perhaps fifty. He continued until the orphanage was empty of children; they had all gone with strangers, with no forms filled out, and the Party Officials seemed afraid to stop them. I have heard that the Party said it would retrieve these children, who were given out wrongly, and they went to these houses but could not take the children, and no one understands why. The orphanage nurse said that there were children there who never spoke, who only stared, but Xao touched them and they tried to speak, and intelligence returned to their faces. I am not going to say what I think this is, as I do not wish to be detained, but a miracle has happened, and Xao is gone, and someone else has taken his place. I cannot say I am sorry. Xao and I were not close, although we were married."

"Well hell," Swift said, "that's quite a story. But, you know—probably urban myth, whatever..."

"I've got three more like that, all within a short time—two women and a man who went, in different places, to commit suicide—and it just didn't work. One put a shotgun in his mouth and it fired and somehow the charge never hit him."

"Some kind of blank."

"And then...he went out and miracles followed in his wake. You know those 'bear farmers' in China? They crush bears into these little-tiny cages, and shunt them, take bile out of them that they sell to people—old-fashioned Chinese medicine. These bears live a life of unbelievable misery—just make you sick to see them. So suddenly this guy who's done it for thirty-three years suddenly starts weeping and says he's been all wrong, says he's never *seen* the bears before—like he's been with them but never really saw them. And he turned them all over to a charity that heals them, sets them free—said it started with some spinning lights all around him. Jim, think about that. You ever hear of anybody completely changing their whole point of view on their own business after thirty-three profitable years? It doesn't happen—it's not human nature. But it's happening anyway."

"Yeah, well, that's all hearsay."

Galivant smiled at him crookedly. "I hear tell, Swift,

about a reporter who was about to get himself killed by three Cambode gangsters, and there was a luminous phenomenon and they suddenly changed their minds and they not only let him go but they released people worth hundreds of thousands of dollars to them...and then two of them turned themselves in to the cops. You believe that one?"

Swift sighed. "Kind of believe that one, yeah."

"Tell me, man. That thing, those lights—they didn't affect you? You know what I mean. Inside."

"It was like I was on the edge of it, just the...I don't know. Now you've got me all suggestible and big-eyed."

"Drink your beer, it helps that big-eye shit."

"Finally, a sensible suggestion from you."

"You see this thick pile of documents here? These are all stories just like the one you told about the Cambodes. Miraculous, impossible changes in behavior. In Russia—immigrants held as virtual slaves in a factory—beaten, overworked, rarely if ever paid— suddenly their bosses start weeping and shower them with money and beg their forgiveness. That's *not human nature*, Swift, people don't change like that.

"Here—check this one out: the Philippines, hundreds of children held in child prostitution houses there, suddenly released by the local authorities after years of looking the other way."

"That's so great, man, it's—we should just feel good about it..."

"And just accept it? Like you don't want to know what's going on? Look at this one, cops protecting drug lords in Mexico suddenly take these scumbags prisoner and bring them in—and then turn themselves in, confessing corruption. Not every corrupt cop did it—but a surprising number, man. Lots of 'em. Four American senators abruptly return campaign contributions, saying they'd been voting the way their donors wanted them to."

"Saw that one on the wire. I thought maybe it was an overdue attack of conscience..."

"Four guys at once? It's unnatural. And look here at this

one, bunch of Mexican illegals working in a slaughterhouse in slavery conditions were moved to an empty apartment building owned by the president of the meat-packing company. He's helping them get citizenship, tripling their salaries, reducing their hours, taking them to doctors—it's like Scrooge and what's-his-name, Bob Cratchit, but in Texas. Look here, four LAPD officers turn themselves in, they were taking bribes from crack dealers. They turned themselves in as a group! There are dozens more. *Dozens!* They talk of visions, lights—"

"Not much in the national media about all this—not as a phenomenon. The senators, yeah, but this other stuff—"

"That's mysterious too, isn't it? Lot of rumors that OBM is pushing to keep this stuff down—they've got some corporate deal with Time-Warner and Fox..."

"OBM? Why them?"

"I don't know. The thing's freaked them out. Big media or not, the stories are getting out. Blogs, Web sites, tweets. Everything I've shown you I passed on to the Fortean site— they're getting *millions of hits*, corroborating stories from all over the world! Now some you could explain away—but all these events happening all about the same time? How do you explain that?"

"Well..." He could think of explanations. But they rang false to him. He remembered those people in the doublewides, in Fresno.

"I...can't explain it."

"It's *justice*, man—an epidemic of justice. And there's something else, Jim—check it out. Here's a timetable. I've got it worked up right here. These incidents are happening faster and faster...and closer and closer together. This thing is coming to a head, Swift. It's coming right at us like a runaway freight train..."

6

Washington, DC

BIRCH tugged at the window in the hot waiting room. It wouldn't budge. He felt tense, restive. "Damn window seems to be sealed shut. Here it is, this old fashioned window, made for opening up on a hot day, and it won't open."

"It's sealed shut, Frank," Ellen said: Ellen Meyers, OBM's lobbyist, sitting across from Meredith in the small waiting room. Birch knew Ellen from meetings in New York when he'd prepped her on OBM's new nanomaterials-deregulation push; she was a brunette with a glossy hook of hair falling over one shoulder; African-American blood showing in light-cocoa skin, full lips. A pleasantly plump, busty woman in a pale blue dress suit—the skirt cut fairly short for a suit—she was very familiar with "the corridors of power"; she knew her way around the Beltway, even the peculiarities of its heating and air conditioning. "It is hot in the Senate offices—they always have the air conditioning on when it's cool, the heat on when it's warm out. The senators complain and a 'maintenance order' gets put in but it's never quite fixed. Whew, it really is too warm…" And she unbuttoned the top button of her blouse.

As Ellen undid the button, Meredith sat up very straight, pursed her lips, her icy blue eyes fixed coldly on the lobbyist.

"It *is* stuffy, isn't it?" Ellen went on. "It's a lot like the doctors' waiting rooms I used to be stuck in, in my old job, right down to the outdated magazines."

"Yes," Meredith said, her voice brittle, "I'd heard you used to work for the pharmaceutical companies—women sent in to chat up male doctors..." She looked at Ellen with studied ingenuousness. "Did it really work?"

Ellen blinked at her, just as if she didn't understand. "Oh I didn't actually *sell* the pharms. I was just someone to let them know what the latest pills were." She glanced at her watch. "The senator's late coming back from lunch. He's usually pretty prompt."

Birch looked back at the window. "Why do they seal the damn windows shut? Doesn't seem safe."

Ellen made an eloquent gesture that said, 'Go figure'. "The whole building is sealed, the whole Capitol complex. They coated the outside of this building and the White House in that plas-seal stuff. Supposed to preserve it from everything from fungus to rockets. Preservation of historical landmarks and all that. Looks weird, about sunset—all glossy, like it's wet when it's not."

"Sealed in..." Birch muttered, unsure why he was saying it. He put his hands in the pockets of his gray suit trousers, immediately felt uncomfortable that way, and took them out again. He paced over to the waiting room's magazine rack, read a headline on a *US News and World Report* cover:

Reports of 'Sky Messages' Bring Derision, Ambiguous Video

He decided he didn't want to know what that was about, paced back to the window, aware that both women were watching him, Meredith's head swiveling like a machine tracking him on her long neck.

He thought about what sex was like with Meredith. The way she twined him, like a pipe cleaner toy his sister had as a child; she'd twist it around his GI Joe. *"See you escape from that, GI Joe!"* The toy shaped like a vaguely feminine human figure, Twisty Terry.

Now he was dating Twisty Terry. It wasn't that he didn't like Meredith. He just didn't really trust her, not fully. He trusted the raw need he felt in her, when he held her. That was real. He liked her long slim limbs, even the desperate quality in the pumping of her hips, her blond hair swishing rhythmically like a benediction over him when she straddled him—it was as if she were trying to make contact in the only real way she could. That brought out something tender in him.

No, Meredith wasn't what was bothering him. Nor the stultifying room. It was the agenda. It gave him a pinched feeling inside that kept him awake at night. He had trained himself not to ask, *Are we doing the right thing?* He had learned not to ask it—even mentally. But the question never went away.

"Let's go over it one more time, since time is what we seem to have," Ellen said lightly, opening her Powerbook, tapping at it. "And Frank is new to a lot of this, we've got to bring him up to speed. So, the Senator Baxter file and...there it is. Two things, the proposed nanomaterials regulation, and this new, um, 'Wi-Fi enhancement' process."

"About that," Birch said, hearing the nervousness in his own voice—which sounded annoyingly high pitched to him—"I got a text message from Griffin, something about this 'control group' process of his, some church group— we're not supposed to mention it anywhere, so don't bring it up with the senator, I guess."

Meredith gave him a faintly reproachful look, and tilted her head toward Ellen, as if to say, *She doesn't know.*

Why did the control group thing have to be such a secret? Birch wondered, looking at the framed photo of Senator Baxter on the wall: the senator's perfect smile and regular features counterbalanced his feeble comb-over; the dimple in his chin compensated the old acne scars.

Ellen peered at her Powerbook file. "So—OBM's nanomaterials division... Congress has witnesses claiming these, um, super-small particles pass easily into skin cells from lotions, clothing and the like, get into the air, into lungs, an effect like asbestos—we need to reassure him our research has shown they're safe and..."

"We don't have any research to speak of on their safety," Meredith said sharply. "They're too small to be dangerous."

"Some people are afraid it's the opposite," Ellen said, shrugging. "They're so small they're dangerous."

"We can say they're demonstrating their safety every day," Birch suggested, feeling that pinching in his stomach with the words.

"They'll say that's using the public for guinea pigs," Ellen said. "But we'll dance around it."

Suddenly feeling like postponing the whole thing, Birch said, "You sure Baxter's the guy for this? Maybe some other senator?"

Ellen nodded, her eyes lazily half-shut as if to say, believe me. "Baxter is on all the right committees. He can kill the regs for us before the bill gets to the floor. As for the Wi-Fi connection," she added, "we've got to try to get him to call the FCC, see that we get the frequencies we're going to need. The thing to remember about the senator...well..."

She gestured for Birch to come closer. Patted the chair beside her.

Birch sat. Meredith's hands balled on her lap.

Ellen bent close to Birch, almost forehead-to-forehead and whispered, "The senator from Rhode Island is a Democrat— he is very conscious of maintaining the appearance of being... unattached. You know, for the sake of his constituency. It got out that he's playing ball with credit card companies in his state—he backed that bankruptcy bill they wanted— and he's worried now it'll come out how much money we've given him for his campaign. Well, we spread our donations across the board, Republicans, Dems and Independents. But still—he's touchy. So he wants to pretend to go after this nanomaterials thing in Congress."

Birch was almost shocked. He hadn't thought of it as being anything so blatantly duplicitous. "He's planning to support it...but only after he pretends to oppose it?"

"Right. We have to get him to 'reluctantly' change his mind. I've got the expert testimony right here..." She tapped a folder on her lap under the Powerbook. "That'll be a

walk through. But the FCC thing, the wi-fi experiment—
that's going to take some convincing. He's going to have to
make calls for us and if it gets out that he intervened..." She
lowered her voice. "... hard for him to get away with."

"We really shouldn't be talking about this in the waiting
room," Meredith said, barely audible between clenched
teeth. "If we—"

She broke off as the door to the inner office opened and a
slim young man, with neatly trimmed blond hair, a perfectly
tailored blue suit, and the faintest lisp, said "The senator
just got in, I'm sorry to keep you waiting, I think you can
come in to the—"

The young man was startled, his mouth dropping open, as
Senator Baxter, in shirt sleeves, shoved him aside, stepping
into the doorway. The senator's eyes were wild, and he was
almost panting. The wildness looked particularly odd on
a man of sixty-five. He had his charcoal jacket bunched in
his hands; his blue tie, with a crooked flag clip, was askew
at his open collar. "I'm...no...no I can't talk about that stuff
today..."

"Are you okay, sir?" the assistant asked, putting out a
slender hand to touch the Senator's shoulder—withdrawing
it at the last instant.

"Yes...Actually—I don't know. No. Not really okay. I was
in a private room at the restaurant, and we were having
a working lunch..." His lower lip quivered. "Something
happened." He pushed into the waiting room and went to
the window, stared out at the sky. "Did you see anything...in
the sky? I've heard stories. I didn't see anything up there..."

"You mean, sir—like a missile or...an attack of some
kind? A plane? Terrorists?"

"No. No no no. Uh-uh, no, it's just that...I've *heard* things.
And then I was eating my London broil and...it turned into,
like, mud or clay in my mouth, and I tasted blood on the
clay, and I looked around and I could see everything in the
room so...so sharply. I could see something *in the air*. This
gorgeous yellow light, this sort of...*spinning* shape, with
points, and where the points connected this...this beautiful

smell and this feeling sort of vibrated out. And...and it changed colors. And...I realized that *everyone was lying!* Everyone around me was lying about every last thing they said!"

Birch and Meredith looked at one another. She stood up and mouthed: *The influence.* Birch nodded.

Baxter passed a shaking hand over his head, disordering his careful comb-over. "And then the others realized it too, and we all...stopped talking. And Joe Hensley—I mean, we're talking about Old Joe, thirty years in the Senate! He started bawling like a baby and he ran out, calling to his wife. She's in the fucking hospital with a stroke, what does he think he's going to do for her right now, for Christ-sakes? And Darby was laughing. Just laughing like an idiot!"

"Oh my God," Ellen said, snapping her Powerbook shut. "Someone drugged you! They put something in the food!"

Baxter looked at her—strangely, intensely. Suspiciously. Suspicious of *her*, really. "Do you think so? Something in the food?"

"It really sounds like a drug experience."

"Almost. But—it wasn't. I just...don't think so. God I'm tired—I feel heavy. Like my chest is made out of a big lump of lead..." He put his hand to his breastbone.

"Maybe you should go to the emergency room, sir," Birch suggested. He was glad of a chance to get out of the meeting, but spooked all the same.

"Emergency room? Maybe. But...I don't know."

"We can reschedule, sir!" Ellen said, coming closer, touching his arm.

"Reschedule?" He stared at her, drawing back. "About that nanomaterial business? You can forget that. Forget using *me* for that little scam. Uh-uh. That's over. I'm out. That stuff is criminal. You people are using us all—using us as guinea pigs. From what I've heard there are already people getting sick. You thought we had a deal? We did! Do you think we have one now? We don't! All deals are off. I'm resigning. I don't want to live in this hell anymore. Not me. I'm done with that. I'm going home to Rhode Island. And if you people try to block that bill I'll blister you in the papers from here to LA and back up to New York. I'm getting out of here, Sandy—" This last to the assistant. "You can come with me if you like."

"I...I can?"

"Yes. We have a lot to talk about."

Baxter rushed back into the inner office, saying he wanted to get some photographs from his desk, and then he stepped back into the hallway between the waiting room and the office, and his eyes were wilder than ever, there was terror and horrified realization in them. He looked like a man running from a juggernaut, from some terrifying presence looming over his shoulder, and then—

He stopped in his tracks and stared at them in shock. His left leg wobbled, buckled, and he went down on his left knee. Then he fell sideways against the wall, still awkwardly half-kneeling, clawing at his chest, gasping out, "I can't... there's a big weight...it's all coming now...it's all here."

Birch and Sandy rushed to him, as Meredith called 911. But within the hour Senator Baxter was dead of a massive heart attack.

Sacramento, California

"Give me this again now," Swift said, spreading his hands in bafflement. "Where are you going?"

Linda didn't answer immediately. She looked out the living room window at the mid-morning sky.

"Do you think that cloud is...?" She was thinking aloud as much as asking him.

He stepped close enough, just close enough, to look past her at the sky. "No. Not every funny looking cloud is...a sign. I'm not even sure what I saw that day. It could've been a technological trick. Maybe suggestion. The video is... ambiguous."

She looked at him in disgust, shaking her head.

Swift shrugged. "Where is it you're taking her, Linda? She's my daughter too, for heaven's sake."

She looked back at the sky and said, "There's a camp sponsored by that company, OBM. There's a...I think his name is Mr. Griffin...who arranged it. His sister is in the Church. They have a retreat, you see. The OBM corporate retreat."

"O'Hanlon Business Machines is giving your church a retreat?"

"They said we can use it. This Mr. Griffin said they were very interested in our using it. He said...it was of..."

"Of what?"

"Of...scientific interest. Or something. It doesn't matter. I'm lucky we were invited—it's only certain people in the church."

"Where is this place exactly? In California?"

"That doesn't matter either."

"You're not going to tell me? You're just taking my daughter and not telling me where you're taking her? I just have to trust that these end-times lunatics at the Church of the Revelation in Jesus—"

"—In Christ!"

"Whatever. I have to just trust that they're not going to go David Koresh on my daughter?"

She turned savagely to him, eyes narrowed. "Are we going to talk about trust?"

"Linda..."

"Where's the trust I'm supposed to have for you? I'm the one who can be trusted here, not you. Let's review, shall we?"

"Can I just see my daughter, please?"

"She's not back from school yet. What, you want to avoid this discussion?"

"We already *had* this discussion."

"We did." She crossed her arms over her chest and, still facing the window, looking washed out in the light, she turned her head to look at him like someone trying to decide if they're going to cross the room to squash a spider on the wall. "But apparently we need to review. You had an affair with a chickie at work, I found the credit card receipt for the motel, there were tearful confessions, and swearing off all such, and then less than a year later you got drunk with some woman who thinks she's a goth rocker and—"

"That was only once." Or, really, two, no three times. "I tried to get rid of her from the start—"

"And she kept calling the house and hanging up and finally it all came out and then you were gawking at that woman at the awards banquet and I'm supposed to pretend you didn't have a thing with *her*—"

"We *didn't* do anything. We talked a lot, that's all. By Facebook message. Not even in person." That wasn't entirely true but she already had enough in her "file" on him. "It's not as if you had no part in it, Linda." Seeing her mouth drop open, her eyes widen in outrage, he put in, "I mean, you froze me out and you admitted it. You were trying to find yourself and you decided giving yourself to me was a—a self betrayal and you just *isolated*. We hadn't been intimate in a year—"

"It wasn't like you were there *anyway* when we...when we were intimate, Jim. You were..." She flicked a hand dismissively. "Imagining someone else maybe. You were doing it like it was urinating or something, just getting the fluid out."

"That's pretty harsh, Linda. You should have communicated—anyone can get...distracted, lose touch with...you know."

"Jim—I did try to talk about it."

"I don't remember that. And what I remember is that you weren't that interested anyway. You were having your political fantasy then, Linda—running for city council and when you weren't elected you sulked all winter, and then you went into your self-discovery thing, you got into yoga, you went to that balding guy on PBS, and then one day you came home with 'It was right in front of me all the time— I'm born again!' and now my daughter is being taken off to some *compound* somewhere..."

"It's not a compound, James, it's a retreat."

"If it's so innocuous," Swift said dryly, "tell me where it is."

"I don't want you coming around disturbing things."

"Linda, I can find out anyway. OBM's not that hard to track. I work for a major newspaper. I'll make a few calls."

She smiled in cold triumph. "This place is brand new, the public doesn't know about it yet. Almost no one at OBM knows where it is. And I happen to know they want this to be on the QT."

"They do? And why, Linda, huh? Doesn't that raise a red flag for you? Doesn't that make you wonder about this... *Graffin guy?*"

"It's Griffin. I think. Anyway we...haven't decided to go yet."

"No?" He looked at her a long moment, and decided she was lying. She'd made up her mind to go. "I want to see my daughter. I can get a court order, Linda. But I already have the right to see her."

"You have the right when I say so."

"Daddy?" Erin was just coming in with a backpack slung over one shoulder, her hair tousled by wind, her skirt way too short for his liking. "Dad—Mom says I can't go to Spring Homecoming. Can't I go to Homecoming?"

He expelled a long breath as he looked at Linda. "You're not going to try to push her into home schooling again? Or that Christian school? We had a discussion about that, we talked to lawyers, you can't just *do* that—"

"I'm going to take her with me, Jim. It won't be necessary to defend it in court. It's all going to be over soon."

"See, now you're sounding like a cult-drone—"

"Jim!" she interrupted sharply. She glanced at Erin. "You're going to scare her. I'm not talking about anything but what God will do in His own time, His own way. We just know it's coming and we have a place where we will wait for it together. You saw for yourself, the other day—the signs! There've been a lot of other things happening. A lot of things. There's a Web site collecting them, signsofwitnessdotcom, go see for yourself."

"Dad, she's freaking me out with this stuff—"

"You hear that, Linda? Why don't you go to your retreat and let Erin stay with me for a while? When you get back, she can come here."

Linda shook her head gravely. "There won't be any 'coming back'."

Erin's lower lip trembled. She walked to Swift and stood behind him. "Daddy..."

"You're not going anywhere, button. I'm gonna go see a lawyer right now. I'll bust in on his meetings if I have to. I'll be back."

He kissed his daughter on the forehead and rushed out the front door.

Swift's lawyer, an earnest young man named Irv Steinmetz, agreed to see him during his lunch hour, eating a sandwich at his desk as they spoke. He couldn't get a court order "just like that" but he wrote a letter of warning to Linda, specifying that a court order had been requested— which wasn't quite true, the paperwork wouldn't be filed till the following day—and Swift hurried back to Linda's house in mid-afternoon, only to find it locked, and her car gone.

Feeling like there was a bruise on his heart, Swift broke in the back door, and went to Erin's room.

Her bureau drawers were open, a lot of her clothing missing. So was her suitcase. Linda's suitcase was gone too. Her closet a mess, dresses, still on their hangers, fallen on the floor.

They had simply gone.

In the kitchen, he found a broken glass on the floor, Erin's backpack beside it. He thought: There was a struggle here. With someone else beside Linda.

They'd taken his daughter with them by force.

PHASE TWO

THE SWORD INTRODUCES ITSELF TO THE GORDIAN KNOT

"I'm only human—and I regret it."
—Mark Twain

7

Houston, Texas

F. NORRIS Frasier looked at his watch. Nine a.m. exactly. He strode up to the head of the boardroom table, surveyed the five expectant faces—some of them with "this better be good" looks at having been called here for an emergency meeting—and simply stuck his hands in his pockets. He didn't sit down. He just stood there, looking at them, for almost a full minute, before speaking.

"Ladies and gentlemen—to make a long story short, I'm dissolving the company," said Frasier, with cool, rehearsed confidence. Normally he didn't have to rehearse what he was going to say. Normally, he was imposing and confident, and he knew it. The CEO of Energy-World Incorporated, Frasier was almost six-foot seven, a one-time college basketball player, going paunchy now, balding, eyes watery blue, cheeks jowly. Usually he dressed casually at work; this morning he wore one of his best blue suits, exquisitely tailored, because he wanted to make a formal statement in everything he did today. He'd been up for a couple days, mulling what happened, and he was tired, but he was quite certain about what he wanted to do. There was no doubt about it. And what a relief it would be.

Not everyone had been able to make it on short notice, but there were enough, all of them looking at him with expressions of shock, confusion, bemusement—Gary Osborne, sleek and blond and casually dressed at just thirty-nine, smiling conspiratorially, was definitely taking this as a gag of some kind, the old man trying to make a point, wake them all up.

"Gary thinks I'm kidding," Frasier noted dryly, "and he is quite mistaken."

"You can't dis-sholve anything," said Mary Ambrose, with one of her smug little snorts, tossing her flip of glossy auburn hair. She'd gotten more smug, more condescending, as she'd gotten older, Frasier reflected; recently she'd had a series of Botox injections and her face was largely frozen, her upper lip rigid as a mannequin's. When she spoke, the syllables were slightly mushy because not all the muscles of her mouth responded anymore. "It's a big elaborate pross-sesh..."

"Oh, but I can. I spent most of yesterday, through one means or another, through shells and reps and a half-dozen means I learned right here, buying shares of the company. Check your by-laws. I can do this. It won't take effect immediately but I can make it happen."

"I'm just going to wait for the other shoe," said Doug "Beachboy" Huskitz, a onetime surf-music enthusiast, still showing 1960s damage, including the loud shirt and the Grateful Dead tie; but the lines in his face were mostly from drinking and blow in the eighties, before he'd gotten to AA. He was on the board because his parents had bought a substantial chunk of shares in the fifties. "Other shoe's going to drop, and bang, we'll all jump in our seats."

"This is both shoes," Frasier said. "I'm dissolving the company so you can say *sayonara* to the money. Bang, bang."

"Yo there," Huskitz said. "If you bought my shares, whatever, I get the cash from the buyout. Like my kid says, 'I ain't trippin'.'"

"True enough—but you won't get any more out of this company after that."

Stan Beeman, a fox-faced man with a puzzled expression even when he wasn't puzzled, tilted his head and said, "I... expect you're going to explain why this is a good thing, Fred—I mean, yes, you're going to make a big pile of cash in the liquidation, but in the long run we stand to make more money holding on to the company. Why should we stand by—"

"As for your standing by, you don't have a choice, and as for money I'm going to make on it, oh, I'm donating all of that to various charities."

Beeman blinked. "Donating? What percentage of it?"

"I said *all* of it. What part of *all* don't you understand, Stan? Hm? All of it. I have a list of charities. I'm giving it to Amnesty International, because we pushed our friends in Congress to help General Hafez hold onto power a few years ago, when his death squads were dragging whole families to massacres—"

"Here now!" Lou Tottenham objected. Close on Frasier's right, Tottenham was a pop-eyed man with a nose like the prow of an icebreaker, a receding chin, club ties. His Brit accent came out when he was upset. "This is a bloody farce! You know damned well all that stuff about Hafez was cooked up by the Marxist wankers running about in the jungle like a lot of bloody monkeys—"

"Actually, no, it wasn't," Frasier interrupted. "Senator Baxter briefed me. He's dead, did you know that? But of course you heard it on the news—he died yesterday of a heart attack, not two hours after I had lunch with him. We all left that lunch quite changed—he was so changed it killed him. Now..." He took off his coat, slung it over the chair in front of him, stuck his hands back in his pockets, and rocked on his heels, looking at the ceiling, smiling oddly. "Where was I? Amnesty International, yes, and then I'm giving a great chunk of it to the American Cancer Society as our refineries have caused a fair amount of lung cancer—"

"Oh, come on, you don't believe that!" Mary snorted.

"Oh, but I do—our own studies confirmed it. I just never showed them to you. I had some clumsy little justification for suppressing the studies—we gave a lot of people jobs, that sort of thing—but what with the layoffs and outsourcing and mechanization, I can't really claim that one anymore. Another portion is going to the Sierra Club—"

Horror at that one.

"What!"

"You can't be serious!"

"But I sure as hell am," Frasier said. "We have a lot to make up for. Manipulating energy markets in California, buying politicians, having that little understanding with the regime in Burma about our pipelines...slave labor, people forced to give up their land, all of it at the point of a gun."

Osborne winced at that, looked down at the table. "I heard something about it...1 was hoping..."

"That it wasn't true? You didn't bother to check, did you, Osborne? Well I told our friends in Burma to do whatever it took. I said I didn't want to know. I made it clear. I knew... but I didn't try to stop it."

"So you're having a bloody attack of conscience," Tottenham said, "then make some changes—but you'll send the market into a tailspin if you try to go all the way with this."

"No, we're going to make a clean breast of it," said Frasier, coolly. "I'm going to tell the country, in a press conference, what I'm doing and why I'm doing it. And I expect there'll be a call for prosecution. But..."

Beeman shook his head in dull wonder. "Frasier—what the fuck happened to you at that lunch?"

Frasier chuckled. "I imagined explaining it to you. Impossible. Things are happening around the world—things that have our friends at OBM panicking. But I welcome it. I couldn't bear it much longer, I can tell you—I was not sleeping much and I didn't know why. I was impotent. I was losing my appetite—for life as well as food. And then— the shining thing came, and it woke me up and showed me myself, and I saw things, just saw them. I saw what was eating me, what was making me weary and limp and dead inside. My own conscience."

Mary rolled her eyes. "You fool, you've been drugged."

"No. Drugs wear off, Mary. This hasn't. Insight is insight."

Tottenham was on his headset cell phone, muttering. "Yes—meet you in the hall outside the boardroom."

"Calling your broker, Tottenham?" Frasier asked. "Your lawyer? Waste of time. I've got this sewn up."

"Oh, have you?" He stood up, his face red with anger. "No one leaves this room! Don't do anything rash, any of you! Don't call any lawyers, don't call any brokers, and I'm not going anywhere, I'll be right outside that door."

Tottenham stalked out the door, and, shrugging, Frasier walked to the window, smiling gently out at the silvery, haze-dulled skyline, the leaden gulf beyond it. "I feel much lighter now. I feel like anything is possible. Like all possibilities are gathering, right here on our world—the possibilities are having a conference, deciding amongst themselves which of them we need most, but they're all there, not one possibility is excluded from the conference. And do you know who's running the conference? Who the CEO of that boardroom is? The Impossible. The Impossible is calling the shots, at the conference of the possible."

"He *is* drugged!" Beeman whispered. "Or just...gone off his nut."

"Let me try to explain what happened to me," Frasier said, turning a sad smile at them. "I was at a lunch with some congressmen, one of those meetings we like to deny ever take place, and we were working up the outline of the country's energy policies for the next congressional session, and these, sort of, big glowing cones appeared in the air, one pointed down and one up, touching at the tips, spinning in opposite directions, and from the place where they touched this...this something came out...I don't know what it was... it was intelligence, a vibrating intelligence, but it was an intelligence that could touch you, you could feel it like you feel a wind, and..."

They gaped at him as he went on, and on, and only firmed up their conviction that he had gone mad, until Tottenham returned with Roger Mergus, the ex-linebacker, ex-Special Forces, who was head of Security, subcontracted from an O'Hanlon company. He was a flat-topped, barrel-chested man in a gray suit that seemed too long for him in the trousers, too tight around the torso. The suit had a little OSI logo on the kerchief pocket: O'Hanlon Strategics International. He had a headset on, and he was muttering into it as he circled the table to stand behind the CEO.

Frasier looked at Tottenham, who was smiling nastily, and past him to the three other men he didn't recognize, coming in the door behind Mergus. Big men, who worked for Mergus, he assumed. They all wore the same blazers and carried the same type of guns on their hips.

"You're all in this," Tottenham said to the board. "He isn't going to bugger *me*. And I don't want to hear, later, if it comes out, it was all Tottenham's doing. *It's all of us.* Frasier here is going to have an accident. Today. Do I hear any objections?"

"Uhhhh..." Osborne began. Then he pursed his lips and looked at the table.

"This isn't going to work," Frasier said. "I've—"

"We'll deal with the ownership issues later," Tottenham said. "Mergus?"

"You're sure about this?" Mergus said. "You understand about my shares? The cash? And the money for these others?"

"Swiss bank accounts, whatever you want. Do it now, Mergus."

Frasier turned to look at him. Mergus drew his gun and gestured.

Somehow, Frasier didn't have it in him to fight. This seemed...right. He had to pay a bigger price than he'd planned. Too bad if they stopped the donations though, he reflected, as he let them take him down the elevator to the parking garage. But he suspected it wouldn't matter soon. Money would become irrelevant.

He was still thinking about that, trying to imagine what manner of world that would be, when they drove him in the limo to the marina, to his own motor yacht, the *Destiny*.

And he was still thinking about it when they'd gotten far enough out to sea—and Mergus brought the butt of his gun down hard on F. Norris Frasier's head. There was very little pain, surprisingly little, even when they dropped him overboard, and the drowning began.

Now I can really begin to see, Frasier thought, as he sank into the Gulf of Mexico, and died.

Sherman Oaks, California

"Are you an angel?" Ama asked, feeling stupid but also feeling like she had to ask the question. She crossed her legs on the chair, the motion slow and subtly provocative. At least, she hoped it was subtle. She didn't have much practice. She wanted Boyce to notice and thought: I don't usually act this way around men. What's the matter with me?

She'd lived with her ex, Joey for about six months, and had gotten used to the intimacy, the release, the ease of having company night after night. And then, wham, he'd broken up with her and moved to Hawaii with that long-legged, strawberry-blond airhead who "just wanted to be a housewife and have kids, you wouldn't understand, Ama." Oh, bullshit. She was kind of glad he'd gone, after that. But it had been lonely.

Hoping something would happen with Boyce, though, wasn't so much about wanting to fill a void in her life. It was just plain hard to keep her hands off Boyce. There was an electricity around him. Not that she was ready to jump in the sack with him. But it'd be nice if he took her in his arms and...and what?

Boyce leaned back on the sofa in the living room of her bungalow. He seemed to be reviewing something in his mind. "Angel. Am I an *angel?* No, I'm not mythological. I'm quite real."

"But—maybe you're a real angel. Maybe there's a sort that's not just mythological."

"No," he said thoughtfully. "I don't think so, no. There might've been some misidentification, at some point. But no."

Ama gazed at him. She was sitting in a desk chair, turned toward the closed sofa bed where he'd spent the night. He was still dressed, except for his shoes, which he'd left outside the door at her request—a holdover from her Asian upbringing. It was almost eleven at night. She still felt the paradoxical mingling of fatigue and exhilaration; was still reeling from what he'd done yesterday in the animal testing lab—and today, when he'd taken her to a series of homeless camps, and simply *changed* all but the most hardcore people, in minutes...

Two thirds of the homeless had walked away from the encampment, heading for shelters, family, treatment centers they'd ignored till that day.

"Excuse me," Ama said now, "I don't mean to be rude, but I have to do this." She turned on the gooseneck light curling from her desktop, and twisted it around to point at his face. "I have to know...yeah, I'm not mistaken. You look way different from yesterday. Same face but...younger."

"Yes." He reached out, blinking, and turned the lamp away. "I expect I've repaired this body a good deal. The process has begun; it will repair even more."

She tried to stay cool around him, aloof but friendly. But he there was a feeling she got from him—she felt it radiating from him as clearly as heat from a stove. Something she felt in her midsection, and lower at times. It made her squirm in her seat. But it might be that she was feeling it sexually because her body just didn't know how else to understand it. A strange thought...

"So Dennis...are you...an alien? From, you know—another planet?"

He didn't seem surprised by the question. "No. I'm not from 'another planet'. I'm from...*this* planet as much as I'm from anywhere in particular. But then, I'm not from this *world* as you think of it. This world is incomplete. I'm from the *complete* world."

He frowned, as if trying to think of how to explain. That confusing emanation seemed to increase...

She imagined his hands on her; the feeling shimmering from him going directly into her throat, her breasts, the skin of her waist, her hips.

This is nuts, she thought. I'm cautious about men.

Suddenly this guy is in my house, taking over my life. Just when I'm starting to get my own direction together...

Nine months before, she'd dropped out of college after two years of business admin, classes she'd taken because her father wanted her to come into his import firm. He'd pushed her into it when he saw she'd had no idea where to go with her life—she only knew that she didn't want to "just get married and have kids". But every day in business school felt false to her. There were really nice people at the community college who were perfectly happy in it, and she envied them. She'd felt a disconnection, a feeling of climbing a steep, slick hill every time she forced herself to go to the class.

So when a car hit a terrier, and she had to sit there and hold the dog as he convulsed and died in her lap, she realized she wanted to do something else. She dropped out, found a job as a waitress and got into animal rights—something she'd always felt a connection to. That felt good, and she'd started to think she might become a lawyer, to do something in court about these companies using animals—and people— as guinea pigs. Life had just started to have some meaning— and then someone hit her in the head with an existential baseball bat, a bat with "Dennis Boyce" printed on it.

I ought to throw him out, right now, she thought. But she just sat there, looking at him. Finally she asked, "So –I don't know what you mean, about where you're 'from'. This planet, not this planet. How about...*Dennis Boyce?* Where's he from?"

He nodded. "Dennis Boyce is originally from Long Island. He lived in Los Angeles for most of his adult life."

"Come on—you're not that guy. I found him online. I googled him, saw his picture on an old Web site for a radio station. Kinda looked like you, kinda didn't. There was a statement from him. It was...like, shallow."

Boyce shrugged. "His substantial being—his core self— has moved on. Is no longer here. I'm not from Long Island, myself, any more than I'm from any other place."

"So let's try this again. You're from...where?"

"I'm...from everywhere."

"Oh come on, that's hokey."

"Hokey. Yes, I remember. I see. And it's certainly not very clear. I'm from...if not everywhere, then everything."

"Oh please!"

"That's as close as I can come to explaining it—" He broke off, frowning again. "Thing is, Boyce doesn't have much vocabulary. If you'll wait a moment, I'll get some more from the collective mind. Have to specify contemporary English..." He stared into space, for a moment, blinked, shuddered, and then said. "There. More words. But I'm still not sure there's a word for where I'm from. I'm from all-things-in-totality. It was noticed, at that level, that things were wrong here, the wrongness that's outside the accepted ratio."

"It was noticed, was it? Why now? Why not a few thousand years of human confusion and misery earlier, Boyce?"

"It's as if—as if you had a tumor growing in your leg, say. You wouldn't notice it for a long time. But finally you do, when it grows big enough to create pain...eventually you feel it."

"You *felt* something was wrong...with this world. My world."

"*We* felt it. There was someone here trying to keep us from feeling it, or we'd have been here...in the sense you understand...a bit earlier. But finally, we felt something sourced on this lower part of the universe, this ball you live on. We felt several distinct spikes of suffering, at certain unprecedented peaks. Very sharp peaks, over the last eighty years. And since your population has gotten big enough to create high levels of this distress, the emanation it created was transmitted to us—through your appointed transmitters, people of..." He thought about it for a moment. "You call them holy. They have more-complete-sentience. Most people on this planet have only partly developed their awareness. You, Ama, have more complete sentience than many, but these few men and women have fully developed inner selves—as fully as they can develop them, at the level of a human being living physically in this world. Most of them are undeclared, I understand, but they are among you. We've found that virtually everyone who claims to be 'holy'—isn't."

"You say *holy* like there's quotation marks around it. Like you don't quite mean that."

"The word carries mythological connotations. It implies the supernatural. The supernatural doesn't exist."

She stared. "So—there's no life after death, no spirits, no—"

"I didn't say that. The notions people develop of those things are primitive, tied to ancient superstitions." He scratched his head. "I'm sounding pompous, aren't I?"

"Kind of professorial."

"I'll try to sound more...like a regular guy." He cleared his throat. "At any rate, I can't tell you about life after death. I'm not allowed to. Except—I can tell you that 'heaven' and 'hell' are myths. There is only being close to the...what you would call the Divine...or being further away from it. If you're away from it, you're not under its protection and you can be preyed on by whatever's out there."

"But—will I still be myself after death? Is there reincarnation? Is there—"

"Ama? I really am not allowed to tell you anymore about what happens after death."

"Why?"

"I'm not allowed to tell you why I can't tell you, either. I can only tell you that there's something more than nothingness, after death—but it's not what people imagine. That knowledge is something that has to be earned."

"What sort of body did you have before you were here? A purely...uh...spiritual body?"

"In effect. But—no. It was something you might describe as a thinking, feeling, complex field of energy, and you'd think of it as not embodied. But it has its own bodily contours. There are lots of beings you would think of as disembodied in the universe—but they do have bodies. We have bodies. It's difficult to understand from a lower-dimensional perspective. Their bodies are intricate fields contingent on the fields they move within. And they go through many stages of evolution. So in a sense I'm only about six years old, as you reckon time."

"Six years old!"

"But I'm around a hundred thousand years old if you take into account all the permutations I've gone through."

"You mean incarnations?"

"No. More like transmutations...only after a time one transmutes again, and yet again...But, I shouldn't say any more about that—I'm in danger of treading in proscribed areas." He frowned. "The tone I'm speaking in is still tiresome, isn't it? I could talk in the vernacular. 'Their bodies are, like all vibrationally weird, from here, so you can't really...' Hell. I don't think Boyce had a vernacular term for comprehend that isn't out of date. *Dig it* sounds wrong for the current—"

"Dennis?"

"Yes."

"Just talk the way you were before. Whatever seems clearest. You were explaining about the supernatural. Spiritual bodies."

"Very well—though the word 'spiritual' promotes misunderstanding. The truth is, there *is* nothing supernatural, there is only the invisible natural. There are people who are in genuine conversation with the invisible natural. They feel the suffering, and act as transmitters, sending the information—though only some of it got through to us, for a long time."

"Information? It's just information? I thought you could feel it."

"We feel information, yes. All feelings are information."

"Huh. There's suffering every day all over the planet. But you say there were spikes. Do you know anything about... geography?"

"I have absorbed some from Dennis Boyce and more has been transmitted to me. I had to correct some of his assumptions. He seems to have supposed that Sumatra was part of China. That's not right, is it?"

"Ha! It's not right. So do you know where these spikes of suffering were from?"

"One was from Europe. There was apparently a mass extermination of human beings by others..."

"The Holocaust. And the others?"

"From Cambodia, Russia, Africa, China. Rwanda in Africa, and something in the area of Darfur was the last spike."

"The Killing Fields...Stalin's pogroms, Mao's purges... Rwandan genocide, Sudanese genocide. So you guys, whoever you are, were, what, indifferent to the Terror in France or the Black Plague or the genocide of the Armenians in Turkey, or to, oh, the Inquisition, or the slaughter of whole cities in ancient history or to millions starving..."

He gestured—borrowing one of Boyce's—as if to say, *Hey, what can I tell ya?*

Then he sighed. "I know it's fucked up. But harsh conditions are in the nature of the universe. Especially this universe. We're selective about our corrections."

She smiled. "It's 'fucked up'? Yeah. But—why deal with some suffering and not the rest?"

"Because we were supposed to regulate only what puts the... the race with the 'potential for full consciousness' in danger of extermination. Up to a point. We are like... referees. We had left a referee *here*, to see to it that the game was being played fairly."

"It's a *game*?" Her mind was spinning with all this input. She wanted to put thinking aside, do something physical— he was more and more attractive to her, as she looked at him—but a certain fascination kept her listening.

"Only metaphorically," Boyce was saying. "It has rules, it has a playing field. But no, suffering certainly is not a game. Still—we cannot interfere in *all* suffering. I may heal someone, if I encounter them, just to reduce the general background of suffering, and because it's in my nature, but on the whole we allow the natural processes of worlds under our guidance to proceed. This means that destructive volcanic conditions, tectonic conditions, weather, dangerous microorganisms, dangerous animals, all these things are supposed to be there, to exert pressure on you, so that you evolve. Struggle, stress—these things predicate evolution. Difficulty, darkness, pain—it's all part of the machinery, art of the whole picture. War also is to a degree quite natural. But there are levels of injustice and cruelty here that aren't supposed to be here—and diseases that aren't supposed to be here, like Alzheimer's and AIDS. Someone has..." He searched for the phrase. "...fallen down on the job. Maybe deliberately."

"Someone? You said something about a referee who was supposed to be here?"

Boyce sighed. "Yes. It's aggravating as all hell. We're investigating to find out what became of him. Possibly he was damaged and hid the damage from us. We're not all-powerful; we can be damaged, after all. He seems to have...I say 'he' because he chose a male form...he seems to have succumbed first to megalomania, then to a...a sort of narcosis."

"You talking about...God?"

"I understand he called himself Jehovah, in some cultures. Gave himself other names in other cultures. He told your prophets he was a god. But he shifted about, and became by turns vindictive and...reclusive. He keeps pushing things out of balance, in a kind of fury—with a diabolic purpose. He's *become his own opposite*—what you call the devil. Creating problematic genetic types—certain serial killers, for example—or suppressing awareness, empathy, in people enough so that they don't struggle with their animal natures. There is such a thing as useful animal nature of course—even what appears to be cruelty can be useful to a primitive race—but you were supposed to've moved past that about two and a half *millennia* ago. On the contrary, he encouraged it."

"Then—we're not responsible for the evil in the world. So whatever you are, you can't punish us for it."

"This dark influence was just an influence—and many transcended it. But others seemed to enjoy the excessive selfishness, the cruel appetites, the dehumanization he fostered. They cultivated it, in themselves. We *do* hold them responsible—but we won't punish them, not really. We'll simply painlessly *remove* them or...or give them a certain choice, at a certain time."

She was shaking her head. It was all too much. "You're saying that God...*became* the devil? He created the world and then...fucked with it?"

"No, no, this so-called God didn't create the world. Nor the universe. The being I was talking about was never the *real* God. Not that any of the ideas about God I've seen in Boyce's mind, or in most of your literature, have anything to do with reality—there isn't a supernatural 'God'. There's a consciousness...but nothing like the usual notion of 'God'."

"So the God we think we know is, like, the...the 'UnderGod'?"

"As good a term as any."

"And you say there's no real God?"

"There is a great mind that is an expression of the universe itself—that tries to ease suffering, in its way, with an almost infinite slowness. You can call it God for now if you like. It's mind that lives pervades the sum total of all things."

"It didn't create the universe? Neither of these 'gods' you're talking about created the universe?"

"No. *The universe created 'God'*, Ama. 'God' is evolving, as we are. 'God' was created—by the Uncreated."

She wanted to ask him a good deal more, but he sniffed the air. "I think I am in need of...a shower. That's exactly what it is, a *shower.*" Something respecting social protocol seemed to occur to him. "May I? Shower?"

"Sure. By all means."

"Thank you...for your hospitality."

He undressed right there, in front of her. He had definitely changed his body since yesterday. He'd had a little paunch yesterday.

"Gone over *night*," she said, aloud. "You're looking good."

"*Hell* yeah," he said, peeling off his socks. "Ah, I'm getting the vernacular. In the morning, I'll—"

She watched him undress, enjoying his complete immodesty. "Boyce? Um—can I take a shower too? With you?"

"You like to be thrifty with the water? That's good. Good stewardship of resources. We like to encourage that. Please do."

"You sure you're not an angel?"

"Not an angel, no."

"Good." She took off her nightgown, flung it on the bed. Was a little insulted that he didn't look at her, naked, as he went into the bathroom. She had a good body, after all.

He adjusted the shower water, frowning a little as he did it, as if remembering the process, and they got in.

In a few minutes—the warm water flowing over them, the soap sliding, the warmth communicating between them—Boyce had a natural physical response.

"Shall I help you with that, too?" she asked, her heart pounding.

I shouldn't be doing this, she thought. It's not me. But he's no ordinary man. Okay: Understatement.

"I can't recommend that you—that you help me with that, Ama. *It* wants you to, of course. That's in the nature of Boyce's body."

She blew soap bubbles off her lips. "Man, you are a buzz kill."

There was a note of apology in his voice as he said, "I'm not capable of *true* intimacy with you, Ama. I can couple with you using Boyce's body, but if I were to try for any deeper intimacy...you would not survive it. The energies you saw me use at the animal testing lab were...*different.* Of a quite different order. The energies that are involved in the equivalent of intimacy, amongst my kind—are explosive. I mean—I'm afraid you'd trigger the intimacy that my *real* body wants—the body hidden within Boyce's. And in the discharge of energy, your essential self would be forever flung from your body, spun away into the ether. Your body would fail."

"You mean—you'd kill me?"

"No. But you might die as a side effect of sex with me. It would at least damage you. And for me it would be...what kind of comparison can I make? It'd be like a kazoo."

"A *kazoo*? Having sex with me would be like a kazoo?"

"I'm having trouble finding the analogy. Ah—a kazoo compared to, let's say, a perfectly coordinated orchestra of one thousand instruments played by perfect musicians."

"Oh *thanks*, pal!"

"I seem to have fucked up our interpersonal protocol. Dennis Boyce had foggy ideas about women. This problem of scale is not...particular to you. Oh, I mean: Don't take it personally. It isn't you in particular. It's anyone in these little monkey bodies you have. The sensations are so...tiny. Simple primate wiring."

"It's...almost like *bestiality* if you have sex with me? Boyce, that's the last time I ever try to have sex with you."

"Ah. Just as you like."

He seemed relieved.

An Airbase in Yemen

"Lieutenant, do you understand the implications of what you're saying?" Colonel Tobin asked, not unkindly. He was sitting in a camp chair, in the air conditioned Quonset hut, and having to speak loudly because the air conditioner was noisy as one of the Model T's his dad had restored. His father, a retired Air Force officer himself, would've been horrified by what this kid Banks was saying.

"I do understand I will probably be court-martialed, sir," said Lieutenant Banks mildly. Like many pilots he was a compact man, alert, well spoken. He had sandy hair; his hazel eyes seemed reddened by lack of sleep. Unlike Tobin, Banks didn't wear glasses. Poor eyesight had kept Tobin from being a pilot, but his job was to give orders to pilots, and this one wasn't taking orders today.

"You haven't been sleeping, boy? You look tired."

"Couldn't sleep for a couple of days, sir. Kind of felt naturally wired."

"You're not doing those buzz-ups? Those pills are only for long flights, they're not to take on the ground."

"No speed, sir. Just...had an experience. No drugs involved."

"This experience have something to do with you refusing to go on a bombing mission?"

"Yes sir. Colonel, I'll go on a mission to attack that house *in person*—on foot, sir. We've killed a lot of non-combatants, with bombs and missiles and I'm not going to do it anymore. I'll fight the enemy—you just show him to me, face to face. We need to go in and see for ourselves who's there, sir. And accept the risk. Retrain me for a Phantom, I'll dogfight till I bust. But I'm not going to bomb some house that might have kids in it. No sir."

Tobin stood up and went to pour himself a mug of coffee. "You want coffee, Lieutenant?"

"No sir. I hope to sleep tonight. In the brig if I have to."

Banks said something else that Tobin couldn't make out, so he turned off the air conditioner—and the room seemed too quiet. "Damn thing. It gets hot in here so fast without it. Banks, you are disobeying an order to attack the enemy, and that's as grave as it gets."

"Yes sir."

Tobin glanced at the young pilot. Banks seemed strangely unconcerned. Tobin would've assumed drugs, no matter what Banks said, or insanity, except that he'd had three other cases like this and he knew that every commander in Yemen was plagued by them. It was getting hard to keep it out of the media.

"So this experience, Lieutenant—you don't seem eager to talk about it."

"No sir. It'll just be misunderstood. I tried already. In one part of it, I saw some lights. Medics say that could mean I had a stroke. But I've never felt better. Except for needing some sleep."

"You saw some lights." Some psy-ops thing? Was the

enemy experimenting on his men somehow? But the Yemeni insurgents didn't have anything like that.

"More like...more like I was given light, sir." He licked his lips. Seemed embarrassed. "I saw things around me, so clear, so incredibly clear. I had some time off, I was walking along, on the edge of town, I could see every grain of sand, individually, at my feet, sir. Time slowed down."

"Time...slowed down."

"Yes sir. And...I saw some Yemenis working on the road and they...when they looked at me it was like I saw *right into them*. And what I saw in them—it was like it was mirrored in me..." He shook his head. "I can't bomb indiscriminately, sir. I just can't."

"I see." Despite himself, Tobin was moved. He decided that he was going to declare Banks a victim of some form of battle fatigue, send him home for treatment. Partly it was sympathy—he understood the boy's compunctions, though his own orientation was for the bigger tactical picture. But also—there was just something about Banks. It'd be like kicking his three-year-old son, little Harry, to prosecute Banks. Not that Banks was childish—but he seemed *pure* in the way Harry was.

Goddamn but he'd like to see Harry right about now.

"Well, I'm going to send you for evaluation stateside. Come on, let's go over to the medic station, I want to talk to Dr. Bernstein. Let's hustle."

"Yes sir," Banks answered tonelessly.

Tobin glanced at the young man as they went out into the brassy, molten sunlight, the palpable heat, the odor of dust and truck exhaust. "You don't seem all that relieved, boy. You ought to be."

"I appreciate not being court-martialed, sir. But it won't matter, you see. I just...know. That it won't matter. Harrison, he had an experience like mine, and it didn't hit him as hard as it did me. He doesn't *know*. Some of us—we get it clearer. We get to see things. And I see it, sir. *It's not going to matter.* It's..."

"Colonel?" It was Sergeant Blaylock, a stocky black man,

wiping sweat from his forehead as he strode up, assault rifle slanted across his chest. Behind him was a Yemeni, in a turban, sandals, and dishdasha, wrists tied behind him, and two Filipino MPs, with their white helmets and guns at ready, clearly escorting the local.

"What is it, Blaylock?"

"Sir, this man here says he can lead us to three weapons caches. Says he can locate a bunch of explosives and timers the insurgents are planning to use."

"Another insurgent push? I thought that was pretty much over."

"He says no. Says they've just been biding their time, sir. Says there's all these caches..."

"I speak English," the man said, with an Arabic accent, only a little halting. "I can speak for myself."

"Very well. You are one of the Mujahadeen?"

"I was. I was Mujahadeen Brigade. I helped to make bombs, suicide bombs. We were planning many new bombings, planning all together. But I saw that it was not right —because we kill the people. We do not so much kill the occupiers. We kill the people, our own people! My mullah, he says we have to do it, he says he knows they're all martyrs, all are going to paradise—but something happened to me, and when next I listened to him speak, I knew he was lying." There were tears in his eyes then. "Lies. He made many lies to me. The people are not going to go to paradise because we blow them up and we are not going to go to paradise for killing them. I am a Muslim. I saw that this man who says he is a mullah was not a true mullah and not a true Muslim. He thinks he is a Muslim. But he is not. Mohammed would not ask us to do this."

Banks was nodding. The Iraqi and the pilot made eye contact. Some indefinable understanding passed between them.

Tobin glanced at Banks, then at the Iraqi. "You two know each other?"

"No sir," Banks said. "Not till this moment." He licked his lips. "But, in a way, we do know each other. This man is telling the truth, sir. He will take you to those weapons. Safely."

"How do you know that?"

"You can see it, sir. He's *not lying.* It's right there, in his face—and all around him. I'd *know* if he were lying, sir. I promise you—this man has seen the truth. The light was given to him too."

The Yemi insurgent nodded, and smiled sadly at the American pilot.

And the pilot smiled back.

8

Sacramento, California

PROBABLY a waste of time, Swift thought, getting out of his car in front of Linda's house. If she had anything in the house that gave the address they were going to, she probably took it with her. Probably the suits at Colbertson's offices were lying. *We really have no information about a retreat, sir. Now if you'll excuse us...*

Hell, they must've been lying—they were packing. They must know where they're packing for. They'll be gone when I go back there...

It was sunny, breezy out; bees buzzed around the enormous white blossoms of an angel's trumpet bush in a corner of the yard, its sickly-sweet smell seeming to continue the day's motif: pretty on the surface with a rot underneath. A beautiful day, but everything he looked at seemed to ache with anxiety for Erin. The beetling eaves of the house seemed worried; the thatchy lawn seemed choppy with worry. Everything worried—even the kid on the front porch.

A tall slender black teenager sat there, on the splintering wicker chair, leaning forward, elbows on his knees, scowling. He was dressed in a hand-painted T-shirt, two sizes too large, oversized green military pants bucketing at the back, his hair in cornrows.

"You her dad?" the teenager asked, looking Swift over with a sardonic appraisal.

"Yeah. You Shontel?"

"I better be. Where they at?"

"Gone somewhere," Swift said, coming onto the porch, looking through the front window into the house. It had the obscure look of a house no one was in, though most of their things were there. "I don't know how long or where, been trying to find out. You really don't know?"

Shontel glanced at the angel's trumpet bush. Somewhere between a bush and a tree, really. "I asked you where they at, you think I was frontin'? Lying, pretending, I mean."

"I know what frontin' is. No, I don't think that. I'm just getting desperate. I got some definite 'frontin'' from the dumbass fundies at that megachurch her mom's been going to."

"Her mom tried to get me to go. I wouldn't go. You see that angel's trumpet shit, there? People make tea out of that shit and smoke it and make themselves sick. Erin told me about that. I never heard that till she told me. They think it's gonna make them high."

"She been getting high?" Swift made it sound like a casual question.

"Erin? Naw, man. I'm trying to figure it out, work out where they went. I've been here all morning, came over twice last night looking for Erin."

His heart warmed to Shontel. He seemed genuinely concerned about Erin. "It's that church, Shontel. That megachurch took them somewhere. I don't think Erin went voluntarily. But I talked to a cop friend of mine, he told me that unless I got some strong evidence that they were kidnapped by the church, Linda can pretty much insist on taking her underage daughter to 'church camp' or wherever—"

"Cops," Shontel snorted. "Going to get *lots* of help from cops. You think she's at church camp?"

"Not exactly. They're calling it a retreat. Being very mysterious about it. You never heard 'em mention any retreat place—any town?"

"Nah. Shit. Not that I can remember. How we going to find it?"

We? "I'm going to try a guy I know at OBM—apparently they're sponsoring this retreat, according to Linda. He'd have heard where the corporate retreat is. Then I'm going there myself."

Shontel stood up and stretched. "How long we going to be gone? I got to get a change of clothes?"

"I can't be taking you away from your family on what might be a wild goose chase."

"You got no choice, brewd, I'm going."

"Or..." *Or what?* What good would it do them to get in a pissing contest? It occurred to him that Erin might've gone voluntarily after all, might be persuaded to stay with the sect. If he had Shontel along, that'd be further persuasion to get her to leave.

Was he really going to find this place and crash it? Was he making a mistake? Maybe it was a big damn to-do over nothing. Maybe they'd spend a few days praying there, nothing would happen but boredom, and they'd come home.

But it didn't feel that way. He'd heard about Christian end-times sects who'd gone to Israel, to "help bring about the Day of Judgment," back in the late twentieth century. The Israelis had expelled them—the "Armageddonists" had been hinting about violence. Who knew how crazy Colbertson was?

There was no choice, really. He had to find Erin.

"Yeah, whatever, Shontel. You can go if you want, if you're legal to go. Bring more than one change of clothes."

Washington, DC

The President of the United States was at the window of his office, looking out at the White House lawn. Trees leaned in a breeze, straightened, then leaned again. A flock of pigeons circled. The President's thoughts circled too.

"I just don't know," he said. He hated to admit he didn't know. But there was no denying it today.

"This OBM Shield has national security ramifications, sir," said his aide. "Some would say it's a threat to national security—the OBM people say it's protecting us from a threat to national security."

"Suppose it's protecting us from...Judgment? Suppose these things they're worried about are some of *the Signs*? According to that report...well, they might be."

"Kind of funny, that report, sir—like he's losing his objectivity. Great deal of that going around."

"But just suppose... suppose we're trying to stop Judgment Day?"

"If it's God's work, sir, nothing can stop it."

"True. We might be punished for trying, though."

"Far as I understand it, OBM is simply trying to block a certain high energy particle phenomenon."

"A what?"

"A transmission of some kind, sir. Now, if it's God—does God 'transmit' in anything human beings can pick up on their instruments?"

"That's a damned good point." The President took a long breath. Made up his mind. "I guess we'll let them go ahead. You read all these reports?"

"Yes sir."

"I'm kind of shook up about all these soldiers refusing to take their orders. Anyhow it's like they're insanely particular about their orders. Some they'll take, some they won't. Six suspected insurgents released from detention in Yemens—with no authorization. Just, whoops, out they go."

"They didn't let them *all* go, sir."

"No. It's just—where do they get off making these unilateral decisions?"

The aide thought that the very question had been asked about the President more than once, but he kept his peace.

"We've got about a third of Congress suddenly absentee," the President went on. "And the ones who are still there are saying crazy things. It's getting into the television news, now. Media's not taking directions anymore. Who the hell do they think they are?"

"I don't know, sir. Chief of Staff says that if we want to regain control we'd better let OBM move ahead—and help them out if we can."

The President nodded briskly. "That's what we're going to do. That's just what we're going to do, by God..."

Coldwater Canyon, California

The Man was coming upstairs. Cliff heard him coming.

This was the time The Man was going to hurt him in the *big* way. Till now, there'd been only the abduction, the binding, The Man slapping him. But Cliff knew the big, hard, bloody hurt was coming. And then: being dead. He knew it with a loneliness that filled all the universe. He wondered if his parents were still looking for him. He knew they'd never find him. The Man had explained that; had explained why; had told him about the others. And Cliff believed him. "I'm telling you this so that you can be ready to do what I want and maybe not get hurt as much. We'll see..." The Man had said. The Man had seemed like a big machine in the body of a person; he'd seemed like he was being operated like the remote control truck Cliff had gotten for Christmas...

The Man was coming up into the attic. He was pushing open the trapdoor. He climbed up, singing a song to himself that Cliff didn't recognize.

Cliff felt the crying feeling start up in him and tried to keep it down because he knew The Man would punish him for it. The Man might like it, though. The Man seemed to like it when he cried even though he was hitting him for crying.

Cliff wanted to shout, "YOU DON'T MAKE ANY SENSE!"

But the leather gag in his mouth prevented him from doing anything but whimpering; the handcuffs on his wrists prevented him from trying to get away as The Man leaned over him. The Man smelled like eucalyptus leaves and cigarette smoke.

He was a dark shape, outlined by the light from the trapdoor, and he had no face in the shadows at all.

"Time to play, Cliff," said The Man.

"You sure this is the block, Dennis?" Ama asked, as she drove onto a cul-de-sac of bungalows shaded by eucalyptus trees. They were just half a mile from Ama's place in Los Angeles.

"I am sure, yes."

"You know, there are other animal experimentation centers. I could take you there."

"They're being taken care of."

"By who?"

"By others like me. And a greater cleansing is coming— the great sweeping light, which we have summoned. It began in the Sudan today. It is going around the world at a fairly slow rate, and it won't get here soon enough to save the one in this house, so we'll do it, you and I. Some we will not be able to save at all, in some places...but perhaps most. Perhaps."

He seemed preoccupied as he spoke, looking at the only two-story house on the block, and she sensed that he was talking to someone else at the same time. Telepathy, or something even more powerful than telepathy.

She parked and looked at him and found herself wondering yet again, almost the way she had when she'd followed him into the animal-testing lab, what the hell she was doing here. Oh, she knew he was for real. But lightning was real too; did you stand on a roof in a lightning storm, waving a metal rod?

He started to get out of the car, then turned to look at her, grave and decisive and very present, so that when you looked at him you thought he seemed more real than anything around him, more real than the car, than the street, the trees, the houses.

"Ama? Did you want to stay here, wait for me in the car?"

She did—and she didn't. She could let him get out and then drive off and let him go about his business, and just let it all happen. She could at least be removed from it—not feel this grim responsibility, this feeling of being the first to see the tsunami coming and not knowing whom to tell first. She could just let the transfiguration of the world simply—unfold. What could she do to stop it?

Why would she want to stop it?

But she realized she almost *did* want to stop it. Even though he was a vector of...of justice? So he seemed: A living vector of justice. But something in her wanted to stop it. Because it meant the whole world would be redefined, would become something presently unimaginable, and even though that might theoretically be a good thing, it terrified her.

At last she said, "No. I guess I'll come. What are we going to do here?"

He didn't answer, but strode away from her, and she thought of a Patti Smith song, "Stride of the Mind". It was like he was striding through her mind as she watched him.

She got out of the car and followed him up the walk, under the eucalyptus tree. The lawn was neatly cut; a white-painted lawn-jockey stood in one grassy corner up against the house. Hooks for a porch swing protruded from the ceiling of the wide front porch, but there was no swing.

She expected Boyce to knock, but he simply opened the screened door and put his hand on the doorknob. She could hear the front door's lock click open. He opened the door, went in, and she followed, feeling a shudder go through her at the flagrant illegality of what they were doing. At the lab, she could've said it was civil disobedience, but what was this?

Inside Ama smelled a certain mustiness she associated with the houses of people who rarely went out. The living room contained a brown sofa, a brown leather easy chair, an abstract painting over the sofa, a yellow-brown carpet, and nothing else except an ashtray on a table beside the chair, with a single crimped cigarette butt in it.

"Dennis, seriously, I'm scared. I don't want to get shot and I don't want to go to jail."

"You won't be shot. Or arrested."

"If you say so. Where are you going now...?"

"Upstairs. They're upstairs. You can feel them, if you open up your attention enough, Ama."

She followed him up the narrow wooden stairway to an upstairs hallway, itself narrow, with a linoleum floor, no wall decorations. At the far end was a wooden ladder, leading to an open trap door in the ceiling. There was a little plaster dust on the floor around the base of the ladder.

A muffled, choked, squealing sound came from the trap door. The sound made Ama feel cold; it made tears burn in her eyes and she didn't know why. She wasn't at all sure what made the sound. Then there was a dragging noise— something was being dragged overhead.

Boyce went to the ladder, and shouted, "Mr. Winsock! Ross Winsock! Bring the boy down here!"

There was a long frozen moment of silence. Then hissing noises of warning. Whisperings. Footsteps coming closer to the trap door.

A creak as the man up there crouched to peer down at them. Ama saw only his feet. Then she heard a distinctive sound that she'd only heard before in movies. But it was that exact sound, oh yes, there was no doubt: the click-click of a gun cocking.

"Dennis—?" Ama's voice was just a squeak. "Dennis I think—"

Boyce raised a hand for silence. He kept looking at the square of darkness in the ceiling. Then he tilted his head forward, almost the way her father would when he would bow, a little, to another Japanese businessman. Boyce seemed to be aiming the top of his head at the trapdoor. She waited...

There it was, that thrumming, that drumming in the air, that seemed to spread out from the crown of his head, and she had to put out a hand to keep her balance when it washed over her.

She heard a thump and the man above them came tumbling down through the hole, the gun clattering, the man sliding bumpily down the ladder to land on his rump on the floor.

Instinctively, Ama rushed forward and snatched up the gun—a large revolver—by the crosshatched metal butt and, backing away, she tossed it down the hall behind her.

The man was ordinary looking, his graying black hair cut close, the top of his balding head tanned, marked with spots from the sun; his face was lined, his mouth down-turned, his eyes small, his nose stubby. He was wearing a sleeveless T-shirt, and trousers and sneakers. His fly was unzipped. He had a gold alumnus ring on one hand; his nails were exactingly manicured.

His gray eyes flicked dazedly, right and left, then up at Boyce. "What'd you use to bring me down, some kind of microwave thing? I've read about them."

He looked at Boyce's empty hands in puzzlement.

"Move away from the ladder," Boyce said, his voice even, but commanding.

The man—Winsock, Dennis had said—looked like he was going to tell Boyce to go to hell, and maybe rush him.

She expected another one of those strange emanations—but it didn't come. Instead, there was a subtle sense of disclosure in the air. As if something invisible was saying, *Look here, see how things really are.*

She saw it herself, then. Boyce seemed in that moment like a man carved of some incredibly compact, hard material, like a diamond—and Winsock seemed like a little piece of dirty, corroded wire, with grease on it, something you'd find in the trunk of a car and toss away in irritation. The room seemed to bend toward Boyce, in some way, like gravity bending toward a black hole; and Winsock seemed hardly even there.

Winsock made a small, frightened animal sound and covered his eyes. Then he got onto his hands and knees and crawled away from Boyce and Ama; crawled off into a corner.

"It won't help to try to run," Boyce told him.

"I know," Winsock said, huddled in the corner. "I'm dead, aren't I? I died. I had a heart attack, that it?"

"You're not dead yet," Boyce said, turning to Ama. "There's a little kidnapped boy up there, named Clifford Robert Fishman. Winsock probably the keys to his handcuffs up there."

Winsock murmured, "It's all there."

"Oh my God—a little boy?" Ama was already partly up the ladder as she said it.

She found Clifford wedged in a corner of the attic—a small boy in his underwear, close beside his wadded-up jeans, bruised but not badly hurt. She found Winsock's key ring hanging on a nail; she located the little handcuff key, and unlocked the boy's restraints, then picked up his jeans and helped him—both of them weeping—across the attic, down the ladder.

When she got down she found that Boyce was gone —but no, she sensed him nearby. He had taken Winsock into another room.

"What's your name?" she asked the boy, helping him into his jeans and making herself stop crying.

"Cliff. It's Cliff Fishman. It's...I'm from..." He was hyperventilating and couldn't say anymore.

"Relax, relax, you're safe now. My name's Ama and you're gonna be okay now...we'll get you back to your folks..." She held Cliff a few moments, till he calmed a little, then handed her cell phone to him. She thought it'd be good to give him something to do. "Run downstairs to the porch and call 911, tell the police what happened—that the man took you and we found you and tell them your name, I'm sure they're looking for you. Look at the street address and tell them where it is. Finch Street. Okay?"

The boy nodded, snatched the cell phone and ran down the stairs.

She found Boyce and Winsock in a bedroom nearby, Boyce standing against a curtained window, Winsock kneeling with his back to him, hand clutched against his chest, completely helpless, though Boyce was neither armed nor apparently threatening.

"Is there a hell?" Winsock asked, voice trembling.

"The question is irrelevant to you, Winsock. You have nothing that would survive death. That part of you was strangled away at some point."

"I have no soul?" Winsock shut his eyes. "That would make sense..."

"I did not say that. You have a part in the mind that underlies things, as all living beings do. Even a cricket partakes in it. But the part of you that can feel for others—the part that could survive death—is dead, or as good as dead. That part of your brain did not develop; so that part of your soul didn't either."

"So it wasn't my fault!"

"It's not so simple. You knew. You could have struggled with your sickness; could have reached for fullness, and you didn't. You preferred to feed your appetites. How many children did you destroy?"

"Not so many. At first I let them go—but I had to move, then, and it was risky and...I learned that I liked killing them even more. If you let me live, I can tell you where the others are. The ones still alive. I gave them to someone. Sometimes we trade..."

"We know where the others are, now. We know all that you know and all that is known by everyone you know. We have your *type*, and we sweep for it. All the others will be found very soon. Every one. No child on this world will ever be hurt in this way again." He reached toward the top of Winsock's head. His hand seemed to vibrate in place, like a tuning fork. Boyce had a look on his face like a man working in carpentry, or like an electrician laying a line. He was concentrating, but there was no emotion involved, unless there was a faint sheen of job satisfaction.

"That's...that's...a good thing, eliminating those others too..." Winsock seemed almost to believe it.

The vibration of Boyce's right hand grew more pronounced, so that it blurred. His hand seemed transparent for a moment.

He reached down into the top of Winsock's head, the fingers penetrating without breaking skin or bone, and clutched at something. Winsock gave a childish cry and flailed his arms. Boyce drew his hand out, clutching something—it was like a deflated dummy made of some ectoplasmic substance. It wriggled and flapped, and then burst into fragments—which became smoke, but not smoke. It dissipated without a trace, and Winsock keeled forward, stone dead. Boyce's hand returned to normal.

Ama found that she felt very little, seeing Winsock eliminated—snuffed out, almost literally like a candle-flame.

She thought of the little boy downstairs. She and Boyce went to comfort him, Ama wondering how—or if—Boyce would explain all this to the police. "Boyce—how do we explain our part in this?"

"Some of the police are now conscious. We've arranged for one of them to respond to your call. He will know what I am. There will be no problem."

"When Winsock died—did it hurt him?"

"No."

"Too bad," she said, thinking of children bound in attics.

"You're opposed to hurting animals, but not people?"

"People too. But some guys...I'm sorry it didn't hurt, in his case."

"You're still a savage people," he said, without any real censure in his voice. It was just an observation. "Even the gentlest of you."

They found Cliff on the corner, huddled against a lamppost, chewing his knuckles, his eyes flicking wildly about. The boy ran to Ama when he saw her, and she took him in her arms, and held him as they waited.

She felt a sudden joy, then, remembering what Boyce had said:

No child on this world will ever be hurt in this way again.

London, England

"Mr. Cohn McGee," intoned Judge Bracegirdle, at the inquest, adjusting his pince-nez on his long nose to see McGee better with his rheumy eyes. "What have you got to say for yourself, Mr. McGee?"

"Did what I had to, didn't I?" said the little man with the broad shoulders; he had a shock of black hair, in odd contrast with his red eyebrows, his spray of freckles. He adjusted the coat of his blue suit, apparently not used to it, and unconsciously rubbed with a thumb under the handcuffs around his wrists.

"Stand still there, you," growled the bailiff.

His lawyer, a bored-looking woman with a pointed nose, half-glasses, and a pile of glossy black hair on her head, whispered to him. McGee nodded and stood very still.

"Come sir," Bracegirdle said, spreading his hands, "you can't say you had to steal an airplane full of someone's goods. You had no crying need. You were a pilot working steady. I understand you had a nice little cottage, two cars. Perhaps you had no great wealth, but according to the prosecution's brief you did not have a grievous need for money. No children suffering from cancer, needing treatment, none of that tatty drama. So then, what drove you to this?"

"Mr. McGee—" his lawyer began, looking at her watch, "was possibly mentally incompetent due to—"

"Miss Berrett, is it? Counsel, let him speak for himself, if he so chooses. I'm curious about this case."

"Like to speak for myself," McGee piped up. "Regarding the grievous need, sir, wasn't my need, not mine specific. Except as how everyone's need is mine. It was them children, sir, it was their need. I saw it on the telly, your honor, how they were starving by the tens of thousands in Bangladesh, after that flood, and I was to fly over that country with a plane full of food! Full of rice and soy—bloody damn tons of the stuff—"

"Here, watch your dirty mouth!" the bailiff snapped.

McGee's lawyer whispered to him again. "Sorry, squire," he said to the bailiff, in a small voice. "Well sir, your lordship, after what happened to me, I couldn't do that again, flying over all them hungry mouths carrying just what they needed. I've been flying cargo in Asia since I was a boy, my Da, he was a freight pilot, we never gave a thought to our cargo except what was they paying for it. But your honor, I knew I could land that rice and soy, and give it to the Red Cross there, and say it was a donation, and they took it right enough—and it wasn't enough yet, so I went back and got another load, and took that to them too. And sir there was children alive after, who wouldn't have been had I not done it."

"Another load! *Did* you, by God!" the judge exclaimed, shaking his head in wonder. "You know, I find it hard to fault the, um, spirit of your enterprise, Mr. McGee, but you might've used your *own* money to feed people, if you were so bent on this—sold your house and..." He shrugged and looked at McGee skeptically over his pince-nez.

"Your honor—" Miss Barrett began.

"Let him speak, counsel!"

McGee nodded. "I've already got me house on the market for that purpose, your honor—was going to sell everything and help how I could, but of course I was arrested and, well, sir, you know the rest."

The judge sniffed. "I don't know what's to become of you, McGee. Greater India Produce Limited means to prosecute you. But then, they can't, if they can't find you."

"Sir?"

"I myself had...an *experience*, McGee."

They exchanged a knowing look. "Oh indeed, sir!"

"Yes. This is as good a time to retire from the bench as any—there will be an uproar, of course, when I let you go. In fact..." He stood up and removed his gown and cap. "I believe I shall go with you. Bailiff, release him."

The barrister looked back and forth between them, her mouth open. She was stunned into abject silence.

"But what will you do, sir, if you're not a judge?" McGee asked, as the puzzled bailiff complied.

"Oh, I'll do whatever I can—in the time that remains."

"The time that remains, sir?"

"You don't know, McGee? You will. Some got that message, some didn't. It was all a bit overwhelming. Well... shall we go round the local and have a pint? You coming, Bailiff?"

OBM Retreat Grounds, Northern California

"Birch? You have a reason to be at this facility?" Griffin barely glanced up from his electronic clipboard as Birch and Meredith walked up. "This is pretty need-to-know, here..." He was speaking rapid-fire, the words tumbling over one another. "Things to do, don't need people stumbling around, bumbling into things..."

Birch managed not to roll his eyes. "O'Hanlon asked me to come."

Griffin didn't seem to hear that. "...asking inane questions, every frequency must be monitored...but now you're here, of course, you have to stay, no choice in the matter..."

Taking out his sunglasses to ease the bright sunlight, Birch considered Griffin, thinking: He's *on* something.

Birch put the sunglasses on, and the sky, barely darkening, took on a deeper tone of blue; the grass of the broad open space that had once been intended as a football field was a darker green; the tall fir trees ringing the field became shadowy. But the glassy, wire-strung, forty-foot-high columns, each rippling inwardly with rings of light, seemed brighter; they were placed at intervals around the field, in an oval. Birch counted twenty-three of them, all but one the same distance apart, the twenty-third looking like a goal post with another column at the south end, and several standing rather crookedly.

Griffin was in front of an improvised control center, laid

out on a tarp, under a dusty orange awning that looked like he'd pulled it from his garage. He was hunched over, fluttering his fingers over his digital clipboard that threw faint green light on his face.

Meredith strolled up close beside Birch, her arms crossed on her chest, a pose some women struck to show they were neutral observers. She leaned close to Birch and whispered, "Those circles of light going up those columns—they seem like they're just...decoration."

"I heard that," Griffin said, almost running the three syllables into one word. He didn't look up from his clipboard as he went on, "And you are correct. The circles of light are showmanship. O'Hanlon needs to *see* something happening, heh, but these columns and the other ones in Australia will do their job, they're not just a lot of trumpery, pally, no sir, uh-uh, this is the shit. The lights are fake but the guts of the device—that's real."

"Australia?" Birch asked.

"Yes, yes, yes, you have to bounce it back and forth, hither and yon, off the Earth's core, and then through your other receiving station and—never mind, forget it, just forget it, there's some sandwiches in the...the whatsit, the Event Tent, that big tent over there, some Gatorade or some shit..."

"What, no open bar?"

But Griffin had ducked his head under the awning to go into the control area, peering at the clutter of blocky consoles and instruments set up on portable tables. The whole thing was wired to one of OBM's new, prototypical hydrogen batteries

"Those lights move up the columns almost like the 'Jacob's ladder' bursts in Tesla coils," Birch said, "I think it's supposed to remind you of Tesla's gear. And just to—look like it's doing something."

"You don't think it does anything, really?"

He lowered his voice, as O'Hanlon walked by, in close conversation with the Elder Colbertson, a man in a double-breasted suit; the elder Colbertson had a broad face, mossy eyebrows, long hair tied back, so that he looked like some acquaintance of George Washington. "I don't know if it does or not. And how'd he get it built so quickly?"

"He's been working with a big team, two hundred technicians, night and day—literally. Sent them home two hours ago. The whole thing still looks thrown together to me."

Birch glanced over his shoulder at the "End Timers" crowd gathered in the bright yellow canvas Event Tent, thirty yards away, murmuring and grazing on canapés and juice. They didn't look like religious fanatics, particularly, but they were chattering happily, looking out the open sides of the tent at the sky. Waiting for the coming of the End of Days. A few of them lined up at the blue port-a-potties to one side of the tent. They could be at an ordinary company-wide picnic. He judged there were several hundred in the core group of faithful around the Reverend Colbertson and his charismatic son. He could see George Colbertson standing at the center of the group, orating.

Birch glanced at the sky himself. He'd heard stories of the "signs" and he'd seen some inconclusive video—you could make anything with CGI—but hadn't seen anything miraculous himself.

He wanted to be back in his apartment, in New York, or better yet at a baseball game. He forgot his self-consciousness at a baseball game. One of the things he liked about Meredith was she knew the odds between the Sox and the Yankees. She sat patiently with him during the games—they'd only been to a couple, but she'd been great at both of them, never complaining when it ran into extra innings, though he could see she was tired.

She'd only marred their trips to the games once, by veering into politics, between innings, talking about how the New York subway system should be privatized. He had almost pointed out that privatization of a public service was historically disastrous, but he knew how the conversation would go then, she'd say "oh in time competition would force them into efficiency," and he'd say "it ends up in a monopoly, then there *is* no real competition," and then *she'd* say...

Instead of going down that rutted road, he'd changed the subject. It was better not to talk politics with Meredith.

"You know," Birch murmured, looking at Griffin, "I'm really starting to wonder, Meredith, about this whole 'influence' thing—I mean, if it was an illusion to start with. There are, you know, social movements, that come and go. Labor movements, the so-called Summer of Love, and so on. They ripple through society, they wear off. So maybe all this behavior that O'Hanlon has got everyone worked up about is just one of those. Maybe it's spreading through some... some Wi-Fi Internet underground thing. Like, what do they call them—flash gangs or whatever that is."

"Flash mobs," Meredith corrected him. "And what about Baxter?"

"Someone probably *did* put something in his coffee..."

But surprising Birch with the matter-of-fact conviction in her voice, Meredith said, "Something's happening, all right, and not just a social movement. I've gotten a lot more information—the President is all worked up. The Pope. The Prime Minister of England. They're worried."

He looked around at the crowd. "So there are probably government agents here? NSA, people like that?"

"Sure. So be careful what you say."

He looked at her to see if she was joking. She wasn't.

"Well, if Griffin doesn't get a grip—" He gestured at the glassy, flickering columns around them. "This thing could melt down, short circuit. Who knows what that equipment really does? He could fry us all while he's supposedly saving us. I mean, Griffin is—well look at him!"

Even from here they could see sweat running off Griffin's forehead, dripping onto the back of his hands as he sat in a folding chair typing furiously on a keyboard, his face drawn, his body rigid, eyes staring.

She nodded. "But O'Hanlon thinks he's our own Merlin and he's going to trust him."

O'Hanlon isn't King Arthur, Birch thought, watching his

CEO waving his arms, pontificating at three dazed, trapped-looking men in business suits, ranting about how the Chinese were behind this, it'd all started with regulations, the Chinese had financed the Democrats, surely, through some front organization, to regulate American industry so it couldn't be competitive with their Communist industrial machine...

Birch shook his head, thinking, *How'd I end up here?*

9

Sherman Oaks, California

AMA felt a dull disorientation, threatening to become panic, when she returned home with a bag of groceries in her arms to find Boyce missing. The blankets were flung on the floor beside the sofa—there was no other sign he had ever been there.

Maybe she'd imagined the whole thing. Maybe in a few more days she'd be in a mental hospital trying to explain to a therapist why it had all seemed so real.

But the blankets were there—and a curly brown hair on a pillow.

Stop it, Ama, she told herself.

And whatever he was, she reflected, picking up the blankets, he had either adopted some slovenliness natural to Dennis Boyce or he didn't understand housework. He used a toilet properly, and once, in a dreamy way, he had carried his dishes to the sink. But that was about it. He'd never asked about clean clothes, and she'd had to peel his clothes off him to wash them.

Ama went into the kitchen, calling his name, or anyway the name he had borrowed, and found it vacant but for a single housefly, describing elliptical circles in the air. She put the groceries away, thinking she'd drive around looking for him. He wasn't from "here". He might be lost, or...

The front door banged, and she rushed into the living room to find him sitting on the blankets she'd folded on the sofa, staring into space. He looked even younger today—a nineteen-year-old boy.

"I hope you're not going to get even younger than this," she said. "I'd hate to have to change diapers."

"No," he said, distantly, "I think I'm in the optimal format."

She sat in the rattan chair across from him. He seemed to re-organize the room, just by sitting in it. Things that seemed out of place a moment ago—a magazine lying open next to an easy chair—now seemed to have fallen into the perfect place: the order in disorder. Details leapt out at her; the air hummed with subtle energy. She had learned to blunt some of her sensations when he was there, to draw back, close down the aperture on the camera, so to speak. It kept her sane to do that. She focused on Dennis Boyce, now, as an ordinary human being—though he was that only physically.

"You look like...like something's bothering you."

"You were asleep when I left."

"Where've you been?"

"I had a—it would seem like a dream to you. It was a cry for help from somewhere nearby. Only about six blocks from here. There were a number of houses affected by an addictive toxin, sold in the area. Two such toxins, actually—one of the houses was infested with the amphetamine variety, the other by another toxin—they call it 'crack'."

"Uh-huh. Good old crack. Were you able to help?"

"Up to a point. I cured eleven people of their addictions—"

She stared. "In...a couple of hours? Just cured them? Dennis...it's the plague of the world—I mean, one of them. One of the worst. Can you...?"

He held up a hand to forestall the questions. "As you'd expect—as it is in any world—there's a complexity behind these things. The household that summoned me was headed by a single mother. She had become a prostitute. Most of the money she earned went to her addiction. Her children were undernourished. They were badly injured, psychologically—or perhaps neurologically is the word. These injuries, these deep feelings of abandonment, are printed in the very tissue of the human brain. *He* saw to that, of course."

"He...Oh. *Him.* The UnderGod." She watched Boyce closely as he spoke, looking for traces of emotion, or personality. But he showed these only if they seemed called for, socially. His air was of a workman, a technician. He seemed almost chillingly objective. Not cold, though—more like a kindly veterinarian, coolly removing an impacted tooth from a dog.

"The woman's history involved her own abandonment, first by her father, then by her husband. This in turn appears to be the result of trauma that goes back generations, poverty putting too much stress on families, tribalism—racism, you call it—enforcing the poverty, itself the legacy of a period of slavery. I cannot erase that history—we are not allowed to remove all trace of the negative from a person. Something must be there for a person to struggle with. There is a reason for the need to struggle inwardly with...negative tendencies. But I was able to remove the cravings and cure her of a dangerous retrovirus—"

"HIV, Dennis? Did you...you cured her of..."

"Yes, though she didn't have the symptoms yet. But we plan to end HIV. We're already curing AIDS patients—the UnderGod came up with that one, and it is so unfair to so many. Children born with it, people getting it from a blood transfusion. AIDS will be history."

"Oh god..." She had to sit down at that. Felt herself dissolving, emotionally. "Can that be true? That's..."

"Why are you crying?"

"Oh, Dennis, my best friend as a teenager was a gay guy. He's dead, he—Dennis why couldn't you have come sooner? Why did he have to die but not these others?"

"We came as soon as we could," he said gently. "I wish we could've helped more people."

"What..." Ama paused to wipe her eyes. "What happened with the crack addicts?"

"When I left she and the other parents were begging their children to forgive them—and I eased some of the trauma in the children so they could accept their parents again. But she will continue to have a tendency to medicate herself, to muffle emotional pain. She may not be able to remain free of addiction unless she's given guidance."

"So...will she? Be given guidance? I mean, there are Twelve-Step groups, there are therapies. But you could really guide her..."

"Her specifically? Your species as a whole will receive the guidance, if that decision is made. We can restore some semblance of justice—the expression is, *a level playing field*, and then we can withdraw, or we can monitor Phase Three with guidance."

"Phase Three? What's that? What...what phase are we in now?" She was aware of her heart pounding. She was going from an enormous emotional high, thinking about no more AIDS in the world, to sinking into a welter of fear. Boyce was gravely delineating the transfiguration of her whole world...

"Phase One was the arrival of 'consciousness lamps' to begin the process, lay the groundwork, in certain carefully selected places—in something like social pressure points—so what came after would not be too shocking; so that there would be people who could guide the others when the second and third phases began. Phase Two began with the arrival of myself and a few other...*Adjustors,* you might call us."

"Adjustors? Like insurance adjustors?"

"Sort of. Only you can count on us. We redress certain wrongs, follow the lines of relationship to other wrongs of the same kind, in other parts of the world; we learn by doing, for a time. To be just, we must integrate. Phase Two's conclusion has already begun: the Hand of Light is beginning to sweep through the world—like a net, or a comb, combing out the worst parasites. It will take twenty-four hours, following the sunlight."

"The Hand of Light? Is it God's Hand?"

"Nothing so literal. It is...when it gets here it will resemble a *wall of light*, arriving just after dawn. That is the culmination of Phase Two."

"A wall of light? And...Phase Three?"

"This final phase may last many years. It is...complex. But it begins with a great sundering: an end to the human world as it is known now. Those who remain after the Hand does its work will be again sorted through—and some, who are fixed in their mindsets, like ticks in skin, will be left here to face their ultimate end, which they will bring about themselves. Some of those will be given a choice. Many—perhaps a little more than half, including nearly all children—will go safely to—"

He broke off, turning to stare at a Japanese print on the wall—a stormy wave crashing from the sea—and after a moment she realized that he wasn't looking at it, but through it. "Let us eat something, and then...there is another place I have to visit."

"Dennis—I have so many questions. Like about this *guidance*—when does it start? What will it be like?"

"We haven't decided on it yet, we need more information. You may be left on your own after the primary issue of Phase Three."

"But if we are guided— What'll it be like? And what's going to happen exactly, in Phase Three?"

"No more questions, now. I have something I need to do, Ama. If you wish me to go and accomplish these things alone—I can." He must have seen that she was crestfallen, at that. "I don't mean to imply you aren't any use to me."

She looked up at him. "How am I of use—besides feeding and...and sheltering you. I mean—I've been wondering—why me? Just chance?"

"No. You enhance the process."

"That's something I haven't heard from a guy before. I enhance the process. You'll turn my head, Dennis."

He smiled. "You're ideal for that enhancement. You're a suitable field for tilling—and the seed falls on you. But I can do it without you if you feel...hassled. Or—maybe a better term is *burdened*."

Looking at him, she was feeling increasingly disturbed to think that she'd almost been sexually intimate with him. There was nothing monstrous about him—it wasn't that. But he *was* something inhuman—or, perhaps-beyond human. He wasn't 'alien from another planet' inhuman. He was something even stranger than that. And it disturbed her. But there was no way she was walking away from this...

She stood up. "I don't exactly understand, Dennis, but...I'll make us something to eat. Only please—explain what you can, when you can. Okay?"

He nodded distractedly, and turned to look, once more, through the print on the wall.

Studio City, California

They can call it a hospital if they want, wrote Max Drydel in his journal, *and like so many things it's true while it's a lie. They can call them medications if they want and like so many substances they're medicines and they're poisons right at the same time. They can call them doctors if they want and like so many people they're what they say they are and they're something else—something worse. Something terrible. I hear their hearts beating under that starchy white cloth: two hearts for each one of them! Double beats! Thus do I know they're Reptoids!!! That double heartbeat is a chink in their illusion, revealing their alien reality!!!*

Max glanced up from the crafts table where they let him do his "therapeutic writing." The big red-haired psychological technician, Mike, standing near the door, freckled hands in the pockets of his white jacket, was watching him closely. Probably because earlier Max had been poking at the skin on the back of his hand with the pen. Max knew Mike was human because he'd given him the Test, looking at him peripherally with one eye closed, and Mike had stayed human. But the doctors and the nurses and the therapists all turned into Reptoids when he gave *them* the Test.

Max put down the pen and looked through the door at the rec room television mounted behind Plexiglass up on the wall. He couldn't hear what it was saying but he could see it was tuned to the show "Cops". That show seemed to go on forever because there were always people to arrest. To take to mental hospitals. He supposed that there would be a message for him on "Cops", as usual. Victims of the uniformed bad-wearing Reptoids would say something in code to try and warn him, and people like him, as they were being carried away. A white trash type guy, on another episode, said, "It's my cousin's car, I don't have my license on me but he got it, dude, that car's not stolen, that my cousin's car. That [bleep—probably 'shit'] in the trunk belong to him, I don't know nothin' about it."

Cousin's car = Sarah's car. Sarah was Max's own cousin. There was some Reptoid control device—or possibly a *mind bomb*—hidden in her car. He must never ride in Sarah's car again.

The door from admitting burst inward and two people came in, a young man with curly brown hair and an Asian-looking girl, followed by Jessie, the other psych-tech on this shift. Jessie was a large dark-skinned man with short dreads and decorative gold teeth, every other one in front was gold. He wore civilian clothes under a white jacket, but around his neck was an ID on a cord, which of course had a monitoring device hidden in it, a micro-camera watching him, so that Jessie—also a human—would be the unwitting carrier of Reptoid observation drones.

"Who's this?" Mike asked, mildly, looking at the two people with Jessie. "It's not visiting hours."

"They're...I'm not even sure who they are," Jessie said, shaking his head. He looked like he was breathing hard. Was Jessie stoned? He sometimes smoked pot, Max knew, he'd smelled it on him.

"How'd they get in here?" Mike asked as the two strangers approached Max.

"I can't explain it. I let them in but—I can't explain why."

Max stood up, heart hammering in panic. These two strangers with Jessie must be a Reptoid Assassination Team, come to take him out! They'd used some mind control ray on Jessie!

Max backed away as the woman said, "Listen, it's okay—I'm Ama, this is Dennis, he just wants to help..."

Max decided he'd jump to the top of the table and then jump from there over their heads, come down running for the rec room. Once in the rec room he could wedge chairs against the door.

He took a running start, jumped up on the table, landing on his journal—it slid under his foot and he fell heavily onto his back on the tabletop. The air was knocked out of him and he wheezed, flailing around, trying to turn over, to scramble off the table. But it was too late, the young man with the kind face—a perfect camouflage, that face—was reaching out to him, and something *pulsed* from the top of his head and from his outstretched hand, and the pulsation rippled through Max—a death ray of some kind, it was too late, too fucking late. But...

But death wouldn't be so bad. At least the torment of knowing the world's secrets would be over, the voices would stop. There would be an end to the series of traps that was his life.

He didn't try to fight it. He let the pulsation sweep through him...let it ripple into him from the stranger with the curly brown hair, the soft gaze.

Something *changed*. It was like the axis of the Earth had shifted. Max realized he wasn't dying. He felt stronger, and impossibly relaxed, yet gently alert—like when he was a boy, before the voices had started, and he'd wake up in bed, look out the window and think about the leaves falling from the tree, and wonder if there were blintzes for breakfast, and if his dad was home this morning...

He felt like that boy again, though he was lying on his back, on a table in a mental hospital, at the age of—how... how old was he? In his thirties?

The Asian girl helped him sit up. Mike was there, looking on with concern, saying something to Jessie about calling the police, Jessie shaking his head, repeating that he didn't know how to explain.

But Mike and Jessie were in the background. They seemed

unimportant. All that mattered now was the man with the curly brown hair. A young man? Yes. But no. His face was a young man's face but the look in his face was not a young man's look.

Max felt strange—like he could feel every inch of himself.

"I don't feel the meds..." Max said. "I feel all *crisp* and— I...I don't feel...all, like, blurry around the edges."

"I've taken the influence of the meds from you— s well as the disease," the young man said, matter-of-factly. "The higher centers of your brain were not entirely functional, Max. Their filtering capacity had broken down. That allowed other parts of the brain to be over-active. You were suffering from grandiosity, hallucinations, paranoia. It's a genetic disorder triggered by environmental toxins. I fixed it."

"Are you...Jesus?"

"No," the man said. "I'm going by the name of *Dennis*. We knew Jesus, though. He was called *Yeshua* then. We sent a number of messengers—like him but their message has become terribly distorted, I'm afraid."

"This man's from one of the other wards," Mike said, nodding toward Dennis. "Or he ought to be in one. I called Dr. Fenway on the intercom."

Ama smiled. "He does sound pathological himself, sometimes, doesn't he? But he isn't." She turned to the man who called himself Dennis. "There are millions of people who suffer like this man. Can you really help them all?"

"Yes. It's not the kind of disease we allow. Not on *this* scale. But the one you call the UnderGod encouraged it, of course."

Max thought: The UnderGod? These people sound mentally ill, they really do. Probably they are. But...

The door to the inner offices opened and Dr. Fenway came in, scowling. "What's going on here?" He was a man with a sagging, lined face, a toupee, the white coat, the big watch on his wrist, the cell phone clipped to his belt...

"Go ahead, Max. Test him," said Dennis.

Max turned, closed one eye, looked at the doctor in his peripheral vision.

Just an ordinary man.

Maybe...maybe Dennis had done something...to hide the Reptoids, to disguise them...

But Max knew better. He could see things around him as they were: all flat and plain and dull and—real. He felt the concreteness, the quotidian inevitability of things, felt it as definitely as feeling wind or water.

Somehow, he thought...somehow my disease just—went away. I can see I was sick now. How many years did I waste?

He began to weep, to think of the wasted years.

"It's going to be better, after this," said Dennis, helping him off the table. "There are many others here we have to help..."

"What about me?" asked Gerald, coming from the rec room. He was a stocky, doughy-faced patient with drooping eyes, a stained pocket protector with nothing in it, self-mutilation scars on his forearms. "Can you fix me too?"

Dennis turned and looked at Gerald, and an exploratory pulsation made Gerald take a step back, blinking. "Whoa—what was that?"

Dennis shook his head. "Sorry, Gerald, I can't help you. You're merely depressed. It does have an organic basis but—I don't think it's the work of the UnderGod. I don't see it as created by other humans, either. Max here had his youth stolen away from him. He had no choice—the voices came, the delusions, it was like a freeway built through the center of his mind. But depression—it's something you could have struggled with, Gerald, and defeated. I see that you had a great deal of warning, and help and therapy, but you chose to be sullen and withdrawn and hostile and infantile and you chose self-pity and you kept your nose to the darkness..."

"What!" Gerald sneered. "I was supposed to, what, 'keep to the sunny side of the street'? Just fucking 'cheer up'?"

"No. But you weren't supposed to collaborate with your own spoiled inner brat. If you want to be free, you must see those tendencies in yourself, and struggle with them, and see all the possibilities, not just a few...You are capable of it, so it is demanded of you, Gerald."

Gerald swallowed and leaned against the doorframe,

slowly shaking his head—and staring at the scars on the back of his arms. "You could help me if you wanted."

"I just did," Dennis said. "As much as I'm allowed—in your case."

Dennis turned toward the doctor—who was calling security on his cell phone, telling them he didn't know how these people got in but someone was going to be getting a pink slip real quick unless...

"You must stop some of the things you've been doing, Doctor Fenway," Dennis said. "You have been punishing certain patients by over-medicating them, and you've been admitting people you know aren't mentally ill—homeless people, really, who simply drank too much—just so you could raise the number of inpatients and charge the state more money. That's something you shouldn't do, isn't it?"

Dr. Fenway went pale. "Who's been spreading this...this baloney?"

"Remember Jenny Hu? She complained to you that her medications were making her sick, giving her seizures, and you punished her for complaining by doubling them."

This Dennis person, Max noted, didn't speak to the doctor in a hectoring, self-righteous tone. It was more like a defense lawyer giving a client the cold facts. "You have only a little time, doctor, only a day, perhaps less, before the darkness is divided, and the great Hand separates those who will come and those who will stay. But you won't need to take Jenny off those medications. I'm going to get her now, and take her home to her husband. I have just enough time before we drive up north."

Dennis and Ama walked past the doctor, toward the door, and Max drifted after them. He wanted to go and see his mom, and tell her he was better. She wouldn't believe it, but he'd show her.

Mike started to interfere—then a pulsation came through the air, and Mike the Psych staggered back, and sat heavily on the edge of the table, and stared after them.

The locked door popped open, and they went out into the

unfettered world, Max trailing happily after Dennis. Ama asking, "Dennis—what do you mean, we must drive north?"

Near Chico, California

"We going to ride with that big motherfucker all the way north in this little bitty car?" Shontel asked, as Galivant, wearing an unbuttoned trench coat that flapped in the wind, came trotting ponderously toward them from the front door of the Chico Police Department.

"Yeah, we're going to ride with that big motherfucker," Swift said. "All the way north."

"He's coming from the police. We supposed to trust him?"

"We're looking for a missing person, aren't we?"

Galivant got into the small car, jamming himself into the front seat beside Swift. Shontel was seated sideways in the back, knees drawn up. The air in the car was almost immediately warmer with Galivant there. The windows started to steam as Swift drove down the highway.

"Shit," Shontel said.

"That how you say hello where you come from?" Galivant asked, with spurious innocence, looking over his shoulder, as Swift pulled out of the parking lot. "My name's Ed Galivant. You'd be Erin's boyfriend."

"Shontel. Why you come from the police department?"

"I've got a contact there, a cop I know who's a cattle mute enthusiast."

"What's a cattle mute? Trying to teach cattle to talk?"

Galivant looked close at Shontel, realized he was kidding about the talking part. "Funny. Cattle mutilations. Cattle found mutilated in symmetrical patterns. Turned out it was biological war experiment stuff. Anyway this cop gave me the dirt on where this retreat is."

"We already had that," Shontel said. "Swift found it out."

"And I asked him about rumors of some new high-

frequency device being tested out there. He didn't know—
did say that some big trucks went out there..."

"Could've been carrying port-a-potties," Swift said.

"Those too. We got, what, three hours drive north?"

"I get car sick," Shontel said. "Yo, Swift, can you open
the window?"

Chuckling to himself at the meeting of the minds between
Shontel and Galivant, Swift cranked his window down a
bit. Air streamed in, smelling of pine trees and water thick
with algae—they were passing a small lake. "This place is
supposed to be like a few miles east of Lassen. Is that what
you got too, Ed?"

"It is. I've got a map—he drew it on a napkin, but it's
some kinda map."

Shontel said, "Man, cattle mutilations. I saw something on
cable about it. You believe in all that stuff...?" Shontel said.

"No, I check it out, is all," Galivant replied, his forefinger
tracing a "classic Gray alien" face in the steamy window
beside him. "In case any of it's true." He admired the face,
and then blotted it out with the heel of his hand. "Maybe
we get a few saucer jockeys now and then. Maybe. But
mostly not. Mostly it's other stuff. Anomalies. Most of them
explainable if you look far enough. Not all of them."

Shontel shrugged. "Like 'rains of frogs.' That was
just all waterspouts, freak weather, shit like that. And
that Mothman, that was a big bird got his ass lost. They
explained both of those."

"They did. Some other stuff, though, no—like lately you
see anything strange in the skies?"

Shontel didn't answer for a long moment. "Yeah," he
said finally. "I did. You know what it was?"

"Not definitely," Galivant said. "Either a side effect of
something happening—or a signal. Or both. Those are my
theories. I tend to lean toward thinking it was a kind of side
effect. A lot of other things have been happening. These
were a whole series of opera performances, in China, Italy,
the USA, where the singers started singing different words
than they should—words they didn't really understand. In

was their own language but—it was almost like speaking in tongues."

Swift looked at him. "You confirmed this?"

"I did. You hear about the oceanic phenomena? Like, the waves on the sea, *the entire Pacific Ocean*, went glassy for exactly forty-seven minutes every morning at eleven a.m., as that time of day. In all those countries around the Pacific. Happened for three days in a row. Where there should be waves—none. For exactly forty-seven minutes."

"Could be some explanation for that," Shontel said, skeptically, shifting in the seat, trying to get more comfortable. "Anyway you can't know it was the whole ocean, for sure. Who sees the whole ocean at once?"

"I like this kid," Swift said, grinning, elbowing Galivant. "Sharp mind." He looked in the rearview mirror at Shontel. "I'm guessing, though, they took satellite photos of the whole ocean. You hear any stories about gangs changing behavior, Shontel?"

"Why you ask me that? I'm black so I got to be the gang expert?"

"Let's be honest, man, you're going to know more than I do about it."

Shontel shrugged. "Yeah, I heard some shit. Whole crews of Bloods and Deadbrains walking away from their clubs. Some just—disappeared. Peeps giving evidence all of a sudden and not getting their asses shot. I mean—" He shook his head in wonder. "Buncha snitches just...just snitching and—walking away!"

Swift nodded. Galivant asked, "What you hear is the cause of it, Shontel?"

"Don't nobody know. Scary as hell though."

"Scary? Sounds like a good thing, people not getting punished for speaking up."

"Kind of is. But—it's like the world don't make any sense, people making up rules out of thin air. That's scary. Can we stop soon so I can get out this damn car and smoke a cigarette? I'm getting car-sick back here."

10

A small town in Pakistan,
near the border with Afghanistan

HALLIL was on sentry duty, outside the safe house on the corner, in the quiet pre-dawn. The morning light was breaking over the high craggy foothills above the town. A whole night had passed, but the air hadn't cooled much. There was no wind, and the air was damp, muggy after yesterday's rain. Hallil wanted to take off his jacket, but under it was the bullet-proof vest, and that made him conspicuous when the patrols went by, though no one who lived on this street would have thought it strange; he was to keep his Kalashnikov in the van, close to hand, and simply watch for coalition patrols, or Pakistan Army. All he saw, though, was the little old fool, Kalib, toddling toward him, grinning as usual in his black beard, scratching with one hand under his filthy turban, the other twitching the long dirty gray robe he wore—that he always wore, that and nothing else, like a woman swishing the skirt of her dress.

"Kalib, what do you want?" Hallil called. "Do not come any closer to the house, you know better!" An important meeting was happening in the house behind him, hosted by Sheikh Muhammed al Quatar, and it must not be disturbed—they had been up all night, making preparations, because the Great Jihadi was among them. He was known to work for days until the task was complete.

The people of the street—the men who would soon gather

to sip sweet coffee at the splintery old tables outside the café, the teenagers who scavenged old bits of equipment to sell on the street, the old women, covered head-to-toe in black burqas who would soon come two-by-two to gossip under the awnings of the market—*they* all knew better: Stay away from that house. If the patrols come, say nothing about it. Misdirect the soldiers to the other side of town, where the infidel tribes dwelt, and never so much as look at this house—though most of them knew that the First Muslim Brigade made its plans and its bombs right here.

"Hallil," said Kalib, "you are young, you are not yet fixed within yourself, you are one who can be saved from the Hand of God, and I am come to tell you. There will be an end to the Jihadi now, and forever!"

Hallil sighed. He had heard more than one extemporaneous rant from this old man. Kalib was known to be a Naq'sh'ban Sufi, which was just another kind of infidel. It was a surprise he hadn't been made an example of, as yet. "Kalib, do you call yourself a Muslim? Yes? Then do not speak heresy."

"The time when the Naq'sh'ban had to hide themselves away is over, Hallil! A time of joy is here! The Liar God is gone, the True God—the mind of the great universe, whom Mohammed only glimpsed— *He* has sent his djinn before Him, and will sweep the world with His mighty Hand! There is no heresy for those who will soon depart this world! Behold, Hallil! His sword sweeps down the street! Look there!"

Hallil saw that something, indeed, was sweeping down the street toward him.

It was a vast, moving wall of light: sheer, attenuated but sharply defined; a golden light tinged with red and moving slowly but implacably toward him. The wall of light seemed as flat and straight as a razor blade, so high its top could not be seen; so wide it stretched down the cross street, as it came to the corner across from him, extending to the rolling hills to the southeast; it followed the contours of the hills like a fence, continuing on over them into the distance. In the other direction it reached across the plain, visible beyond the edge of town. The wall of light stretched across the plain all the way to the horizon. And it moved toward him the way a wave on the sea would, closer and closer to Hallil.

Hallil gaped at it, frozen in his tracks with amazement and fear. The great blade of light seemed more solid than a rainbow, but he could see through it, making out the bare outlines of the low buildings beyond it...

"The Americans!" he said. Barely loud enough to hear his own voice. "They must...this comes from above...it must be from orbit, from their satellites—some form of surveillance!"

"Ho ho!" Kalib laughed, dancing with glee. "From the sky? No, no! It is from *every direction!* It is from the Every Thing! It is not from any one Where!"

Hallil grabbed his assault rifle, and fired a shot into the sky, to alert the others. He was supposed to call the house on the cell phone but his mind seemed as frozen as his feet, he couldn't think where the cell phone was. In the van? In his coat? He couldn't remember. "Muhammad!" he called, to his sheikh, loudly now. "My Sheikh!"

The wall of light crept closer. Was there a whispering sound that came with it? Voices that never quite articulated words?

The Sheikh and the Great Jihadi and two other bearded men, all of them armed, came out of the house shouting questions. Hallil pointed at the wall of light, and they stopped, staring in awe.

The door of the house across the street opened and a man came out in his robe, barefoot, a cap on his head. "Who is firing rifles? What is going on?" This was Nazir Ahmad, a small dark man with a black mustache and a face carved in sharp planes, who had escaped here from a jail with the help of Sheik al Quatar. Ahmad had been put in jail, awaiting death, for killing his three daughters, because the eldest had run off with a man for love; her love had not been chosen by the family, and she had disobeyed her father. So he had tricked her into coming home, telling her he had forgiven her, and in the night he cut her throat, and then he killed the other two girls, as they slept—this, Hallil had heard—

so that they could not grow up to disobey their father too. To do this was his right, according to the Sheikh al Quatar. This girl who had chosen her own man had been infected with the licentiousness of the Great Satan, and it was good to tear up that weed at the root.

But when he'd heard this story, and seen that the sheikh was helping this man, Hallil had almost left the Jihad.

Now Ahmad stumbled into the street, seeming drawn in fascination toward the wall of light...

"Get away from it!" The sheikh shouted at him, but Nazir Ahmad goggled and fell to his knees, babbling.

"He knows his fate is come to claim him!" crowed Kalib.

The wall of light struck Kalib first, however—he was standing closer to it. He lifted his arms like a man bathing in a waterfall. The light passed over him, and continued on; he shivered and went rigid—and then danced in place, spinning like a dervish, singing a song in a language of the mountains—while the wall of light continued its implacable march, a curtain of illumination dragged slowly, inexorably across the whole world. Now it swept over Nazir Ahmad. Who shuddered, went rigid...

And fell dead. The wall of light had spared Kalib—and killed Ahmad.

The wall of light moved onward, toward the Great Leader, the sheik, and his men—and toward Hallil. He took a step back, and another—and stopped.

"There is no use running!" Kalib shouted, spinning. "It sweeps the whole world! It enters into caves and basements and tall buildings and automobiles and the depths of the sea! Even into the ships that sail under the waves! No one can hide from what is of the Every Thing!"

"Quickly—it is the Americans, one of their weapons!" shouted the Great Jihadi. "Into the van, we will escape!"

Hallil, his feet feeling like they were weighted with concrete, dragged himself to the van, and inside. The Sheikh himself took the wheel, the Great Jihadi beside him. The others crowded in back. The Sheikh fumbled for the keys, hidden in the glove compartment, found them, jammed them in the ignition, had to pull them out and put them in properly.

"Hurry! It is almost here! It comes!" shouted the Great Jihadi. "It is laser light, it is death! Hurry!"

But the van would not start; the ignition only grumbled and wouldn't turn over.

Then the light passed over the van...Hallil closed his eyes.

But the light penetrated his eyelids. He saw it with his eyes and in his mind's eye, stretching away to infinity, in all directions. He felt it taste his every cell...He felt it sort through his mind, his innermost being...

And then it passed on. He opened his eyes—and saw the others slumped in their seats. They were dead. The Great Jihadi, who had made fools of the CIA and the Pakistani Army—dead.

"Now!" Kalib called, sliding the door open. "Come with me! We have to pray, to prepare for the great dividing! You have been given another chance!"

Not knowing what else to do, Hallil went with Kalib. He followed after the mad old fool, whom everyone had mocked.

OBM Retreat Grounds, Northern California

"What did you say he's calling it now?" Birch asked, keeping his voice low and blinking in the smoke from the fire. It was just sunset. The columns were glimmering around the darkening field, rippling electric circles from the ground toward the sky.

"O'Hanlon calls it 'the Shield' but Griffin calls it 'the Griffin Interference Coils'," said Meredith, moving closer to him at the edge of the fire pit. "If it's a big success O'Han will make us call it the 'O'Hanlon Interference Coils.'"

"OIC? As in 'Oik!' That'll be good." Birch watched the sparks spiral up from the burning logs. Ghostly fire-lit faces flickered in a red ring around the fire pit. There were children among them. Birch muttered, "Meredith—I want to get out of here."

She glanced at him, then gestured for him to lower his voice. "I would too. But I don't know if we can," she whispered, leaning against him, the firelight dancing in her long straight blond hair.

"Where are we supposed to sleep?"

"There are tents stacked out back, and sleeping bags. That appears to be the best this multibillion dollar company can do on short notice."

"I don't believe O'Hanlon's going to be in a sleeping bag. I saw a very, very big RV in the parking lot. Meredith—we're cut off from the world and things are *happening*. Who knows what it means for us? And those security guards are making me nervous."

"They aren't really security guards—they're mercenaries, from O'Hanlon Strategies International. Mercenaries in suits. One of them, guy named Mergus, used to be a football player."

"O'Hanlon Strategics? What—that outfit that helped out in...what was it, years ago...oh—Abu Ghraib, right?"

"Keep your voice down! But yes. Exactly. Not people to mess with. I'm not sure they'd—"

"Oh bullshit, I've had enough, Meredith, come on..."

Birch took her by the hand and drew her away from the fire. The evening seemed darker than it really was while his eyes were adjusting after the fire pit. He drew her toward the gravel road that led to the parking lot, beyond the perimeter of glittering columns.

Just inside the perimeter, close to the road, were two large men in suits. Birch spotted others, at intervals, around the ring of columns, each of them with a headset, a white shirt, suit jackets, ties. Their coats looked unusually bulky—Kevlar vests and guns in shoulder holsters, he supposed.

"Hello—Roger isn't it?" Meredith said, smiling sunnily at a man with an OSI badge. Looked like an ex-football player, all right, with his flat-top haircut and wide shoulders. *R. Mergus, OSI*, it said on his badge.

"Yes ma'am, can I help you?"

"Just wanted to keep you abreast of our movements—it's scary out here in the dark, it feels good to have you guys watching out for us," she said, making Birch marvel at her cheery cunning. "We're going to the parking lot, get something from our cars..."

"No ma'am," said the man with Mergus—a smiling, square jawed black man with dead eyes and close-shaved hair. "You folks have to stay inside the perimeter tonight." He had his thumbs hooked in his belt, and he drew his coat back, just a little, as if simply adjusting his stance, so they could get a glimpse of the big pistol.

"That wasn't necessary..." Birch read the man's nametag. "Cullum, is it? It wasn't necessary to show us the gun, Cullum. We're executives at OBM—you work for us."

"No sir," said Cullum, his smile never wavering, "We work for Mr. O'Hanlon himself, and he gave us orders—no one leaves here till sometime tomorrow. Not sure when. Except it'll be when he says so..."

Birch felt his face getting hot. It made him angry that this man had no fear of him whatsoever—and no real respect for him, either. "And if we simply leave—with all these people here, along with our CEO, the man who personally handed us Christmas bonus checks last year, you're going to, what, haul out that piece and shoot us?"

"Oh, I don't think that'll be necessary, sir," said Mergus, his voice a rumble. "I've got pepper spray, and my hands. But hopefully just blocking your way would be enough. You want to have a pissing contest, sir—you're gonna come up short."

"Thanks very much for that vivid image," Meredith said icily. "You not only behave like a thug—you talk like one."

Mergus winced a little at that. But he set his legs a little farther apart, and crossed his arms, and the body language was clear. "I'm sorry, ma'am, I should speak more respectfully. But Mr. O'Hanlon was extremely...I'd call it vehement, I guess, that no one leaves. No one, no one at all. Not till tomorrow."

Meredith took Birch's arm. "Come on, Frank."

Birch was glad of the excuse to save face—he could act as if he was relenting only because she insisted. He shrugged, and let her draw him back toward the main tent.

"Let's see if there's any news," she said, her voice quavering a little.

Birch realized that she was scared, and trying not to show it.

The entrance to the tent was nominally blocked by the two Colbertsons, the elder Reverend and his son, who seemed to be arguing with a compact woman of early middle age, her embarrassed teenage daughter in tow. "I just want to know what those things are, Reverend!" the woman said, clutching her purse to her. "This whole thing is beginning to...I'm starting to wonder..."

Meredith started to ask them to move, so they could get into the tent, but Birch squeezed her arm, shook his head. He wanted to hear this. He had been wondering what Griffin had told these Church of Revelation people.

"It's an experiment of some kind, 'to focus energy' they tell us," said the elder Colbertson vaguely. His voice was roughened by age. "They say it'll help us see the Coming as early as possible."

"Why would we need some technological fix to see God?" the woman demanded.

"Mo-om," the girl groaned, "I'm tired, I want to sit down somewhere, find something to eat...this was all your idea—"

"Erin—be quiet!" the woman said. "Just—go inside. There's food to eat. I want to talk to the Reverend..."

"I was actually wondering about this too, Dad," said George Colbertson, a little apologetically. "They're not doing this like they said they would..."

The elder Colbertson seemed to notice Birch listening, and frowned, his face pinching with the expression. "You folks need to get on by..." He drew his son aside, talking in whispers, and Meredith hurried into the tent. Birch followed, to the bank of monitors set up on the right.

"They don't have a clue," he muttered to her, as they

approached the televisions, the awed, murmuring crowd staring at the only one that was lit up, and that one fuzzily.

"I wonder if *we* have a clue," she said, looking in fascination at the image on the screen. "Look at that!"

"It's...what *is* that?" Birch asked. "Something wrong with the picture?"

"The phenomenon is passing around the world," said the grim voice of the newscaster, "seeming to select out individuals, many in some communities, sometimes only a few; sometimes people we think of as important, and sometimes it's the less important. To our knowledge, twenty dictators in as many countries just dropped dead, when overtaken by the...the phenomenon. It does not help to hide in a bunker or hunker in an attic. The phenomenon has been described as a wall of light, or a blade of light, and in some places it has been called the Sword of God. It is moving east, roughly ahead of what is called, oddly enough, 'the terminator', the line of light marking the coming of dawn..."

"Nothing wrong with the television," Meredith said. "It's a big...a big wall of light moving in a straight line and..."

"It kills people," said the voice on the television set, finishing her sentence for her. "And so far as we can find out, many of these people have something in common —violence in their pasts, or some crime of terror, or some connection to a terrible brutality—from cruelty to children, to torture in a political context."

Birch stared in fascination at the television image, piecing the situation together as the story went on. The wall of sheer, golden-red light seemed to stretch uninterrupted through the great city it was passing through—was that Moscow?—as if it went into the buildings, right through the walls, without damaging them. Indeed, it could be seen through the windows, combing through the rooms. Other news shots showed crowds running from the wall of light in panic. When it caught people—in an overcrowded city square, on a train platform, in their cars—only a few of them died as the light passed over them.

Was the killing random? Birch wondered. Or was it that certain key individuals were dying, as the newscaster implied?

The commentator continued, with a rustle of paper, "Ah...Professor Cohen of MIT spoke to us ten minutes ago by telephone. We didn't get a good recording of the call but I can quote him here: 'This is certainly not a supernatural force, unless God deals in high energy physics. We're getting readings off this thing that indicate it is a very complex energy transmission, with an internal pattern of particle-wave forms, some familiar and some unfamiliar, that suggests intelligent origin. That is, we believe it is designed *by an intelligence,* and is not some geophysical or astrophysical phenomenon as some of my colleagues first supposed.' Well professor, it seems to us here that God must be an intelligence—and who's to say He wouldn't use high energy physics? It seems to me that might be God's own high technology."

At this, a number of the Revelation in Christ churchgoers moaned, some in fear, others in the peculiar psychosomatic ecstasy of the evangelical. "Praise God! The day is come!" shouted a rotund woman with thick ankles, thicker eye makeup. She wobbled and someone had to catch her, as some notion of the spirit of God transfixed her. "Ai-yee-ho-ba-sa-eena!" she howled, speaking in tongues, raising her hands over her hand.

Birch stared at her. Could she be right? Was this really judgment day?

But it wasn't happening according to the Book of Revelations scenario, with Gog and Magog at war, the Antichrist calling the faithless to him, gigantic beasts rising from the sea...

No, it wasn't. But if it wasn't the *Christian* apocalypse... Whose was it?

A State Park Near Lassen in Northern California

"What you going to do with all that beer?" Shontel asked, yawning, as Swift opened the trunk of the car, which was pulled up under the single street light over the forest-fringed parking lot.

In the trunk of the car was a case of beer, an empty backpack, and a flashlight.

"What you think I'm going to do with it?" Swift said. "I'm going to drink it. Judiciously, I mean."

"You going to *share* it?"

"Normally, not with an underage guy. But after what we heard on the radio—drink up, pal."

He pulled a can of Heineken out of the case, and tossed it to Shontel—who jumped a little as a bat fluttered over them, squeaking; an owl hooted somewhere in the dark woods outside the street lamp over the parking lot. "Lotta weird fucking animals out here," he said, after taking a pull on the beer.

"There's bats and owls in the city, people just never notice them, Shontel."

"Swift?" Galivant said, coming around to the rear of the car, tilting the compass in his hand to catch the light from the single lamp over the parking lot. "We got to get moving— we've got a good four miles to hike before dawn. And it's not going to get us there faster if you two are drunk."

"Just one or two beers," Swift said, glancing at his watch. "My nerves are shot. Couldn't sleep in the car much..." He popped the top on a beer.

"You plan to carry the beer in that backpack?"

"Yeah. So?" He took a flashlight from the trunk and switched it on.

"So it'll get all shaken up. And warm. And it'll be heavy. Slow you down."

Swift sighed. It was true. And getting there faster could

matter. Who knew what was happening to Erin and her mother?

He and Shontel each drank a beer, tossed the empties in the trunk and, Swift sighing, slammed it shut.

Shontel laid a lightly restraining hand on Swift's arm. "Brewd—"

"Do me a favor, Shontel, call me Jim."

"Okay, okay, *Jim*—what they were saying on the radio. Some big beam of light killing people, going around the world, people changing overnight, the signs in the sky...You think that's, like, the start of...*the end*? I mean, on the radio they were hinting that, it might be the end of the world, you know? And...I love my girl, but my mama's got to be hella scared right now. All my peeps. Maybe if it's the end...I should be with my family."

He seemed embarrassed to be talking about his "mama", about family. Expressing his fears openly. He looked down the road they'd come in on, toward the south, as if he could see his family down there.

"I don't know, Shontel. But you notice that the wall of light only kills some people. They haven't had much time to check, but it appears to be taking out only certain kinds of people. Fucked-up people. Your mom's a good woman, right?"

"Yeah. *Hell* yeah. She never did nothing scandalous. She always there for us."

"Then—if it's true it's only certain kinds of people—she'll be all right."

"And if it's not," Galivant put in, "what could you do for her anyway? Nothing stops the phenomenon."

"I could be there with her, man."

Galivant nodded gravely. "You got a point. But—chances are, it's too late. We're too far away."

"And Shontel," Swift added, "I can't go back now. Main road up to that retreat is blocked off by OBM's hired thugs. So we've got to pack in the back way—going to take time. I've got to find my daughter. I can't even give you the car— because I might need it to get her away from these people.

They're cultists, man. You know? Like that Jim Jones guy."
He paused, thinking that over. Probably it was going too far,
comparing Colbertson's flock to Jonestown types. But who
knew how bad it might become, with all the hysteria. "We
can't get to your mom, Shontel, not in time—but maybe we
can get to Erin in time."

Shontel looked down the road once more, then he put
out his hand for the flashlight. Swift gave it to him and,
Shontel leading the way, flashlight beam darting ahead, they
plunged into the dark forest trail.

Chicago, Illinois

Huffy was camping in the subway station with Gidge. She
was drinking, in her tattered sleeping bag, under the bench;
he was lying on top of it, on a double layer of cardboard. He
heard the shuffle sound of someone coming down the ramp.

"The bulls coming down?" Huffy asked, seeing the
shaggy, ragged outline of Marv, his distinctive shambling
gait, hurrying onto the station platform.

"Nah, it's not the cops, it's something else, it's something
else, Huff, it's...I dunno, some crazy shit. But not the cops..."

It was late, the subway station was technically closed, but
they had ways to get in. It was cold down here, the concrete
and steel space echoing, patchily lit, drippy in places because
it had rained about midnight, but Huffy had his cardboard
insulation and plastic tarp set up on the bench, under an
old, peeling poster for Tom Cruise in something about
Impossibilities, a subject on which Huffy was an expert.

"They should have asked *me* to write about impossibilities,"
he told Gidge, right before she dropped off from the dope
and the wine.

"Yuh," she said. Pretty quick, she was snoring under the
bench. He could smell her under there too. A comforting
smell, though some people didn't like it.

Huffy pulled out his pint of E&J, looked at it, drank off

half, and handed Marv the rest as he shambled up, bringing with him the distinctive *eau de Marv*—he knew Marv would kill the brandy. Marv drank, and tossed the bottle to crash on the subway tracks.

"Some shit's going down," Marv said, wiping his mouth, turning to gape wildly up the ramp. "There's a light and it's burning people or killing them inside or some shit."

"Well fuck that," Huffy said, not arguing. Marv said crazy things, and you didn't argue with him.

Marv pointed up the ramp. "Hey the bulls *is* coming!"

They saw the silhouette of a uniformed man, the cap and all, on the ramp, and Huffy, thought of running down the tunnel, but Gidge would hiss at them for it, later, leaving her like that, and there was no getting her up, and this guy might well chase them, and it pissed them off when they had to chase you, and then they'd beat you, most of them, with their batons, or they tazed you, though his friend Birdy claimed to *like* being tazed, said it was a good kick in the ass, so you never knew.

Huffy got nervously to his feet, and then the big cop came out of the shadows onto the subway platform, his boot steps echoing, and it was just too bad they hadn't run, because this was Officer Suffocater—anyway that's what Gidge called him. That was because he liked to cuff people face down in the back of the paddy wagon, in a way that made them suffocate. His real name was Officer Kater, according to his little name badge.

"Fuck, it's Suffo-Kater!" Marv breathed, barely daring to say it aloud.

"There's just one of him," Huffy said, as Kater approached, the cop drawing his gun, grinning. A big frog-faced man with thick eyebrows.

"You bums was warned not to come down here! Get your asses down flat, I got three patrolmen coming down here, I got the disposable cuffs, I'm ready for your dirty...your..."

His voice trailed off as the wall of light appeared. The shine of it made him turn his head to look.

They all stared at it—all but Gidge who was still snoring.

The wall of light, golden-red, was coming down the subway tunnel. It moved slowly but inexorably toward them, stretching floor to ceiling, first in the tunnel and then, a moment later, in the station itself, blocking the way up the ramp.

"Oh—it's that t'ing!" Kater muttered, waving his gun. "I t'ought it was hysteria! That t'ing is real!"

"Why don't you shoot it, Officer Suffo-Kater," Marv suggested, chuckling.

"That the thing you meant, Marv?" Huffy asked. "It's real? It kills people?"

"Not everyone I guess. Not even most. But they say it means the end of the world."

"It does? That's okay with me, bro."

"Me too, man. Been good knowing you."

"You too."

Officer Kater had turned his back on them, taken a few steps, and, emboldened by the benediction of the fantastic, Marv stepped up behind and jerked the gun from the cop's hand, then pushed him down onto the tracks.

"Shit! Ow!" Kater yelled, falling awkwardly on his right side. "I'm gonna make you pay for that, you stinking bum! My elbow's all scraped up!"

Dusting off his hat, the cop got painfully to his feet—and then turned, realizing the wall of light was there. He seemed frozen in fear, staring at the translucent shimmer—and it came onward, it enveloped him, making him dance a comical little jig, before he fell flat on his face.

You could just tell he was dead. Something was missing from him, had been pulled right out of him. Huffy thought he'd glimpsed it, a distorted image of Kater, flattened into the wall of light, flickering by—and gone.

"It killed him!" Marv crowed.

"We're next, I reckon. Should we wake up Gidge?"

"Naw. Why scare her?"

The wall of light came on, and on...

Huffy thought of running down the tunnel, but he knew the thing would get him eventually, it was going about its business in a way that said there was no getting away, and he was just as glad to get it over.

It swept over them—making them glow and tingle inside—and then it had passed onward, and they were still alive, all three of them.

Officer Kater was dead, and they were alive. Huffy thought of a line from the Bible: Something like, *The last shall be first, and the first shall be last.*

Gidge woke up, muttering, "Whattahell wassat?" She was nearly toothless, though she was only forty. She rolled out from under the bench, and sat up, scratching at the lice in her hoody.

"End of the world, Gidge," Huffy said, watching the wall of light continue on its way. "That's what it is."

"Well fuck," she said, reaching into her rags for a bottle. "I'll drink to that."

PHASE THREE

RESET

"It's the end of the world as we know it, and I feel fine."

—REM

11

OBM Retreat Grounds, Northern California

"OH my God, did you hear that?" Meredith said, turning to Birch on the wooden bench next to the fire pit. "They said the Vice President is dead!"

"Is he! You mean the wall of light—?"

"I think that's what they said." She turned to call over her shoulder, "Mr.— Reverend Colbertson! Didn't they say the Vice President has died?"

Hands in his pockets, George Colbertson emerged slowly from the blue-tinged darkness of pre-dawn, his face still in shadow as he said, "Yes, so it appears...He was in 'an undisclosed location', a bunker somewhere." His face came into the light of the fire as he went on, "The wall of light took certain members of Congress, the Vice President, the Chief-of-Staff, a good many lobbyists...remarkable number of lobbyists..." He shrugged. "It's puzzling. The Vice President was a religious man, a conservative. The Lord works in mysterious ways. Some of those people—I just do not understand why they were...Why they..." He glanced back at Griffin, at his workstation, illuminated with floodlights, then turned back to Meredith. "I have heard rumors, ma'am—that these...devices here are not intended to enhance the Coming. I heard a story—that they're here to stop it. Have you—I mean—is it true?"

"Oh-h-h, I really don't know," Meredith said, chewing the inside of her cheek the way she did when she was stressed.

The younger Colbertson looked at Birch. "Have *you* heard, Mr. Birch?"

"No, Reverend, I haven't...I...uh..." Birch found himself twisting inside with the thought of lying about this. All his misgivings came to a head at that moment. He felt a clear-cut division, for the first time in his life: wrongness on one side, right on the other. Or more like—inappropriate and appropriate. If he lied to this man, he'd be out of alignment with something...something indefinable, but strong. He'd be in a wrong relationship to something important, something bigger than he was—something that communicated ineffably with the core of him. At last he blurted, "Actually, Reverend Colbertson—my understanding is that Griffin there has come up with a device that blocks the impulses that have been affecting people. It blocks whatever's making all these anomalous...behaviors. And...and he thinks it will stop the wall of light when it gets to us, too."

"Oh Frank," Meredith groaned, shaking her head. "Did you really have to?"

He looked at her apologetically. "I just...am so sick of lying."

Colbertson stiffened, staring. "He's going to block the wall of light? What is God but light? *The light shines in the darkness and the darkness does not overcome it.* We would be wicked to turn our backs on it!"

"We—don't know what this phenomenon *is* really, Reverend," Birch pointed out gently. "But if it's God, he's omnipotent, right? Isn't that the...doctrine? He can't be stopped."

"We cannot even try to deny that light—or *we* will be denied! We'll find ourselves in the darkness!"

Birch sighed. "It's out of my hands, friend, and to tell you the truth I never understood the whole thing. I'm just a damned employee."

Colbertson snorted. "You were just following orders?"

"I was...by the time it started to show itself as something with a life of its own—something that wasn't, say, generated by the Red Chinese—it was too late, we were all caught up in O'Hanlon's happy little trip out here."

"What's that about O'Hanlon's 'little trip'?" O'Hanlon demanded, startling Birch as he stalked up from outside the firelight. "I don't think I like the tone you were using, there, Birch."

"O'Hanlon, I don't actually care right now," Birch said, getting up. He was tired, weary with a kind of dull anger, and he realized he'd been that way for hours.

Funny, he thought, how you're in *a state,* a condition, without being consciously aware of it, so much of your life...

"Birch, you're tired, I understand that," O'Hanlon began, "but I need to know how you plan to—"

"O'Hanlon? Is this where you pretend to be smoothing things over? It isn't going to happen. Don't you see? If even *half* of what we've been hearing is true, you are flat broke. And all your power comes from money. You see, the stock market's plummeted, O'Han, in light, so to speak, of all that's happened—and people are walking away from OBM in droves."

"Oh bullshit," O'Hanlon sputtered. But he was hugging himself as he said it. He looked like a tired, feeble little old man to Birch, then. "It's...a lot of...a lot of..."

"Can't you feel it, O'Hanlon? *You can feel it in the air...* It's all quite real." Birch turned away. "Come on, Meredith."

O'Hanlon called after him, "Griffin and I, we're going to *block* all that bullshit, reverse the whole thing! We're almost ready, Birch! And by the way..."

Birch kept walking.

"...you're fired!"

Meredith trotted after Birch, took hold of his arm, but her lips were trembling and he suspected she was tempted to run from him, to turn back to O'Hanlon, beg forgiveness.

It couldn't be that the world—O'Hanlon's world—was ending. She couldn't believe it.

But Birch believed it more with each passing minute. "Light's coming up," he remarked. "You see, to the east, over the mountains?"

"Who's that, trying to get past the sentries?" she asked, pointing.

Four people Birch didn't know stood at the perimeter. A tall, stout bald man in a trench coat, a middle-aged man in a suit jacket and jeans, a young, gangly black man in sagging pants, and, just joining them, a fourth man. The fourth was a tall dark-haired man, perhaps half-Asian, of indeterminate age, wearing a bulky green jacket cadged from some army surplus store.

Wanting something to keep his mind occupied, Birch crossed to the group, who had been stopped in their tracks by Mergus and two other OSI men.

"Just look at the ID," said the man in the suit jacket, offering his press card. "My name is James Swift, I'm a reporter—*The Sacramento Bee*. Galivant here's a reporter too."

"Nobody's admitted," Mergus growled. "I'd guess the press least of all."

"Really? Some shit you don't want people to know?" the young black man asked.

"Good question," said the man in the green army jacket, striding up. "Hi Galivant, Swift. How you guys doing?" He shook hands with the young black man. "Lyman Fuji, brewd. You guys walk here? You look tired as hell."

"We *are* tired as hell," Swift said. "You didn't hike in?"

"Guards all split from the road blocks. Freaked out by the radio reports. I moved the gate and *drove* in."

"Shit!" Shontel said, rolling his eyes disgustedly at Swift.

"But how'd you find it, Lyman?" Galivant asked. "How'd you know."

"It's all over the Internet, man! I worked it out, is all. The HAARP connection, for one thing. This is the place to be."

Galivant nodded, yawning. "Yeah, this is the locus of the hocus pocus, my man."

"You guys have ten seconds to start moving," Mergus said, drawing his gun. He kept it discreetly down by his side, so far. "And then..."

"Ah!" Birch said. "You're here! Swift, Galivant!" He had

heard their names for the first time just now, but he did a good job of saying the names warmly, as if he'd known them all his life.

"Oh—yeah, good to see you!" said Swift, shaking Birch's hand, just as if he knew him.

Meredith was squeezing Birch's arm painfully, trying to warn him to stop this charade, but Birch had made up his mind. He was going to get one over on the OSI thugs and, underlying that, he had another motive. He wanted as many witnesses here, from the outside world, as possible. Especially the press. Because he was afraid of what O'Hanlon was going to bring down on them all.

Mergus turned on Birch in cold fury. "Look, sir, no one's authorized to invite anyone here except—"

"Except O'Hanlon and me, Mergus! I'm head of marketing—and these guys are reporters. Get it— marketing, and reporters? See a connection, at all? Here's a clue—publicity. Good publicity. You need to use some goddamn common sense, Mergus—you can see O'Hanlon's in conference with Griffin there. If I have to interrupt him to confirm this, he'll go ballistic."

A small crowd was starting to gather, mostly church-members, frowning at Mergus, muttering angrily—a number of them had already been prevented from going to their cars by the OSI men—and the sentries could see they were going to lose control of the situation.

Mergus chewed his lip—and then shrugged.

"Okay, but it's your responsibility, Birch," Mergus said, holstering his gun. "You four, go on in. But no one leaves till we say so."

"That's appropriately sinister," Galivant chuckled, striding boldly into the field with the reporter from the *Bee*. Meredith and Birch went with them, as if accompanying old acquaintances. Fuji was hurrying to catch up; the black kid came last.

"Welcome to the 'charmed circle'," Birch said dryly, as they walked into the field.

"Come on, Shontel!" Swift said to the youth. "Stick with me."

"Waitaminnut, that kid's no reporter, what's he here for?" Mergus called after them.

"I'm, like, with the church and shit!" the teenager said, over his shoulder.

"Look at these columns!" Fuji said. "Those circles of light going up them—the lights look kind of fake..."

"That's what everyone says," Birch said. "Griffin says it's window dressing on something real."

"You mean you don't know for sure?" Swift asked, looking Birch over in the gathering light.

"I don't," Birch admitted. As Galivant and Fuji went for a closer look at Griffin and his gear, Birch went on, "I mean—I was told they're supposed to block some mind-control influence but how they work or if they do—I don't know. We've lost track of the whole thing—Griffin and O'Hanlon are riding a goofy little merry-go-round of their own."

"Shontel!" a girl shouted, running up to them. "Dad!"

Swift turned and said, "Hey hon!"

The girl ran into Shontel's arms—Swift looked on benignly, but seemed mildly disappointed that she'd gone to her boyfriend first.

Erin, the girl's name was, Birch recalled. He'd had seen her mother arguing with the Colbertsons.

Erin broke her clasp with Shontel and turned beamingly at her father. "God I'm glad you guys're here!"

He took her in his arms and kissed her on the cheek. "Baby, I'm so glad to see you're all right."

"Oh God, Dad, I'm so *tired* and they won't let us—"

"Erin—don't take His name in vain!" called the girl's mother, stalking up to the group. "Jim, what are you doing here? This is really inappropriate, you hunting us down like this."

"And you," Swift said, "are very confused about what's appropriate right now, Linda."

She raised a small New Testament bound in green

imitation leather, shook it at him, as she spoke, looking at him with a flat, artificially pitying expression. "No Jim. What's right is plain and obvious and that's what I'm doing. But you know—there's still time for you to accept Christ." She walked over to Erin and took her by the wrist. "Stay with us, honey, stay over here—you can talk to your dad later..."

"No!" Erin jerked her arm free and stepped behind her dad.

"Not going to happen, Linda," Swift said. "But I'll tell you what—go to your car, drive to your lawyer, get a court order saying she has to stay with you."

"Dad—no!" Erin put in, looking at her mom over his shoulder. "I don't want her to go anywhere—unless we go, too. I'm so goddamn scared."

"Erin!" Her mother snapped.

"I'm goddamn *scared*, Mama!" Erin shouted, crying.

Linda turned away and walked angrily back to where her church group was beginning a liturgical reading.

Swift held his daughter till her shoulders stopped shaking, and she said, "Let's go sit by the fire, Dad..." Shontel, Swift and Erin went to stand by the decaying bonfire, and Birch watched them go.

He thought about the wall of light they'd seen on television.

"Meredith—it's bound to come here pretty soon. You know that?"

"I know. I'm cold, Frank. Let's go to the fire too..."

Rubbing his eyes as the smoke got in them, Swift thought he ought to try to take his daughter out of here—but where would they go, now? Her mother was here, and she didn't want to leave Erin. Plus, getting past those thugs at the perimeter would be risky—maybe impossible.

"Do you have anything to eat, daddy, they're running out of food here, they're being really stingy...And they're keeping a lot of it for these weird OBM people."

"No hon, I...oh wait, here's an energy bar, in my pocket,
I only took one bite, have that." He handed it to her and
smiled, watching her eat hungrily, like a little girl given a
treat.

"They taste like vitamin pills but I'm so hungry..."

Birch and the blond woman who clung to his arm came
to the fire, and Swift asked, "O'Hanlon—he's here?"

"Yeah, over by the tent." Birch smiled. "He just fired me,
actually. It's amazing how much I don't care."

"What's going on in the world?" Erin asked. She had one
hand on her dad's arm, the fingers of her other hand twined
with Shontel's. "We've heard a lot of weird stuff..."

"That's to put it mildly," Birch said. "Latest we got over
the satellite TV—it was pretty unsettling. I mean—it was
good news in a way, but...it makes you feel helpless too.
Like you're just waiting for some lab to tell you if you have
cancer or not."

"More weird deaths?" Swift asked.

"Yeah. When the wall of light hit Africa, thousands of
Sudanese Janjaweed just dropped dead, like bugs sprayed
with pesticide. In Russia too—*bunch* of Russian industrialists
dead in the light. Sixty-two guys associated with the Russian
secret service, in the Ukraine and Chechnya. Most of those
fascist cocaine-running militia thugs in Colombia...dead.
And a great many middle-level party officials in China—
flopped over dead as doornails."

"We didn't see anything much, coming here, ourselves,"
Swift said, "But the radio said where the wall of light hits
the highway, you get certain cars crashing—the people dead
at the wheel. Just a minority of them but...they just keel over
and the cars spin out."

"Oh God—" Erin burst out, her fingers tightening on his
arm. "Is that the Rapture?"

Swift shook his head. "In the Rapture the people are
supposed to disappear *bodily*. Besides, this thing is mostly
leaving the fundamentalist types behind—it's killing
selectively. We heard on the car radio, eight guys who've been
sitting on death row, in different prisons, just keeled over—

but so did four of their guards! Just under fifty people in
the Pentagon died—but there are thousands of people who
work there, and most of them went untouched. It seems to
have its own rules, not connected to any religious affiliation.
Couple of famous televangelists—killed 'em dead. Other
evangelists, didn't touch them. Just making an inference, I'd
guess it's about how destructive people are, in the world, in
a practical way. If they advocate racist killing, they're about
hate crimes—the wall takes them. They advocate suicide
bombings and violent Jihad, boom, it takes that bunch too.
If they counsel patience and praying for people, it *doesn't*
kill them. It's not about religious people—if they're decent,
humane atheists, it doesn't seem to kill them. If they're
murderous atheists, they die. What it all portends in the
longer run—I'm not sure."

"But..." Erin said, in a hoarse whisper. "What if it *is* the
end of the world? What if this is just the first part of it?"

"Doesn't seem to be ending so far," Meredith said, trying
to reassure the girl. "Everything's still here. Even the port-a-
potties. That's our world, all right. But it seems like there's
a—a big change of some kind coming."

"It's a funny thing," Swift said musingly, as they stopped
by the fire pit, its smoke dark gray against the muted, azure
light of early morning. "If this is really the end of this
world—curious to think of all the people caught by surprise.
Millions of people looking at the ground all their lives, in a
way—suddenly they're all looking up at the sky." He picked
up a piece of tree bark, lying on the edge of the fire pit,
and tossed it onto the embers, watched it flare up, the little
woodchip consumed as he spoke on: "People are looking
up, all startled, from their driven little preoccupations. Just
imagine—people working at the Shopping Channel! What
do they do now? People on Wall Street...or some peasant
in China who just got his first half-acre to farm, till all this
started he was happy as hell about it—*now* what? A sitcom
starlet excited about her new agent; a woman holding her
new baby. Some guy got a sandwich shop franchise in
Florida, thinking he was starting a new career. Millions

of kids graduating from college, excited about their plans. *What* plans? Politicians staring at their campaign posters, wondering if they have any meaning. Some guy just got a job at a videogame company; somebody else just got a bank loan to keep their business going—*now* what?"

"Sure," Shontel said, putting his hands out to catch the last heat from the fire. "But there's people who ain't gonna beat their wife no more. There's cops ain't going to step on some brother's neck no more. I got a cousin, he's in Juvie, gets beaten up every other day, man. I got a text-message on the way here: the doors just popped open at Juvie and the guards walked away and my cousin walked on home. Maybe all this—maybe it's all good."

But he looked as if he was trying to convince himself. He was frowning, worried. "Where's the rest of your family?" Birch asked him.

"My family, they're back in Sac, man. I'm...hella worried about 'em. I got some messages but I can't tell much from that...And I can't get any more messages up here..."

"You tried calling them, Shontel?" Birch asked.

"My cell's not working. What about yours?"

"It should..." Birch found his Blackberry in his coat pocket, took it out, turned it on. No signal. He tossed it into the fire pit.

"Frank!" Meredith said, shocked.

Swift wasn't shocked, though. He could feel it, too. Cell phones would soon be irrelevant.

A commotion at the awning in the center of the field drew their attention, and they saw Griffin, visibly agitated, arguing with the two Colbertsons, the Reverend and his son. O'Hanlon was striding toward them, a glass in his hand slopping over with whisky, if Birch was any judge, his other hand gesturing violently for the OSI men to join him at Griffin's control center.

"Come on, Meredith," Birch said.

Swift turned to his daughter. "Shontel—you guys stay here, all right? Or go in the main tent. Just keep an eye on her, Shontel, all right?"

Erin looked at her dad, smiling. Pleased he'd accepted Shontel to take care of her. Then something else occurred to her. "Dad—I don't need some guy taking care of me all the time. Keeping an eye on me."

"Sorry. But stick with Shontel, I'd feel better."

He turned and hurried after Birch, found Galivant and Fuji joining the crowd around the control center. Griffin was standing with his arms spread in front of his equipment, his eyes wild, mouth twitching. "Just back the fuck off or we'll take you down, you fucking medieval assholes!"

The older Colbertson and his son turned their heads, as one, in equal simultaneous startlement, to stare at Griffin, stunned by his language. "This man is out of control!" George Colbertson said, as O'Hanlon walked up, whisky slopping over his wrist.

"What's the trouble here?"

"You people have been deceiving us!" said the older Colbertson, his voice uncharacteristically shrill. "This man has admitted to me that these...these *devices* of yours are here to keep out the will of the divine—to stop the changes sweeping through the world! Those changes are the first step in the Day of Judgment! You said you'd give us a place to wait and pray in private!"

"You've had your prayer, you've had your seclusion," O'Hanlon growled. He knocked back a slug of amber liquid. "And you can pray your little asses off. But just stay away from this equipment. You're here as a control group, more warm bodies for the test is all..."

As he spoke, the men from O'Hanlon Strategics shoved their way through the crowd, and formed up in front of the equipment that controlled the Griffin Coils, guns in their hands, the weapons pointed at the ground but no less threatening for it.

"Oh Lord," said George Colbertson, under his breath. "Armed men."

"You want to know what's happening here?" Galivant said suddenly, coming to the front of the crowd.

George Colbertson winced, seeing him, remembering the hill where they'd watched the Signs. "Oh great. *You.*"

"The phenomenon has extended itself to more and more people, Colbertson," Galivant went on. "The smarter members of the Christian right have been changing their tune, all over the country. You'd think they'd be congregating in the churches, wailing for the Rapture, with the signs in the sky. But some of them had experiences like my friend Swift here—sudden shifts in perception, a keen mindfulness washing over them. Some of them have been letting go of doctrine and just looking around to see what they could do to help the world. And Griffin here knew that. He needed a group that was likely to attract the vector of change—so he let you bring your hardcore followers up here, so he could see if he could keep the influence away from them."

Birch nodded. "That's probably right, from what I've seen. I wondered why he picked this bunch..."

Galivant turned to glower at Griffin and his control setup. He shook his head grimly. "This is...just wrong. This shield of theirs is something sick. It just feels wrong. They shouldn't be allowed to do this, Swift..."

"Nothing we can do about it, Ed."

Galivant grunted. "Not so sure about that."

"You seem to know a lot about what's happening in the world," Birch said, looking at Galivant curiously.

"I write about...the miraculous. Sometimes. Most of the time it turns out to be wishful thinking."

"You think this is...the apocalypse? The wall of light makes me wonder..."

Galivant rubbed his bald head meditatively. "The word *apocalypse* has come to mean doom to people. But it's from the Greek *apokalupsis.* Means revelation—or a disclosure. Something coming to light. And the thing is, we've all known in the back our heads, that life is just *an amazingly strange thing in itself.* Ordinary life. Dust, organizing into cells, into DNA—cells organizing into discrete bodies, and minds, walking around. Dust feeling, thinking, creating. Matter with feelings! Even a hardened atheist had to know that *something* strange was back of it all. Right? So really—we've all kind of unconsciously been expecting this. So it's late, so what? People knew it'd come for them or their children or their children's children. It's here now. You can *feel* it. And—it doesn't feel like it's a bad thing."

Birch nodded, slowly. "Wish I hadn't given up smoking. Because I sure as hell want a cigarette right now."

Fuji smiled and gave Birch a cigarette.

Swift was struck by something Galivant had said. *You can feel it. And—it doesn't feel like it's a bad thing.* Galivant was right. He had known in the back of his mind since that day at the trailer park that world-wide change was coming. He had *felt* it, however much he'd resisted it. And it did not feel like something he wanted to stop. It felt as welcome as spring after a long cold winter...

If they were going to put a stop to something, maybe they should try to stop Griffin and O'Hanlon...

Griffin, Swift noticed, had gone back to work behind the shield of security thugs, tapping away on the keyboard, muttering to himself, listening to music on his oPod as he worked. Taking a pill from a shirt pocket, popping it dry without even looking up from the computer monitor. Wires extended outward from his workstation like web from a spider. An open box of tools sat at his feet—it presented certain possibilities, Swift thought.

"If it's God sending all these changes," Galivant shouted, turning to glare at the church members massing behind the Colbertsons, "then you people have been cut off from God's will exactly where you came to receive it! But I'll tell you something...Everything you think you know is wrong! Our trying to understand the spiritual reality is like an ant trying to understand the Internet! It's way, way beyond us, people!"

"Oh, yes—!" Linda Swift called, her voice hoarse with anger. "Go on and mock! And when we vanish you will stand here with your mouths open and you'll pray to God—and it'll be too late!"

There was a general murmur of approval at that from the End Timers, until Galivant summarily informed them:

"Your 'Rapture' notion wasn't even a part of Christianity until the nineteenth century! It was manufactured by one lame, confused, half-hysterical evangelical, guy named Scofield—it's all out of the Scofield Reference Bible and it's just his little fantasy! It's not even real Christianity!"

"Whatever!" O'Hanlon barked, tossing his empty glass into the dirt. "Just get away from this tent, and go about your business! Only nobody leaves. You're the control group, we need you here! Anybody tries to leave, we're gonna have to bring 'em down!"

The elder Reverend Colbertson glared at O'Hanlon, his jaw working, hands shaking. Then he turned toward Griffin. "I don't know about the Rapture—but I know that the Day is come and I will have no part of even an attempt, however futile, to try and stop it! Who is with me?"

So saying he marched toward Mergus, raising a Bible in his right hand—Cullum shoved the old man back. They glared at one another.

"Mergus!" O'Hanlon said, between gritted teeth. "Shoot him or tackle him!"

But Mergus was staring at the gun in his own hand. He had an odd look on his face. "I don't know why I came here...I had enough money to retire after the job we did on...but..." He looked up at the sky. "I guess I knew..." He lowered the gun, and walked away, sat on the grass—even as the elder Colbertson started toward Griffin again.

"Dad—don't!" his son shouted.

Colbertson kept going, pushing past Cullum, the black OSI man—who grabbed Colbertson by the collar, spun him around, shoved him back again. "Just stay back, old man!"

Colbertson started forward, his son close behind him, shouting—

The gunshot was like the crack of a baseball bat against a metal pipe, to Swift's ear. He stared at the pistol in Cullum's hand—at the dull, detached expression on Cullum's face—as some part of his mind registered the old evangelical staggering backward, a bullet hole through Colbertson's forehead. The old man fell back, caught by his son, who lowered him gently to the ground.

The crowd scattered, Birch drawing Meredith off to the side, some of the End Timers running, the others backing away, wailing.

"Cullum did what he had to," said O'Hanlon, his voice a croak, sounding as if he were trying to convince himself of it as he stared at the dead man.

"Fucking hell," said Birch. "Meredith, you see? You see what's going on here?" She was weeping, staring at the body, one hand over her mouth, shaking her head. "That's murder, Cullum!"

Cullum shook his head. "Presidential order. I only work for OSI as a cover. I'm NSA." He reached into his coat, drew out the specialized ID with his free hand, waved it, keeping his gun up, pointed in the general direction of the End Timers. He put the ID away. "I promised the President personally I'd keep an eye on this thing. Make sure it came off..."

O'Hanlon gaped at him. "Why you sneaky little..." Then he caught himself. "Well—I guess the President knows what he's doing. I guess...an example...had to be..." His voice trailed off as he turned to look at the dead man.

Swift came out of his shock, and thought: I have to find Erin. People are firing weapons around here...

He turned to look for his daughter—and saw something else. A curtain of light was sweeping toward them.

Swift grabbed Galivant's arms and nodded toward it.

"Oh my gosh," Galivant muttered. "Fuji—look!"

They stared at the wall of light, extending earth to sky, running south to north, through the trees, following the slope up the hills, making Galivant think passingly of one of Cristo's walls of fabric, but far bigger, and glowing with energy, shimmering with illumination, all golden-red. It was still outside the perimeter of Griffin's Coils.

What would happen when it hit the columns? Would they really stop it?

A shriek of mingled ecstasy and horror arose from the

End Timers, as they saw the wall of light moving toward them, and Swift found himself running to his daughter, who was just then emerging out of the Event Tent with Shontel. Time seemed to telescope, and it took far too long to cross the thirty yards separating them.

At last Swift came puffing up to her, wishing he'd brought his beer along—if this was going to be the end, it was hard to face without beer—and Shontel, swallowing as he stared at the wall of light, asked, "You think there's any use running? I mean—we don't know for sure if it's gonna pick us..."

Slipping an arm around Erin, trying to catch his breath, Swift shook his head. "No. You can't hide from it. Not even deep underground."

"Daddy?" Erin's voice a squeak, as the wall of light approached.

"I'm sure it's not going to hurt us, hon," Swift said.

But he was not sure at all.

12

"THE wall of light's just getting here," Ama observed, glancing over her shoulder as she and Boyce walked up to the flickering columns at the edge of the field.

"Yes," he said, distantly. "Look at this artifact..." He reached out, ran his hand over a glassy column. "They're testing it at a low gain, at the moment. Can you feel it—the drumming on the air? What a marvel it is. Unprecedented, in my experience. Really, you are a resourceful set of primates."

"Um—thanks. I guess." She was watching as the wall of light marched up toward them.

He backed away from the columns, ten steps outside the perimeter—just as the light reached them.

"Should I be scared, Dennis?" she asked, hurrying to stand near him.

"No. You won't be harmed."

I wonder, she thought, if he's as angelic as he seems—suppose he's capable of lying?

The wall of light came to Ama then. A warmth seemed to nuzzle the back of her neck. She closed her eyes, and felt the light come tinglingly over her, saw it shining behind her eyelids. Seemed to see a horizontal continuum—or was it vertical? It was both—stretching away to infinity. She saw the wall of light heading toward some unknown center of the universe, some center that was everywhere at once...

And then it moved on. She opened her eyes and saw

the wall of light reaching the perimeter of columns. A stadium-sized bubble formed in the air, encompassing the field, delineated by the perimeter of columns; a bubble of negativity where the wall of light simply wasn't. The wall of light passed over the field, missing it, and moved beyond it...

Touching no one inside the bubble of negativity. Affecting no one. Eliminating no one. Killing no one.

The wall of light moved on, leaving the field behind. The Griffin Coils had worked.

A cheer went up, from some half a dozen men standing around computers set up on tables in the center of the field, under a dusty orange awning.

But there were several hundred others, groaning, muttering, weeping near a larger tent, to Ama's left. "Who are all those people?" she asked.

"Oh those? They're a core group of Christian fundamentalists, I think, so-called 'End Timers'—that's the report I'm getting, though this interference pattern is making input a little indistinct. They represent a much larger church. They seem frightened, I'm sorry to say." He didn't sound sorry, but it was hard to tell—maybe he was.

The sentries were in close anxious discussion near the center of the field, and didn't see Ama and Boyce walk past their perimeter, Ama and Boyce walked toward the cluster of people and equipment at the orange awning. A man in an oversized army jacket looked at the sky, spinning in place to take in the horizon. "They're gonna be mighty pissed off, with us killing one another here."

"Who's going to be pissed off?" Boyce asked, walking up. The End Timers were arguing with the men under the tent. Someone was waving a gun. A man was kneeling by an old gentleman, a few yards away, praying. The old gentleman looked like he might be dead.

"Who?" the man in the green army coat said. "The aliens, brewd, the ones who sent the wall of light. I'm about ninety-percent sure they're from the Sirius star system—the Sirians have been watching us for centuries. They've gotten tired of our bullshit, squandering our resources, fucking people over. We're, like, their little project—we're their ant farm."

Boyce seemed mildly amused by Fuji. "You're almost right," said Boyce, with a confidence that made the other man look closely at him. "All except for the part about space aliens and Sirius and ant farms. My name is Dennis Boyce. You are Lyman Fuji, I think."

Fuji's eyes widened. "You know who I am? You with NSA, like that fucker that killed the old man? I was right—you bastards have been monitoring me!"

"No, I'm not with the..." Boyce thought for a moment. "The National Security Agency? Yes. I mean—no. I'm not."

"Dennis?" Ama said, staring. "There's a man lying there with a coat over his face-and there's blood soaking through it. I think he's dead!"

"He is, Ama," Boyce said, his voice respectfully hushed. "That man Cullum, over there—he shot him." He sighed. "You'd better get used to it—a large percentage of the present human race will be gone soon—even the ones who aren't killed by the wall. We won't kill them, though. They'll kill one another."

Fuji gaped at Boyce. Ama was still trying to grasp—emotionally—what he'd said. A large percentage of the human race...

"Who the hell *are* you, dude?" Fuji asked.

Dennis pointed at the wall of light, which was moving onward, passing over the trees around the field, heading west, leaving them behind. "I'm with the ones who brought...*that.*"

Fuji looked at the receding wall of light, then back at Boyce.

Swift was curious about the fresh-faced young stranger with the mature air about him, and the petite young woman at his side. "Who's that talking to Fuji?" he asked Galivant. "The guards are slipping up..."

"I don't know the guy," Galivant said. He led Swift, Birch,

and Meredith over to the strangers. "Something odd about him..."

"Good to see those OSI guards losing their edge," Birch muttered.

"Frank, keep your voice down," Meredith whispered, chewing her lower lip.

Approaching the strange young man with the curly brown hair, Swift had the odd feeling he was back in time at a rock festival he'd gone to in the 1970s. He'd been pretty young then. What reminded him of the rock festival? Then he had it: he'd been on LSD there. He felt like he was on acid, if only half a hit, as he walked up to the two strangers.

Fuji nodded toward the stranger. "Dennis Boyce. Says he's part of some group of visitors from Elsewhere, sent us the wall of light, those cone things...The lady's name is Ama..."

Swift looked at Boyce, frankly assessing him. What was it about him? Why did he feel so odd standing close to the guy? Get a grip, he told himself. *So he's charismatic. Probably a would-be cult leader sensing an opportunity.* "You claim to be connected to the wall of light? I expect there are lots of people around now making lots of...claims."

"Yes, that's likely the case," said Boyce lightly, his gaze wandering over the crowd. More of the evangelicals, heads bowed, were praying over the body of the old man.

"And I expect a charlatan would say 'that is likely the case' about there," said Swift dryly.

Boyce nodded distantly and then cocked his head, as if listening. "Someone is about to shoot themselves."

Looking at Boyce, Swift thought: If he's a charlatan he's the best I ever saw. Understated, completely unworried about what we think. And there's almost a visible aura...not quite. Almost.

There was a gunshot, then, this one from the crowd of fundamentalists. Fuji, Swift, and Galivant looked at one another, then at Boyce—at Boyce with a new respect—as they followed him over to the crowd near the old man. A woman was lying on her back, there, a smoking pistol in her slack hand.

"It's that woman I argued with on the hill, Swift, remember?" Galivant said, trotting up to the body. "Jeez if I'd known she was so fragile..."

"It was in no way your fault, Ed," said Boyce.

Erin and Shontel walked urgently up to Swift. "Mr. Swift," Shontel said, "this is boosht, man, we got to get out of here. People getting shot." He shook his head in disgust. "You white people think the ghetto is dangerous? That's *two* now."

"We need to know what's going on, Shontel," Swift said, his voice low. He glanced nervously at the OSI men. "Anyhow I'm not sure we can leave yet—not safely."

The dead woman had a silvery "High Point" pistol, lying in her open hand, its muzzle leaking a rising thread of smoke.

"Where's O'Hanlon?" Birch said, looking around.

Meredith pointed at the old CEO, hair disarrayed, swaying at the control awning, arguing with Griffin. Indifferent, apparently, to another death taking place just steps away. "O'Hanlon doesn't seem to give a flying..."

"She just stuck that gun in her mouth," someone said tearfully. "She..."

That's when the woman who'd shot herself sat up and looked around. Her head should have been blown apart— but she was completely intact, unhurt. She spotted Boyce, and gazed intently at him. Their eyes locked. She nodded.

"That's how Boyce got his body," Ama remarked. "A suicide...the bullet turned to light..."

Boyce helped the woman who'd shot herself to her feet. "I'm glad they sent you," he told her. "I wasn't sure how much I should interfere with their machinery here." She only looked at him in response. He added, "Let's speak out loud, when we can. It's more reassuring to them."

"Very well," said the woman.

"She doesn't look hurt at all! It's a blessed miracle!" said a young man with the church group, pushing close to look her over. "Praise Jesus!"

Ama stared at the young man. "He looks so familiar..."

Swift leaned close to her, said discreetly, "Yeah you

recognize him—you were flipping around on cable and there he was. George Colbertson...And the unfortunate old guy under the jacket, over there—you can't see his face but you've seen him before too. That's his father. Father and son, both television preachers."

"Judith!" George Colbertson said breathlessly, eyes wide, trying to get a reaction from the woman. "You've been raised up! Give thanks to God! He protected you from your folly!" Something seemed to occur to him. He turned, knelt by the body of his father, set to praying as if expecting the elder Colbertson to come back from the dead. "'And the dead in Christ will rise first...'"

"Ah," said Boyce, picking up the woman's gun, and looking at it curiously, "I'm afraid you're under a misapprehension, George. Your father will not be...resurrected. The lady has not actually 'returned' from the dead." He nodded toward Judith—there was no spot of blood on her. "You see? No blood. Her *body* never quite died. The essential self of the woman whose body it was—her substantial being—*that* is gone. She surrendered her right to the body when she tried to commit suicide. Her soul is quite gone from here. It has departed. It has *split*. It's cruised onward..."

Ama gave Boyce and exasperated look and he shrugged and fell silent.

The suicidal woman dusted herself off; she was a plump middle-aged woman with small light-blue eyes, a cap of dyed-blond hair and a wide, flexible mouth. Swift had seen her earlier, talking to her friends—and this didn't seem like the same woman at all, except superficially.

"The woman—" She indicated herself with a gesture, "—this woman panicked, when she saw the dividing light had passed over the field without making its selection. She thought everyone here had defied God and all were damned, and she shot herself as a kind of penance. She did it out of the kind of fear that plagues humanity. The fear that your leaders cultivate in you. Her name was Judith. I've taken Judith's body, as she surrendered her right to it, so that I can be of more direct use to my..." She looked at Boyce. "...to my colleague, here. Call me Judith, if you like."

George Colbertson stood, took a step closer, and gaped at them. He swayed, seeming about to faint. And then he sat down heavily on the ground, head in his hands.

"I know the feeling, Reverend Colbertson," Ama said. "But you get used to them, after a fashion, eventually."

Colbertson shook his head, and cited Revelation: "These are demonic spirits, forming signs..."

"We are most certainly *not* demonic spirits," said Boyce firmly, putting his hands in his pockets. "But there was a sick entity, dominating this world—some mistook him for a god. He encouraged the misidentification. The UnderGod, Ama here calls him."

"We found him—the traces of him," Judith said, glancing at Boyce.

Boyce looked at Judith inquiringly; she looked back, for a moment. Then he nodded. "I see. Dead."

Ama glanced at the sky, as if she could see a giant corpse floating up there. "The UnderGod is *dead?*"

"Yes. But the sickness he spread through the world goes on. We'll have to take some extreme steps to set things right again."

Fuji smirked. "The UnderGod! Right. And now he's dead. Floating in orbit, is he? Phil Dick would be pleased. How'd God die?"

Boyce looked momentarily puzzled. "A body in orbit? No. It's not something you could see with human eyes."

Judith was looking at Colbertson, kneeling, his eyes squeezed shut, praying, his lips moving silently. She walked over and patted him on the shoulder, as if to comfort him— he shoved her hand away.

She shrugged. "It wasn't really God," she said, turning again to Swift and the others. "Nor did he control the world, entirely. But he nudged it, this way and that. He allowed the worst human impulses free reign. Much of what has happened to the world, in large part—was not supposed to happen. Human sacrifices, the Inquisition, the Holocaust, the Killing Fields, millions starving in famines—all the result of his morbid, even sadistic affliction. He realized that we were coming, to set things right. So...rather than 'face the music' he shut himself down, made himself numb with impulses drawn from...well, you wouldn't understand. For him, it was like taking heroin. And...it killed him."

Galivant stared. "You're saying God is dead—from a drug overdose?"

"Essentially," Judith said. "The person misidentified as God." She shrugged.

Fuji snorted. "So this false 'God' saw the cops, so to speak, coming for him—and he gave himself a hotshot, and died. That it?"

"Close enough."

Colbertson groaned, rocking in place.

Swift looked around—a core group had gathered around "Boyce" and "Judith". Was it just suggestion, people falling under someone's psychological sway—or was there a convergence of lives gathered, here, under an influence, as certainly as metal shavings were drawn to a magnet? The Asian girl, Ama, stood close to Boyce—an attractive woman, eyes glittering with intelligence. Galivant was there too, and the guy who'd called himself Birch, the blond woman with him; Lyman Fuji, Shontel, and Erin were sitting on the ground; Shontel and Erin were leaning on one another, listening. Some of the End Timers were listening too—others were standing in a separate group, arguing in an undertone about what to do and glancing fearfully at Cullum.

Ed Galivant ran a hand musingly over his bald head, coming closer to Judith and Boyce. "If you two are what you say you are..." At this he leaned intrusively close to scrutinize the woman who had been "Judith". "Then— what's been going on exactly, with all the changes in the world? And what happens next?"

Judith looked at Galivant with her eyebrows raised, drawing back a little, as if a monkey had tried to climb on her shoulder. "This will quickly become clear. This very day. Much is happening—and much more will happen."

"A helluva party is what's happening," Fuji muttered, looking toward the road. "Every place but here."

Shontel glanced over at Fuji, smiling crookedly. "People think that wall of light thing means the end of the world—so they're having a big-ass party?"

"Last I heard, yeah," Fuji muttered. "And we're missing it. So I hope this scene's for real."

"I bet they're having riots, more like," said Erin, yawning.

"Riots are a good party," Fuji said, enthusiastically. "I remember once in San Francisco..."

"I can do without that shit," Shontel said. Erin nodded. "I'm just chillin' right now. People shootin' old men, other people shootin' themselves, falling down dead—getting up again." He sighed and hugged Erin—and again Swift felt himself warm to Shontel. "I'm just gonna chill and let it sort itself out. Can't wrap my head around it."

"I'm with you there, friend," said Birch, and Meredith nodded. "I just feel—it's time to wait."

"Those people have murdered my father!" George Colbertson interrupted, with a shout, looking up from where he sat, hugging himself near his father's body. "What will be done about it? Look at them, they just stand there, all smug and casual!" He pointed at the OSI men. "Where is justice, Lord?" This last addressed to the sky.

But it was Boyce who answered. "It will be seen to," said Boyce coolly, pitching the High Point pistol into the underbrush like a man throwing away an apple core.

"What the bejeezus are you shouting about there, Colbertson?" demanded O'Hanlon, walking unsteadily up, his shoulders hunched in anger.

"This is the financier of the shield device," Birch observed quietly, to Boyce.

"Is he? Then he saved his own life, for a time," Boyce said, looking O'Hanlon over. "Justice will come, shortly, anyway—he'll help bring it on himself."

"Who the hell are you?" O'Hanlon snapped, glaring at Boyce. "I didn't authorize this man to be here."

"He's not from 'here' at all," Ama said. "Not from our

world, exactly. From some kind of heaven or...higher plane or something. He and his colleagues sent the wall of light. The influence."

O'Hanlon snorted. "Bullshit. He's some scammer working his con on you people."

Boyce nodded at O'Hanlon, entirely relaxed and unaffectedly benevolent. "A natural enough assumption. I understand there are a great many con artists who make fantastic claims. I could show you some things, Mr. O'Hanlon. I could create a field that would increase your level of awareness—in English you might call the field a *consciousness lamp*. We sent a good many consciousness lamps around the world, and apparently they caused you some anxiety. We cannot expose everyone in the world to them—what is illumination for some would be chaos for everyone. But we can bring one of those lamps to you, Mr. O'Hanlon. Show you others as they are; yourself as you are. You'd be distressed, for a while. But you'd probably survive it without losing your sanity. I can't guarantee that, but...we could try."

And then a hum began to shiver out from Boyce; from the area above his head. Swift thought he could even see the emanation as a distortion of the air, the way heat waves distort the air, but in this case the "heat waves" weren't just going upward but were spreading out in every direction, from a central point.

The air around them reacted, quivering; the grass rustled and rearranged itself; ambient sounds grew louder; the color of the sky took on more depth. A beautiful scent began to gust over them...A conical shape began to form, all of golden light, then crimson, then violet...

O'Hanlon went rigid—then seemed to wrench himself. He backed away. "Bullshit!" He roared. "Suggestion. Hypnosis! I'm tired and...it's been a long night...but you're not going to hustle me, you—"

He raked the air in front of his face with a hand as if to chase away a wasp, and turned, walked in long hurried strides back to the Event Tent: a man in search of a drink.

The colors faded from the air. Swift wasn't even sure they'd been there in the first place.

"What *happened*, just now?" Fuji said, blinking. "You guys feel something?"

"I'm not sure," Swift said. "When Boyce there was looking at O'Hanlon...it was like the start of what I saw in Fresno."

"It wasn't directed right at you," Judith said. "You just caught the edge of it."

"There was *something* there," Birch said thoughtfully, watching O'Hanlon go. "Watch out for O'Hanlon, Boyce. Maybe he'll get his thugs after you."

Boyce shook his head. "He knows if there was any kind of real confrontation, he'd have to face the truth. He's just blocking me from his mind, right now. Pretending I'm not here."

"You didn't answer my question, not really," Galivant pointed out, looking back and forth between Judith and Boyce. "If you guys are wired into this phenomenon, then what happens to us next? To the world?"

Boyce looked at Judith. A silent exchange. Then Boyce looked at Ama expectantly. Her smiled and raised his eyebrows.

"Three phases," Ama blurted. Everyone turned to look at her and she grimaced self-consciously. Swift felt oddly drawn to her, which was peculiar—they didn't know one another.

"Phase One," she went on, "they sent something to change certain people at what Dennis calls social pressure points— so they can prepare the rest of us."

Fuji looked at Boyce suspiciously. "Sounds like mind control to me."

"It isn't, though," Ama said. "There was no control over those people. If you give someone a pair of eyeglasses, are you controlling them? They just gave them the ability, for a while, to see how things really were—how they themselves really were—so they could make up their own minds. They did it by amplifying perceptions. Just increasing awareness in people. On...more than one level. It's something like the awareness that comes from consciousness-raising drugs, only without their bad side effects. Without that stoned bewilderment. You can't stay in the...the waking dream we're in, see, when consciousness lamps open up your perceptions, unless you *fight consciousness*. Like O'Hanlon just did. I guess some choose their old illusions—their old habits. But a lot of people changed direction, in Phase One. And it's all preparation for what's coming. Phase Two is the wall of light. Still going on, even if it passed up our little patch of ground. Phase Three—there'll be some kind of choice, for people who haven't chosen already...And then—I don't know. The end of the world as we know it."

Fuji looked coldly at Judith and Boyce—first one, then the other. "Whatever you are, whatever you're doing—doesn't matter. Why should we accept it? We're on our own, except for myths, for thousands of years. You guys leave us with some super gigantic *asshole* in charge—if you're not making that wack story up—and then you come here and *kill us* for doing what he wanted us to do! We should be furious with you! We should defy you and tell you to go to hell!"

"You have a point," Judith said, nodding. Smiling pleasantly.

"However, Lyman Fuji," Boyce said, with perfect equanimity, "you don't *believe* what you just said. You *don't know* what you believe, or feel—not really. You watched your parents drink themselves to death, and you shut down. You shut down from the day they left you at the day camp for two days, forgot to pick you up because they were both drunk."

Fuji stared. Swallowed. Then he summoned the anger back. "You *are* NSA."

"No, Lyman," Boyce went on. "I know those things about you because I share in the same underlying consciousness you share in. The consciousness that is part of what some here call the ground of being. And I can look from there into your mind—the bottle of mind that is Lyman Fuji. You're angry, you've *been* angry for almost twenty years, and you pick verbal fights so you can discharge that anger. Same reason you never saw a conspiracy theory you didn't like. It gave you an outlet. Something you could feel angry about safely. Like when your cousin Tara died."

"Shut up," said Fuji, turning away. He took several steps away from the group, shoving his hands in his pockets. Then he just stood there, in the grass, staring into the shadows of the forest around the perimeter.

"Those who choose to look away," said Judith, with a mild-mannered sureness, glancing at Fuji, "will have to remain behind."

"Behind? So—where are the others going?" Swift asked.

"Into a remade world—that's the short way to describe it," said Judith. "That's Phase Three. The final phase of the transfiguration."

Swift's ex-wife Linda walked up then, arms crossed around her chest, her hair disarrayed. "Hi Mom," Erin said, tentatively. Linda looked coldly at Shontel, then turned to Erin. "Will you come and pray with us?"

Erin glanced at Boyce. "We've got someone here who can hear us directly," Erin said, surprising Swift. "I don't think we need to."

Linda shook her head. "False prophets, honey. Have you had anything to eat?"

"I'm not hungry anymore. I feel...like I'm in a dream. But wide awake too..."

Linda closed her eyes, and shook her head. "I'm just... going to wait till you're ready to come and pray with us."

Swift nodded. "Best thing for now, Linda."

"Jim? Shut up." With that, Linda walked away.

Erin turned to look at Boyce, shading her eyes against the morning light. "But what'll it actually be *like*—after? Will it be, like, heaven...or, I don't know, hell?"

"Neither," said Boyce.

Judith spoke up, then. "The end we bring lets a large part of the human race begin anew, without the dark influence— and with renewed guidance." She considered a moment. "Judith worked with computers. On some computers there is a *reset* button. It'll be like pressing the reset button, in a way."

"You're *rebooting the world*?" Swift asked, feeling dazed.

"In a sense, yes," Judith said. "We work for the original 'programmer'. The program—and I offer that computer term only as a metaphor—was set to run on its own, without interference. Without intelligent design exactly. It simply had the *probability of life arising from matter* built into it, in a subtle way. But the UnderGod hacked the program on this world. So here, as is sometimes the case on some worlds—a virus cleansing program is needed. And then a reset is necessary. It's that—or wipe the program entirely."

"But—what about all these people *dying*? I mean—the wall of light?" someone demanded, from the crowd of End Timers. Swift didn't see who it was.

Fuji returned to the little group, wiping away tears, his jaw set crookedly, but something else showing in his face too—the beginnings of hope. "Yeah—why did they have to die?" he asked. More curiously than angrily this time.

"They were dangerous people," Boyce said, shrugging. "Fixated on violence, extremes of belief. Some were people who believe that other human beings are essentially meat-animals."

"They were predatory people," Judith put in, "who would not be changed. They had to be removed partly because we must impose some measure of justice—subjective justice from objective truth—and partly because they would interfere with the possibilities of those who will remain behind. Those who remain must have a chance to change course before Phase Three begins. It is a small chance—there are some very dangerous people remaining, and the chance of their changing isn't good—but the choice must be provided anyway."

"Why tell *us* all this?" Fuji asked. "I mean—us in particular. Why don't you announce it to all the whole world?"

"We will speak to the whole world, after Phase Three. Two of us were sent to this spot to see this unusual technology." Judith gestured at the Griffin's Coils. "And to meet certain people here we have decided to...employ. It's not an accident that Mr. Swift was drawn here. There are others here who have a particular part to play..." She glanced at Galivant.

Swift shook his head. *They're trying to get me to believe they're the ones behind all this by pulling me into their little myth. It is not an accident that Mr. Swift was drawn here.*

But...there was something about them...

Swift stared at "Boyce" and "Judith," trying to see that *something* clearly. The woman, theoretically, had come back from the dead, which was extraordinary—but maybe she hadn't. Maybe the gun contained blanks.

Still, when he stepped back, stopped the flow of questions in his mind for a moment, and just looked at them, he could see every detail of their faces, their clothes, with an intense, crystalline clarity. They seemed more *here* than everyone around them. Which prompted him to ask, "But where are you *from*? What your friend here—Ama, right?—what she said was vague as hell."

Ama sighed. "Just try to get clear on where they're from. Good luck with that. They say they're from 'every thing'."

"That's supposed to be more believable than they're from the Dog Star?" Fuji asked, snorting. "Yeah right."

Judith considered. "There is a better term than 'every thing'...Judith's reading extended into the esoteric before she became an evangelical Christian." She turned to Boyce. "Jacob Boehme—wasn't he one of ours?"

"Yes. He was under our influence. There were quite a number, in various cultures. Jesus and Mohammed and Buddha and Lao Tzu and Meister Eckhart and Gurdjieff. A number of others. But the 'UnderGod'—"

"The UnderGod was once called *Ialdabaoth*, by certain mystics, in the time of Yeshua of Nazareth," Judith put in.

Boyce nodded. "Very well. 'Ialdabaoth' saw to it that cultural perceptions distorted the teachings of our messengers. But Gurdjieff had the right idea, in preferring another term to 'God'. He used the term *the Absolute*. The sum total of all things. Judith and I are not from any one place, but think of us as being 'from' the Absolute. We are not the Absolute ourselves—but we are expressions of its outer reaches. We are...well, call us Adjustors. Our purpose is to offer a little help, now and then—to reduce unnecessary suffering. And in this case to completely re-orient this world. Give it a real chance."

"*That's* your agenda?" Galivant asked, licking his lips. "But what's the *big* agenda? God's, or...or the *Absolute's* agenda, if you want to call it that."

And he waited to hear an answer to the one question he'd been asking, in a thousand ways, his whole adult life.

"The Absolute's agenda, as much as you can understand it, involves the development of conscious beings, with which it can commune, and exchange energies—I don't know what else to call it—in a place that is freer than this plane. In the 'higher dimension', if you want to use the pop term. The Absolute calls intelligent beings to it, to engage with it—to become part of it while still being independent of it. Conscious life is precious: Most worlds are not alive, not in the sense that this world is, or they're occupied by lower organisms. You might suppose there are many civilizations in this galaxy, with its billions of stars. No—the odds militate against species evolving that far. Only about two hundred other civilizations exist in this galaxy."

Judith pursed her lips. "Actually—one-hundred ninety-four, at last count. Or..." She looked at the sky. "It may well shortly be one hundred ninety-three. We can't save them all. Some are so savage we can't quite reach them. The Absolute cannot reach them directly—they are shut off from them, their attention insistently turned away, their instincts keeping them bound to things of the lower world. Still, there are those who have evolved—beings like myself. We try to help, sometimes more directly than the Absolute can, and for this we're rewarded. When we're congruent with the Absolute, we flourish; we thrive. So will you."

"You get all that?" Erin asked Shontel.

"Light-weight, I guess, yeah," Shontel said. He squinted up at Judith. "You're not, like, the point man for Jesus, or something?"

Judith smiled down at him. "No. Yeshua was a very good human being—but he won't be coming back. We're not understood by any reading of the...the 'Book of Revelation' mythology. Fundamentalist religion is largely the UnderGod's little...his little *scam*, I guess. It's one of his pet afflictions. The UnderGod was fascinated with addiction—and persecution. He allowed human selfishness to run rampant so that your home—this world—became polluted. Toxified. He allowed an excessive exploitation of people by people—he encouraged brutality. The level of suffering overwhelmed the possibilities for consciousness. At last, the suffering in this world reached a pitch that called out to us. So—*we* came. We cannot interfere in the basic workings of life—some sufferings are needed, some resistance, to drive both the kind of evolution you call 'Darwinian' and to drive the evolution of the substantive being—what you call 'the soul'. But we try to keep some measure of justice in place—to give you a chance. To counterbalance what the UnderGod did. And that's why we're here."

"That will have to be all the explanation we can offer at the moment," Boyce said.

Much mumbling and muttered dispute and half-formed questioning arose from the eavesdropping End Timers—and some of them began hissing about "the Antichrist".

Birch spoke up, suddenly: "My name is Frank Birch—I used to work for OBM. I've got to point out that they've had some success here, blocking your wall of light, if it really was yours...So this agenda of yours is frustrated, at least in this part of the world. And Griffin has a plan for extending that shield to the whole world! Has to do with bouncing it off a satellite and some other station in Australia—I don't understand the whole thing very well...But you saw what he can do just now!"

"Yes, it's remarkable!" Judith said, smiling fondly. "It would indeed, if not interfered with, block the fulfillment of Phase Three..."

"When does Phase Three begin?" Galivant asked. "The end you mentioned."

"The end of this world?" Boyce said, smiling faintly. "Why, that'll be—"

George Colbertson stood up, eyes running with tears, interrupting, "The true end of this world will come when we don't expect it! 'Behold, I come like a thief in the night'! No man knows its time of coming!"

"Actually," said Boyce, rubbing his temples, as if Colbertson were giving him a headache, "I do. It's coming right now. *This minute*. Look—"

A great warping was passing through the landscape—it looked as if the world were painted on a backdrop, and someone had grabbed the edge of the backdrop and snapped it, like snapping a blanket to make it ripple, without physically changing the countryside in any damaging way. The ripple was coming toward them. It was no wall of light—it was more like a wave passing through the otherwise smooth surface of reality itself. Then a bubble of energy formed over the clearing—as the glistening glass columns drummed at the air, and the grass of the field rearranged to duplicate lines of magnetic force, and the bubble expanded, pushing the ripple back...

"They're stopping it!" Ama burst out, amazed.

Both Judith and Boyce looked at Galivant expectantly.

"Well fuck that," said Galivant, suddenly. He started toward Griffin's equipment, under the awning. "I'm not going to let the bastards do it to us this time!" Galivant shouted. "Not this time!"

"Ed! Come back here!" Swift called.

But Galivant was running now with a speed surprising in so large a man. Cullum and another OSI man were stepping out, raising their guns, to intercept him—Galivant darted right, and left, spun, and slipped between them, ducking Collum's swiping arm, scooping up a hammer from the toolbox near Griffin—even as Griffin turned, snarling and hissing at him like an enraged cat.

Galivant shoved Griffin aside and swung the hammer down to smash the primary computer. The crash of his hammer coincided with the crash of a bullet, striking

Galivant in the back. He fell forward over the monitor, and then slid to the ground. He started to get up...

A second bullet fired by Cullum, aimed at Galivant, instead struck a metal box, from which a spider web of wires emanated.

Sparks flew—and the glass columns stopped their flickering and went dark. A third bullet struck...

"No fucking way, no no no!" Griffin shouted. And then buckled, going to his knees, and staying there, eyes glazing. Struck by the third bullet himself.

Falling beside Galivant, who had given up trying to rise. Who was slumping in death.

The rippling of the world came onward, then, unobstructed by the now-lifeless columns.

The Other End was coming. The fabric of reality undulated...

Cullum lowered his gun, staring around in terror, his professional calm shattered.

Fuji rushed toward Galivant and Griffin...

Ama and Boyce and Judith remained with Swift and his daughter, Shontel close beside them. Birch and Meredith stood a little apart, close to the crowd of evangelists. Everyone gazed at the sky, the hills, the trees around the field. The rippling increased its reach...

Judith looked at Boyce, and communicated with him without speaking aloud. But Ama, attuned to Boyce, heard what they said in her mind: *The pattern emerges again: someone sacrifices himself to make a great change possible. Should we tell them?*

That we would have simply made an adjustment, and overridden their equipment? That the sacrifice wasn't necessary? Boyce shook his head. *No, they need their mythologies. They're still children, after all.*

The great rippling passed through the world...from pole to pole of the lumpy, uneven semi-sphere that was the Earth, not creating geological rippling—altering nothing physically—but altering everything existentially.

The world began to suffuse with light—as if light were

emanating from every living cell, and from every atom of
the world, each one individually, starting with half of them,
then going to three-fourths of them, then all of them, the
light building up and up and up...

There was screaming, there were cries of joy. Fuji reached
toward Galivant's body and Swift and Shontel both reached
for Erin, and Birch reached for Meredith and Ama covered
her eyes...

There was a blaze of white illumination, a whiteness as
blank as nothingness—but containing everything within it.

13

On the Border Between Every Thing and No Thing

THEY were in a place made of light, only light—and yet there were shapes in the light; the outlines of faces, of human bodies. Like seeing polar bears in snowstorms, Jim Swift thought.

He saw his daughter's face, near him, then. Her face was made out of light, shaded by gold. He felt no fear, himself, only awe. But there was fear in Erin—he could *feel* it. He drew closer to her.

Dimly seen outlines of other people emerged from the shining continuum—Linda, many of the Church of the Revelation members—and beyond them was an endless continuum of quavering light, and nothing more.

"Daddy?" Erin's voice.

"I'm here, hon. Shontel—is he—?"

"I'm here," came Shontel's voice, close by. "Where're we at?"

"You're on the border between Every Thing and No Thing," said Judith, coming into view. "This is a temporary state. A more familiar one will come shortly. It will be new and old at once."

Her voice was heard by everyone in the world.

"I feel...like when my dentist gave me codeine," Shontel said. "Kind of warm and numb and...like I don't understand where I am. But...it's not bad."

"I feel the same way," said Ama.

"It's a place of choosing," Boyce said. "Many have already chosen to remain behind. Those who are here, are those who can still choose."

"What...what are our choices?" said the blond woman, Meredith, holding hands with Birch, nearby—Swift saw them appear from the backdrop of shining light, like figures coming toward him from a fog. Voices seemed omnipresent, here, heard in the mind more than the ears.

"Choose to go onward, or to go back to the world as you knew it—but with half of the human race to share that world, and with no hope of help from my kind. If you go back there, you will have to proceed with your own evolution, if you can, or succumb to your animal nature."

"Frank..." Meredith said. "I don't want to go with them. I don't trust them. I want the world I knew. We were just starting to get it right, Frank."

A strange cry sounded on the air, rachitic, deeply poignant, so that Swift was unspeakably moved. It was merely the sound of the woman Meredith weeping—but now he seemed to hear it more clearly, more truly, than any weeping he'd ever heard.

He didn't know this woman at all—yet now, in this place of infinite permeability, he saw into her, through the sound of her weeping. It was as if her weeping was a new avenue, an opening into her inner being, and he saw her whole life unreeling before her, incidents like cards riffled in a deck, but each one piquant, resonant, real. He saw her as a child at her mother's bedside; he saw her father, a politician, standing with his hand on her shoulder. He saw Meredith's sorrow and her father's feigned sorrow and Meredith's sadness realizing her father felt nothing at her mother's death. He saw her father leaving her with relatives, a melancholic aunt taking care of her. He saw the aunt committing suicide.

He saw it all in seconds, and he knew that her anguish was as real as the anguish of a mother watching her infant starve. Suffering is suffering—and suffering rings like a bell in people, he realized; from ordinary loneliness, to despair, to fear of abandonment, to physical pain, it resonates within them and sings out sadly to the world, and it doesn't matter if they are rich or poor, empathetic or psychopathic, they all feel suffering, and feel it deeply; so deeply that they hide it from themselves, when they can, they fold it away in the back convolutions of the brain, they hide it under blankets of inattention. But some little part of them feels it and it drives them, from behind, like a man driving an ox with a switching stick.

Swift, in this place of existential piquancy, saw all this in someone he scarcely knew, and felt his heart opening wide— and he turned to his daughter, who was weeping, herself, and—then he hesitated. He knew he could look into her, through the window of her weeping, in the same way, and he could understand her for the first time. For once, the isolation, the gulf that yawned between people would be broken down, and the enigma that was his daughter Erin would be exposed, the doors of that temple thrown wide, and he could walk in and see, really understand...

And he was afraid of that. Why? What was he afraid of?

He looked—and saw his own culpability in her pain. The times he had not been there when she needed him, because he'd put his career first and then because his philandering had split up the family. He saw moments when he'd been distant, only half attending, because of some selfish fix on his own personal, petty little dilemmas.

"I'm sorry," he told her. "I'm sorry, Erin, if I was..."

She seemed to understand what he was apologizing for, without his having to explain. "It's okay, Daddy. I'll be all right."

"Lyman Fuji..." Judith's voice. "You have to choose...You have to trust someone sometime, Lyman."

Swift saw Fuji, dimly, in the continuum of coruscation. "Yeah. I'm coming with you."

"Frank Birch, Meredith—" Boyce began.

"I'm not going!" Meredith said suddenly. "I don't trust them, Frank! Don't you see? If there were any justice, if they were so omnipotent, they could bring my mother back!

They could make this ache in me go away! But they won't do that!"

"No," said Judith evenly. "We won't. Thousands die in an earthquake, and we cannot change that, though it is 'unjust' for those who must suffer without them. Human notions of justice are narrow, constrained. The only objective justice is physics. The relative justice that we offer, in the service of the Absolute, can't be understood in human terms."

"You see? They're 'above' humans! They're megalomaniacs! They're demons or...just like computers, *machines* without feeling! How will they enforce their new world, afterward? Like great benevolent Mussolinis from the Left?"

"No, we'll just show people things, and they'll make up their own minds," Judith said. "The damaged people, the false Guide, will be gone—people will find their way to the new rules themselves, afterward, when they're awake enough to see them..."

"You say that like a voice mail announcement, like a computer voice—not like someone who feels anything for the human race!" Meredith declared.

"We certainly have those feelings, but we aren't *subject* to them," said Boyce. "They're a part of us, and we let them sing, and we listen, but another order of reasoning guides us. We offer that other, higher reason—to you, to everyone. There's freedom in it, Meredith."

"Meredith," Birch said, "I think we should just...trust them. I don't think there's a better choice..."

"He said we can choose to stay! I'm staying, Frank—I'm staying here without you if I have to! I've always been alone and I'm going to stay that way if you won't stay with me..."

"Then...I'll stay with you, Meredith. I'll stay behind with you."

"I love you, Frank. Thank you."

Then Frank Birch and Meredith Hoestine were gone—gone from this plane of light. Decisions of the same sort were being made by thousands, *millions* of people selected by the Adjustors, around the world. Swift could feel them out there. Millions were deciding to come with the Adjustors.

But there were hundreds of millions of others who had not been given that choice. They were those who resisted seeing themselves as they were, who resisted the impulses of consciousness offered to them, who insisted on sleeping. They simply...stayed behind.

"Daddy?" Erin's voice. He looked at her face, shining like an ember. "Where's Mama?"

"I don't know, hon..."

"She was here," Judith said, "but she has gone back. She chose to stay behind. She chose to believe in the mythology she has clung to for some years, though we offered to set her free. She thought we were trying to poison her mind..."

"Mama!"

"Erin," Swift said, "we have to let her go. We don't want to stay in that world. The people who stay will be the ones who made it so dark, so sick, so poisoned. I'm afraid of what they'll do to it."

"Your father is telling the truth, child," said Boyce gently. "And your daughter, Jim—has made up her mind."

OBM *Retreat Grounds, Northern California*

Birch found himself standing in the grassy field, in the cool breeze, in sunlight strong enough to bring out a sweat on his forehead.

He was standing just where he'd been before going into the cusp between Every Thing and No Thing. He saw several footprints on the grass nearby, where Swift had been and Swift's daughter, and the young man with her, and the man who'd called himself Boyce and his companions, a few others...gone.

Already the memory of the in-between place of light was fading, the way a dream does when you're trying hard to hold onto it. Hard to find a place for it in memory: it didn't fit into any category; it didn't belong in any pigeonhole in his remembrance.

"Frank?" Meredith said, leaning on him. "Where *were* we?"

"I'm not sure. But we seem to have decided...to come back here. And here, I think, we stay." He looked around. The fundamentalists were mostly still here, in the same weary world—maybe a few were missing. Erin's mother was there, wandering about, blinking, calling: "Erin? Erin?"

"They're just *gone*..." O'Hanlon said, standing in the midst of the field, breathing hard, looking from side to side. "There was...it was like everything was...wobbling around and...some of the people just...vanished."

"Did they go to...was it the Rapture?" asked Linda, looking around for her daughter. "If it was the Rapture... Reverend Colbertson? If it was the Rapture, why are we still here?"

"Hmmm?" George Colbertson was sitting on the grass near the body of his father, his knees drawn up, arms around them, looking at the sun rising over the hills to the East. "No no, those people—those were the doubters. The Antichrist has taken them to himself...they will...they will..." His voice trailed off.

"Where's my daughter?" Linda said, her voice a croak now. "Where's Erin?"

She wandered off, calling out, "Erin! Erin where *are* you?"

"Shouldn't someone do something with...with those bodies?" said Birch, holding Meredith's hand, walking toward the awning. The OSI men were sitting dazedly to one side, in the sun, their guns in their laps. Cullum was just standing there, staring at the sky, his mouth moving soundlessly. Mergus, sitting on the ground, was plucking blades of greenery, tearing them up in his fingers, plucking more. Griffin's body was sitting up under the awning. And the bald guy in the trench coat was lying beside him. Galivant. Both quite dead. Griffin was staring—in death.

Equipment lay all around the two bodies, broken, wires and computers splashed with blood, monitors spattered with it. Everything Birch saw seemed freighted with symbolism. It was a sweet spring day but wherever he looked, a terrible destiny was imprinted into the air, the ground, the trees. The world was still here. But the world as he'd known it—was over. He felt it with a deep inner certainty.

Flies were beginning to gather on the elder Colbertson's corpse; to feast on the blood pooled in his eye sockets.

"Oh God, someone cover them up," Meredith moaned.

Birch nodded to George Colbertson and together they dragged the old Reverend's body to the awning, laid it down beside Galivant and Griffin. They pulled the awning down to cover the bodies and the broken machinery.

"God, I'm tired," Birch said, coming back to Meredith. "I'm going to lay down somewhere. Come on, Meredith..."

"Okay, then," said O'Hanlon, stalking up, rubbing his hands together. "Birch, you're not fired anymore! You're rehired! We've got work to do! Mergus! We've got to get rid of those bodies! I mean—bury them somewhere."

"You think you're 'getting rid' of my father's body?" Colbertson demanded, standing before the awning, arms spread. "People of the Church of the Revelation in Christ! Come to me!"

Not knowing what else to do, the church members gathered around him. "Pick up my father's body! We're taking it back with us!"

"You want to press charges, is that it, Colbertson? Mergus! Get up!"

Mergus shook his head. "I think...I made some basic mistake somewhere...Just some basic...mistake."

"Mergus!"

Mergus just shook his head. Cullum seemed to shake himself. He took a deep breath, then walked over to stand near O'Hanlon, and pointed a gun toward the End Timers. "What you want me to do, Mr. O'Hanlon. Too many to kill."

"Oh hell—let them go. We'll cover it all up later. We've got things to do...things to do. You with me, Birch?"

Frank Birch nodded vaguely, feeling an unspeakable sense of loss. A world-sized sense of loss...

Dallas, Texas, the Headquarters
of the Christian Cooperative

One month later

The Reverend George Colbertson was standing in front of the big screen television, gazing at it raptly, when the other guiding members of the Christian Cooperative filed into the big, richly-appointed meeting room behind him. The television was normally used for screening documentaries produced by the Cooperative, but Colbertson had it turned to CNN.

He was silhouetted against an image of panicky people running through the streets of Vatican City itself.

"So far as we are able to...to confirm," said the haggard CNN newscaster, "thirty-one days ago, somewhat more than half the people in the world simply—vanished. Again, they do not appear to have been killed by the so-called 'wall of light'—which seems to have disappeared from the world. It looks as if they have simply disappeared. Whole households, men women and children—gone. In fact, so far as we can discover, there are *no children left in the world at all*. No exact cut-off age can be determined, but all children under the age of fifteen or so are gone and there are extremely few people under the age of twenty left. Babies vanished from their mother's arms. Most pregnant women have vanished too. In a very few reported cases third trimester fetuses seemed to have simply...vanished from a mother's wombs. Many of the elderly and ill are gone. Many adults remain, but cities are largely decimated. Those people who remain have much in common, so far as the informal surveys can make out—and much in contrast, too..."

Harold Bromley, an aide to the President of the United States, was among the board members of the Christian Cooperative. He was a short but muscular man with a square face, lifts in his shoes. He reached out for the TV controller on the conference room table, and clicked mute, his Rolex watch glinting as he pointed the remote control at the screen.

"You get your information from CNN, Reverend," said Bromley, "you're going to get the hysterical version. They're losing their, ah, journalistic objectivity."

Colbertson turned, his face streaked with tears. "Well you give me the official version then—who's gone and who's stayed? Because I know for a fact there are no children left in this community! My own two-year-old is gone! My niece, my nephew. Gone! So is my older sister..."

Bromley shrugged. "Well sir, it appears that about two-thirds of Americans are just plain *gone*. No bodies. Just vanished. We have spoken to agencies around the world, done a general kind of survey. Pretty rough, but we have a sort of picture. There's a pattern. In America, well, there were some reports that mostly Republicans stayed behind but we've got some Democrats too, here—and a certain percentage of Republicans vanished. Along with members of every denomination of Christian, Muslim, Hindu—most any religion lost some people. Even some of the Church of Satan went. Some atheists stayed—others went. People who stayed are of a certain...well, let's just say it's more types of behavior, *attitudes,* which seemed the deciding factor, not your religion or your political party or sexual orientation. The ones who stayed are...well, I'd call them 'our kind', even though they're not all Christians..."

Hudson, a scowling, white-haired televangelist with handlebar mustaches, glared at the aide. "What do you mean, our kind? If they're Muslims—"

Bromley grimaced. "The things that have happened—" He shook his head. "It makes you look around, take stock. See things...different. I can see now, we've got a lot in common with everyone who stayed behind. So—we're here with them. If they were fundamentalist, hard-line, inflexible— they seem to have remained right here. Progressive minded people went to...that other place. Wherever it is. Moderates too. Certain kinds of conservatives..."

"That other place? Hell, you mean!"

Colbertson rubbed his eyes wearily as he spoke. "No. My sister was a good person. She was a tolerant person. She was conservative—but she spoke out against torture, Abu Ghraib, that whole thing. She's gone. She...they gave her the choice and she went."

"Lot of in-between people went too," said the aide thoughtfully. "Besides our people, we're stuck with most of the Scientologists, I'm afraid. There are lots of major business types still around—that's on the plus side. Heads of the oil companies, the big chain stores, their management— the ones that survived the wall of light. Our people, I guess. I'm starting to wonder who 'my people' are. I was given a choice, myself, you know—some here probably got the choice—"

Hudson shook his head and looked away. "No. But I heard about it. New rules, changed world—more of the Antichrist's lies!"

Bromley only shrugged.

"Shit, Bromley," said Colbertson, surprising them with the use of the expletive, "your report is no more helpful than CNN. It's vague as a son of a bitch. Come on, dammit, what are you here for?" He tapped the table. "Why'd you come to the CC? What's your real reason?"

"I've come to you folks," Bromley said, sighing and leaning on the back of a chair, "because the President wants your input on this—he figures no one can deny that all this is God's will, one way or another. What the President says is, God has just cleaned out all the problem people. Liberals, radicals, fuzzy-headed people who wouldn't choose. Most of the gays. God sent 'em away, he figures. Maybe to Hell. Maybe to nowhere. Like he just erased them. I guess he wants your, uh, imprimatur on that. He plans to make an announcement—he's going full theocracy with the country. He's going to enforce it with martial law."

Colbertson shook his head. "There are plenty of problem people still in the world. Millions of Muslim fundamentalists are still over in the Middle East. Hard-line Communists— still here. That asshole who runs North Korea? Still here!"

"Could be they're here for a reason," said Reverend Wiggins, an earnest man in a cream-colored suit and a kind of Reaganesque pompadour. "Set up for the last battle! The Lord leaves us our warriors—and our adversaries."

"That makes sense," Hudson said, nodding.

"Well, I'll tell you what I think," said an old man in an Armani suit, taking a seat at the conference table. He sat there heavily, as if he might have fallen over if he hadn't sat down. They all turned attentively to listen—because he was the co-author of a series of novels about Judgment Day. If anyone would know, he would. "I think *we were completely wrong*. I knew it when the best people in my family just— bodily vanished on me. Right in front of me, in some cases. You hear about the libraries and the housing?"

Colbertson shook his head. Just standing there staring, shaking his head, silently. Waiting.

"The libraries, Colbertson. The libraries are sealed off. There's an invisible wall around them—like those force fields they have in science fiction movies. You can't get in. Lots of hospitals and housing, too. Not all of it. But lots of it. Certain roads. All sealed off. Like it's *being kept* for someone. And the children—it's true, they're gone. My own grandchildren..." His voice broke at that. "Gone! No children left on this goddamn planet! Check the Internet if you don't believe it. It's amazing how many people don't seem to give a damn about all the missing kids."

"What's it all mean, sir?" Bromley asked, straightening up, licking his lips.

"Well I'll tell you what I think has happened...what's happened to us all..." He astonished them by pausing and taking a flask from his coat pocket, opening it, taking a long pull before going on, his hands shaking, his voice cracking: "I think...I think we've been left behind."

Washington, DC

Three-and-a-Half Years Later

"Too damn cold in this office," Birch grumbled. "Do I feel the air conditioner, going? Christ it's November..."

"Typical," said Ellen Meyers, distantly, looking out the window at the sky.

People often stared vaguely at the sky, these days, Birch thought. Waiting for something to return. Something that isn't coming back. We had our chance.

But maybe she was thinking about Miami. Might've had family there. Friends. Memories of a town that no longer exists...

Ellen was wearing a tight black sweater. She was as seductive as ever—maybe a bit pouchy round the edges from all the drinking she'd been doing for the last three years. He glanced at Meredith, who was nodding in a corner. Noticed the jowliness around her face, the lines under her eyes. She had taken too many anxiety meds this morning, again, it appeared.

The door to the conference room opened, and a wheelchair rolled through: Dud Turner pushing O'Hanlon in. If anyone could afford a good electric wheelchair it was O'Hanlon, but he preferred to be pushed. He was glaring, spittle gathered at the corners of his sagging mouth.

O'Hanlon swiped irritably at his rheumy, reddened eyes, as Turner pushed him into place at the head of the table, and glanced at the window. At the sky, really. Then O'Hanlon tore his eyes away from the window, tugged his shawl closer around his shoulders, and looked around the table at the others.

"Meredith, goddamn it wake up!" O'Hanlon snarled.

She jolted in her seat, blinking. "I was! I am!"

"O'Hanlon—don't talk to her like that," Birch said, wondering again, as O'Hanlon shrugged off his superficial insubordination, why he didn't just leave OBM. He and

O'Hanlon cordially hated one another, after all. He supposed it was because of meetings like this one—O'Hanlon had maneuvered close to the seat of power in what remained of the USA. Working with O'Hanlon—helping him with the Media Directives, the propaganda releases—gave Birch a chance to be a fly on the wall in the now-smokeless rooms where the power brokers drank their espressos and ate their omelets and issued execution orders. A chance to know what was coming before it came around the curve.

A fly on the wall, he thought. A creeping, verminous little insect. *That's what I've become. Thought I could help. Change things. Became what I was trying to change. Just looking for a sugar bowl now...Climb in and pull the lid down over me...*

"We decided to go ahead with the attack," O'Hanlon announced. "I don't give a goddamn if the President's 'not sure'. We worked out how to use Griffin's Coils the way Tesla hinted at—to crack open the world right out from under our enemies!"

Birch and Meredith glanced at one another.

"The Griffin Coils?" Ellen asked. "We're going to use it, that way? O'Han—do you think we should? I mean—"

"The AMS took out Miami last week, the whole damn city gone—two years is all it took 'em to build up nukes. They'll build more, and fast. We can't slam the world with a lot of damn nuclear weapons—we'll all get the radiation sickness, your nuclear winter, all that. We're hitting Tehran, a few other targets, with neutron bombs—then it's the Griffin Coils. Tesla's little time bomb..." He laughed creakily.

Birch shook his head in wonder. If they used the coils as a weapon, it could wreck the planet. And even if it didn't, how could they know for sure they were destroying the right target? The AMS—the Alliance of Muslim States—hadn't actually taken credit for destroying Miami. "O'Hanlon—the coils aren't an exact science yet, the way I understand it. We..." He broke off, as something occurred to him. "Did you say 'we're hitting Tehran'? You mean *now*?"

More squeaky-hinge laughter. "That's right. No not

now—half an hour ago! And right about now—" He looked at his watch. "The coils will be..."

Right about now...

The building started to shake.

"This isn't right!" Turner burst out, his voice high-pitched, as the shaking increased. "It's not supposed to hit us here! It's supposed to bounce around and come out under the Middle East!"

O'Hanlon shrugged, as ceiling tiles fell, the glass cracked in the window. "Hell I didn't want you scumbags to outlive me..."

Wind whistled through the window and Birch looked out to see Washington, DC shivering apart, the Capitol building falling into an enormous crack in the Earth, a spreading crack that moved toward the building they were in, that sent up plumes of volcanic smoke, a great cloud of ash that blackened all the world...

Meredith and Birch stumbled across the shuddering room toward one another. She was screaming his name.

Their fingers touched—and then the floor collapsed, and they all fell, together, into the molten rock that rose to consume the city...

14

A Forest in a Land Once Called Northern California

W HERE are we?" Swift asked, looking at the thick, deeply overgrown forest all around them. They were in heavy shadow, with a few rays of mid-morning sunlight angling down. They were big, big trees, redwoods mostly. Thick moss, ferns up to their waists. "What happened to the field?"

"It was overgrown thousands of years ago," Boyce said. He was sitting on an overturned tree, arms crossed, seeming in no hurry to be anywhere else. Ama was sitting on the mossy ground at his feet looking sleepily around.

"Thousands of years..." Swift shook his head, leaned on the bole of a tree, gathering his daughter in his arms. Gazing around in awe, Shontel was holding her hand—seeming to need the reassurance at least as much as she did.

Judith and four people Swift had seen with the church group, two women and two men—all on the young side— were sitting on a mossy hump rising from the ferns a few yards away.

One of the young men was Hispanic, the other a blond preppie type; two fresh-faced girls, one Filipino, the other a blue-eyed redhead.

Judith had one knee cocked, her arm propped on it, looking at the woods like a picnicker who knew the spot well. Swift's gaze lingered on her, as he wondered what was different about her appearance. Then he had it: she was far younger, a young woman in her mid-twenties, rather than the well-worn fifty she'd been before. Somehow he was not surprised.

"Dad..." Erin said, "I feel like I'm...dreaming..."

"I do too," Shontel said. "Like I smoked a couple of bong hits."

Swift himself felt oddly detached, a little dreamlike.

"You'll feel like that for awhile, as you adjust," Boyce said. He picked up a wood chip and skimmed it through the air at a tree, like a kid amusing himself

"We have an easing frequency reverberating right now," Judith said.

"It has a tranquilizing influence—just for a little while, to save people's sanity. But that effect will end in a few minutes. We're easing you into the new reality. We realize what a tremendous shock all this is—and there are more changes to come. Everything people need—really need—will be there. And the possibility of luxuries—if you create them. But... things will be different, too..."

"The announcement's going out now," Boyce said, lifting her head as if to listen.

Don't be afraid, said a voice. Swift suspected he was hearing it in his mind, but it seemed as if it came from all around him. What follows is the message as he remembered it, and wrote it down, soon after. But others heard it in slightly different form. The words were sometimes different, but the message was always the same:

> We are the Adjustors, those who emanate from the Absolute; from Aeon; from the sum total of all things. Had we not acted, the human race would have destroyed itself completely within three generations. We have saved much of the human race from self-destruction.
>
> This is the renewed world. You are safe, for now. The renewed world has its dangers, but you will face them later, and most of

*you, a little over three and a half billion
of you, will face them successfully. What
has happened to you is real. You are not
dreaming this, not in any sense. You have
been physically moved, all of you together,
many, many years into the future: about
twenty thousand years. Others chose not
to come or could not come, because they
belonged too profoundly to the old world.
You are here because you felt the wrongness
of the old world; you will feel the rightness
of this, the renewed world, almost the way
a musician hears a wrong note and a right
note—but you'll be aware of it with your
feelings and not your ears.*

*The renewed Earth has largely returned
to wilderness, but many tracts, some
infrastructure and buildings, have been
preserved, together with some electrical
power, modes of communication, plumbing,
and medical equipment so that you can
survive the transition. Other components
of civilization will have to be rebuilt. Still
other areas will remain pristine wilderness.
There are many more wild animals now,
including packs of wolves, wild dogs, and
other predators. There are places in the
world that were once great cities, which
are now swamp, dominated by alligators,
or deserts, dominated by other wild beasts.
Most of the old cities are covered over by
lava fields. People will have to use caution
in moving around the world, now that we
have dropped the protection we put up
around some artifacts.*

*Human representatives have been
chosen to speak for us.*

The changes will be shocking, but you

will find gifts waiting for you, too. Your sick have been healed; your aged made not young again, but younger and strong. A great many physical and neurological diseases have been eradicated forever. Your life spans will be expanded. And most importantly, the dark influence that encouraged humanity's destructive shortsightedness and selfishness is gone from your world. Those who clung to his ways—the intolerant, the religious extremists, those who enslaved others, those who raped the world—were left in the past to destroy one another.

Things will be different now. Old traditions will be tolerated so long as they don't tread on human rights. Men will no longer make women second class citizens, no matter what your religion or tradition. No tribe will elevate itself over another; no race will oppress another; the rich will not enslave the poor; sweatshops are at an end forever. No parent will be permitted to abuse or neglect or sell a child. People unsuitable for parenthood will find themselves incapable of it. And any invention that damages the biosphere will be regarded as incompletely invented. No significant chemical or biological pollution will be permitted, anywhere on the planet. You are likely to choose to enforce these new rules yourselves—you'll be free to choose them, now.

War will be improbable. Disagreement will occur, and will be resolved in other ways.

We are giving you the chance to live, and to grow in mindfulness and compassion.

*Gifts will be given you but much will
be asked in return. Cooperate with one
another and all will be well.*

The last syllable echoed...*well-ell-ell*...and died away.

"Did you understand that?" asked the young Hispanic man, for whom English was a second language. "It was in Spanish."

"English for me," Swift said. "Must be Japanese for Japanese people, Pashtun for Pashtun speakers, and so on."

"That's right," said Boyce. "It referred to you, Swift, and certain others like you. You have been chosen to be a spokesman for us. It's not mandatory, if you don't want to do it. There are other spokesmen and women too, on other land masses."

Swift grimaced. This was overwhelming enough without that kind of responsibility. He asked wonderingly, "We're in the future—twenty thousand years?" He looked at the dizzyingly high trees, thinking of Galivant. "Ed. I wish you could see this."

"He's seeing it from another vantage," Boyce said.

Swift shivered, feeling the tranquilizing effect wear off.

Fuji suddenly sat up into view—he'd been lying in the ferns. "Boosht! Twenty thousand years in the future. Fuck!"

He lay back down again.

"Why...why we go to...this place?" Shontel asked hoarsely. "Oh Lord, my Moms..."

"Your mother, your whole family, is alive—and in this time with us, Shontel," Judith said, smiling.

"They are?" Shontel's happiness lit up his face like a lamp. "Where?"

"You'll see. You'll be reunited. You've trusted us this much—I guess you had to. But trust us a little more."

"But—*my* mom is dead!" Erin wailed. "She is, isn't she!"

"Yes, she is. Everyone who didn't come with us died. But we didn't kill them. Other human beings killed them—"

"I don't care! You could have saved them! You have the power! You could save my mom!"

"We *couldn't*. We have rules. But we gave her a choice. She chose to stay, to remain behind, just as Meredith and Frank did."

"I don't know," Swift said. Still coming to terms with the idea that Linda, the woman he'd shared a large part of his life with, was dead. "People have so much to deal with. They have so much coming at them, so much uncertainty. Linda and I broke up and that affected her—maybe I'm as much responsible for her choices as she was. People just sort of react to things. We're not enlightened—we can't all make the right choices..."

"You can't see *into* people, the way we can," said Judith gently. "They choose their angry little fantasies at some point. Their choice was actually made long ago. The moment was there—and they took a certain path. Once again—we didn't kill them. We shut down the bodies only of those who were so destructive, so corrupt, there was no real hope for them—and justice cried out for it. Murderers, dictators, those responsible for genocides. We also had to shut down corporate polluters who knew they were giving children cancer and didn't care. Even *those* people we simply switched off—and sent their essential selves to immerse in the great sea of consciousness. They felt no pain! Your mother died at the hands of other human beings—"

"*You could have saved her!*" Erin shouted. "*And half the world is dead!*"

She drew away from her father and suddenly ran into the forest, following the first thin forest track she came to.

"I don't think that tranquilizer thing is working," said Fuji, from amongst the ferns.

"She's been through a great deal," Ama said. "She saw two people shot...and then this..."

Shontel and Swift were already starting after Erin. Swift heard the others coming along behind. "Erin!" he shouted. There was no response at first; just a rustling in the brush up ahead.

"Who made this trail?" Fuji asked, catching up.

"Animal trail," Swift said. "Deer, whatever."

"Erin!" Shontel shouted. "Goddammit, hold up! Stay where you are!"

"Daddy!" she called, from somewhere up ahead. "Shontel!" There was a note of fear in her voice. And when she said it again, it was a scream: *"Daddy!"*

They burst into a small clearing, where bunches of grass grew around a tumble of volcanic rock. Perched on the rock was Erin—cringing as a pack of wild dogs came stalking toward her...

"Jesus son of a *bitch!*" Shontel hissed. "Brewd, those are some big ass pit bulls!"

They were pit bulls, seven of them, but even larger than the ones Swift remembered, with bristling ruffs, every one of them with their heads lowered, their teeth bared, snarling, circling Erin...

Shontel ran in ahead of Swift, grabbed a large angular chunk of rock and threw it at the massive animal that seemed to be the pack leader, in front. The dog yipped when the rock struck its big, wedgelike head, and backed away a little—but the pack only spread out more, some of them crouching in a way that suggested they were going to rush.

Swift caught up with Shontel, picked up a rock. Erin dodged behind them. The pit bulls rushed in...

And stopped in their tracks, bumbling into one another in confusion, as Boyce walked up. They sat down, as he walked among them, like dogs heeling; their tongues lolled, and their tails wagged. He reached out and patted each one on the head.

"You should have stayed with me, Erin," Boyce said. "If I hadn't come along, they'd have killed you."

"You brought us to a place over run by wild pit bulls?" Swift asked, watching Shontel take Erin in his arms. Swift was angry, in a perplexed way, that his daughter had come so close to being killed.

"As you've been told, the world is still dangerous," Judith said, entering the clearing. "Much of it is dangerous in the way it was before it was ever settled. But we've modified the ecosystem to some extent. There are improvements. There are gifts we're going to leave for you...when we go."

Boyce pointed to an odd-looking tree at the edge of the clearing. "Lyman—go to that tree, if you would please, and pull down a couple of those knobby looking things on the ends of the branches...They should be ripe and ready to come off."

It looked a bit like a chestnut tree, but the branches were thicker and they had a ropy quality; their bark, mottled pink and brown, was as slick as skin. The leaves were broad, heavy, reddish-brown, and thickly veined. Some of the branches ended in shapes remarkably like antlers; others ended in big, podlike knobs, each one as big as the paddle of an oar, and thicker.

Lyman Fuji jogged over to the tree. "Weird looking tree, man..." He pulled two of the knobs from the branches— and immediately made a sound of disgust, holding them out away from his body. They dripped red fluid. "It looks just like blood!"

"It *is* blood," Judith said. "Those trees are the end result of genetic engineering research that was being carried out by a Professor Wu Ling, in China, in your time. You were about to develop this anyway, so we made it a part of your world. Lyman, toss those pods to the dogs, here..."

Fuji threw the pods to the pack of wild pit bulls and they immediately seized on them, tore them apart, gobbling them up. He threw a few more to the pack as Shontel said, "That looks like...meat!"

"It is," Boyce said. "Professor Ling was using animal stem cells to grow meat-flesh in vats. No brain, no nervous system, just meat. The tree has replaced the vats. It's a hybrid of plant and animal cells...The tree doesn't suffer, when it gives up its pods—as much as a tree can be said to 'like' something, it likes it when you take them. They contain seeds, as any fruit does, to help its reproduction."

Swift stared. His anger ebbed at the marvel of the thing.

"Meat fruit..." Shontel said. "Flesh. Fruit flesh...you could call it *froosh*."

"*Froosh* it is, hereafter," Boyce said. "People need concentrated protein but the way it was provided in the last decades of your civilization increased the background radiation of suffering to unacceptable levels. Industrialized agriculture was cruel and toxic. Now you have a lean meat to ingest—without the poisons or the suffering. No need to slaughter animals."

"Thanks for saving me from the dogs," Erin said, her voice barely audible.

"I just wish I could save everyone who encounters dangers here," Boyce said. "But I won't be able to. We're not creating paradise. Just a new chance—but the rules require adversity. A reasonable degree of danger. Even some suffering."

"Be boring without danger," Shontel observed.

"That's exactly right," said Judith. "Danger creates motivation, motivation creates organization, ideas. And suffering is there for a reason too. But there's mindless, unnecessary suffering—which we hope to help you eliminate, in time. We've already done away with some of it. Shall we head on down toward the settlements, Erin?"

Erin nodded, mechanically. "Whatever."

Shontel took her hand and they all followed Judith and Boyce along the thread of a faint animal trail. Swift was glad to leave the pit bulls behind, the animals still fighting over scraps and leaping at the lower branches of the froosh tree. "Stay close to us," Boyce said. "There are other animals out here. Plenty of cougars and...Dennis Boyce never knew or forgot the name of the big, very big bears..."

"Grizzlies," Judith prompted.

"That's it. There are a good many in these hills now. And wolves."

The little party of humans and Adjustors trekked for miles, getting hot and scratched and tired, and at last came to a place that was more open than the forest around it. Swift spotted broken pieces of asphalt in the dirt, and a rusted, fallen pipe...No, not a pipe, he decided, looking closer, it's what's left of a lamp post...Nearby, there was a hump in the ground, with a little rusty, pitted metal showing through the dirt, barely visible. Swift realized the hulk was in the outline of a car...

"Is that...?"

"Yes it is, Jim," said Boyce. "That's what's left of your car. This was the parking lot you left it in. A great deal of the world has changed its physical outline—much of Northern Europe is now under water, and most of Central America is simply gone. But there are other tracts we worked hard to keep intact. Much of California is still here. Come on... There's a road we kept, a little ways along here...There are only a few working vehicles, but there are wild horses, nearby. I'll persuade the horses to get us to the settlement. There you'll find food—there's enough food for everyone."

"Boyce," Fuji asked, as they set out along another trail that followed what remained of an ancient gravel road. "How'd you get us twenty thousand years into the future?"

"Difficult to explain in brief. Essentially we selected the appropriate people, and we connected them all in one protective field. Then we moved the field and everyone in it— we used a technology that would seem 'spiritual' to people now. It's a science that uses...mind tools, you might say. We moved 'renewed humanity' into the realm of eternity—and then back into the stream of time at the appropriate point."

"I don't understand."

"You descendents will understand—in another sixteen thousand years or so."

"But why'd you move us to twenty thousand years later?"

"That's how long it took for the world to heal from the third world war—a limited nuclear war. And from OBM's destructive machine. Griffin's Tesla plaything cracked a great deal of the Earth's crust. And above all, we had to heal the damage your civilization did to the environment. Global warming, mercury poisoning of the seas, acid rain, the plastic debris in the oceans, nuclear waste, landfill toxicity, pesticide toxicity...and we had to make certain adjustments, changes. The few survivors of the wars died in the release of biowarfare agents, afterwards. We had to kill those germs."

They traipsed on for a while in silence. Then Erin, her

voice hoarse, said, "Mom...Oh God." Tears streaked the dust on her cheeks.

"She died instantly, Erin," Judith said, gently.

"Is she in some kind of...in hell?"

"No, not at all! There's no hell—only the exclusion from the Absolute. Your mother is part of the sea of consciousness, rediscovering herself there. She's all right, Erin."

"All I know is—she was alive a few minutes ago. To me, it was just a few minutes ago. Now she's...her body's not even around for a funeral."

They paused on the trail. Boyce raised a hand—and Erin took a step back, seeming to sense what he had in mind. "Don't make me feel better about it. I want to feel it."

He smiled and nodded. "That's good. That's very good. Then—let's just keep going."

Shontel said softly: "That's what you have to do, when you lose someone, babe. Keep going."

She hugged him for a long moment, and then they went on.

After they'd passed through a meadow, buzzing with bees of a sort Swift had never seen before—they were twice the size of bumble bees, and banded pink and green—he asked, "But if it's twenty thousand years later," Swift said, "what about your own lives, you Adjustors? You just give up twenty thousand years?"

"We normally live outside of the stream of time," Boyce said. "To us time is a constant kaleidoscope of shifting possibilities. No one timeline is defined and fixed. Yet, there are lines of greater *likelihood*—we try to adjust these to the will of the Absolute. When I return to the Absolute, I'll once more be outside the stream of time...back home."

"I'll pretend I understand that," said Swift.

"Best I can do. You'll understand—Or your descendents will—"

"I know. In about sixteen thousand years...Damn I'm thirsty."

"You left a case of beer in the trunk of that car," Shontel said, chuckling. "You going to dig it up?"

"Don't torture me, Shontel. Hey Boyce—you grow any beer trees?"

Shontel laughed. Then he fell silent. Frowning. At last Shontel articulated what the other human beings present were thinking. "But—how is everyone spread out over the world, now? Are they in houses? What are we all going to do to live? Is there...television?"

"You'll see," said Boyce, smiling. "No television at present. But we've set things up so you can all find shelter, and take care of one another—and start over. Some—unusual technologies are waiting. They'll seem strange to you, anyway. Everyone is currently located as near as possible to the place they were when the transition occurred. But there are a great many challenges to face."

"People will be bringing their old prejudices into this...this renewed world, with them," Swift pointed out. "Their old spiritual superstitions, their attitudes toward the opposite sex, toward other races..."

"Yes," Judith said. "But a great many people were changed by the consciousness lamps—and others, where necessary, will be illuminated by the lamps. We have to do it by degrees or it's too disruptive. Even so, some will resist, or be afraid—or be simply confused. There'll be challenges. You'll have more time to meet those challenges, because your lifespan will be on average almost four hundred years."

"Four hundred years!" Erin burst out. "You mean—we'll live to four hundred years *in good shape?*"

Boyce actually laughed at that, surprising Ama. "Yes. In good shape. People won't reproduce as easily as before, so they won't overpopulate the world—but you'll have a chance to have some children. You and your children and grandchildren will meet all those challenges. Once you're on your feet, we'll leave you to go on alone."

"Alone?" Ama asked, looking at Boyce. "We'll just fall into our old ways."

Boyce touched her shoulder. "The worst influences are gone. What's good in you has a chance to emerge now. We have faith in the human race, Ama."

Swift shook his head. "I'm not sure I do. I can't imagine what it's going to be like, now. How we're all going to find our way in the world, with all that's happened to it..."

"No," said Boyce. "You can't imagine it. You'll just have to wait and see."

"The dark guide is gone," Judith said. "And that means that the responsibility, once we're gone, in a few years, will rest on *you*. On human beings alone."

Then they emerged from the forest at the edge of a paved road.

They stepped out on the road into brilliant sunlight and Swift heard the brisk clatter of horse's hooves, approaching...

Epilogue

*T*HEY *can't confirm his death?* said the being known as Judith.

Not only that, some suspect he didn't die, said the one who'd been known as Dennis Boyce. *What we took to be his remains was a semblance. Of course, he could have made it for any number of reasons. He might have been manufacturing a new body for himself and failed to complete it. But the high-vibrants think that it was never occupied by consciousness.*

So he could still be alive, hiding himself from us somehow. But no one can hide from the Absolute.

The Absolute knows, but it does not tell, because it cannot see one thing as separate from another. The Absolute takes an age to speak a sentence. We will get no help there, only ambiguous hints.

If Ialdabaoth is still alive, he may return to their world, once we have left them.

Must we leave them?

We must, they will not break into the next growth cycle, otherwise.

But if we leave them, and he comes, he may assert himself again and lean his weight against their minds; he may again distort their perception.

We can only hope that if he returns, they will be awake enough to perceive the truth; awake enough to feel the truth; brave enough to embrace the truth.

ABOUT THE AUTHOR

John Shirley is the author of more than a dozen books, including *Demons*; *Crawlers*; *City Come A-Walkin'*; *Really, Really, Really, Really Weird Stories*; and the classic cyberpunk trilogy A Song Called Youth: *Eclipse, Eclipse Penumbra*, and *Eclipse Corona*. He is a recipient of the Horror Writers Association's Bram Stoker Award and the International Horror Guild Award. Shirley has fronted punk bands and written lyrics for Blue Oyster Cult and other groups. A principal screenwriter for *The Crow*, Shirley now devotes most of his time to writing for television and film.

EBOOKS BY JOHN SHIRLEY

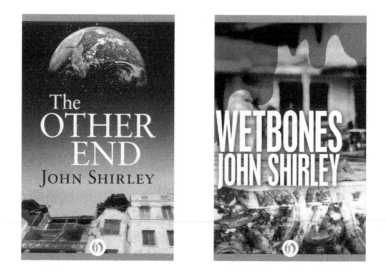

CPSIA information can be obtained
at www.ICGtesting.com
Printed in the USA
LVHW101047201222
735616LV00015B/69

9 781504 021807